"Sherri, I'd like to see you sometime..."

Neill then added, "Socially, I mean. Dinner perhaps?"

How could Neill possibly think he could make up for the past and what they'd lost by inviting her out to dinner?

Yet his voice, his openness as he looked at her and his uneasy smile—they were all so familiar. Sherri waited to see if he'd rub the back of his neck after running his hands through his hair.

When he did, a rush of feeling—long held hostage by her fear—flooded to the surface. It was as if he'd never been gone. She stepped back in shock and disbelief.

How could he still have this effect on her?

She had to stop herself from reaching for him, for everything his love had once offered her. "Dinner? That's hardly necessary," she said over the blood pounding in her ears. She leaned against the wall for support, hoping he didn't notice her apprehension.

When would she ever be free of these feelings? It had been twelve long years since she'd seen him... since he'd seen her. And still, he held the power to make her want him.

Dear Reader,

Having friends enriches our everyday experiences by encouraging us to be who we are and to share our lives with those who believe in us. Yet finding a true friend means trusting another person to care about us despite our shortcomings.

Neill and Sherri had been best friends in high school, a friendship that over time became a love affair. But loving someone doesn't guarantee happiness. Sherri and Neill's love would have been lost forever but for the friendship they'd shared *before* they fell in love. The memory of how much they'd once trusted each other becomes the starting point from which they're able to rekindle their love.

The Doctor Returns takes place in Eden Harbor, a fictional town on the coast of Maine, and begins what will be a series of stories about the lives of those who live and love in a place of magnificent beauty and shared family values.

For those of you reading this book, my one wish is that you have been blessed with close friends who have made your world a brighter place.

If you'd like to contact me, I would be delighted to hear from you. My website is www.stellamaclean.com and my email address is stella@stellamaclean.com. I can be found on Facebook at www.facebook.com/stella.maclean.3 and on Twitter, @Stella__MacLean.

Sincerely,

Stella MacLean

The Doctor Returns

Stella MacLean

HARLEQUIN® SUPER ROMANCE®

Recycling programs
for this product may
not exist in your area.

ISBN-13: 978-0-373-71877-1

THE DOCTOR RETURNS

H HARLEQUIN®
™ www.Harlequin.com

Printed in U.S.A.

ABOUT THE AUTHOR

Stella MacLean has spent her life collecting story ideas, waiting for the day someone would want to read about the characters who have lurked in her heart and mind for so many years. Stella's love of reading and writing began in grade school and has continued to play a major role in her life. A longtime member of Romance Writers of America and a Golden Heart finalist, Stella enjoys the hours she spends tucked away in her office with her Maine coon cat, Emma Jean, and her imaginary friends while writing stories about love, life and happiness.

Books by Stella MacLean

HARLEQUIN SUPERROMANCE

1487—HEART OF MY HEART
1553—BABY IN HER ARMS
1655—A CHILD CHANGES EVERYTHING
1817—THE CHRISTMAS INN

Other titles by this author available in ebook format.

I dedicate this book to Debbie Macomber, author, mentor and friend.

Acknowledgments

The best books are those carefully encouraged and skillfully edited by professional editors.

My heartfelt thanks to Paula Eykelhof and Lara Hyde for their guidance and support in bringing *The Doctor Returns* to readers everywhere.

CHAPTER ONE

JUST ANOTHER FEW steps and he'd be there. "Hang on, sweetie," Neill Brandon pleaded over the thrashing movements of his little girl's body. Fear tore through his heart, fear driven by dread that he'd let his daughter down.

His feet thudded against the concrete of the driveway leading to the hospital emergency doors, while his lips moved in silent prayer that this was not the beginning of a reoccurrence of Morgan's epileptic seizures. That he wasn't somehow responsible for what was happening to her.

He'd picked Morgan up after school and taken her with him while he checked on a patient at the hospital. They'd been sitting in the car in the doctors' parking lot when Morgan began arguing with him about being allowed to have a sleepover at her new friend's house. Morgan's grandmother approved, so why couldn't he?

He hadn't wanted to part with her so soon after their move to Eden Harbor, but his nine-year-old daughter's plea had turned into a tearful demand just before her body was overcome by the tremors that announced the arrival of a seizure.

The seizure had been milder than the ones she'd had before they'd found a stable dose of medicine for her, and he was thankful for that. He was relieved she'd still had her seat belt on when the seizure began, which made it easier to control her shaking.

He hugged her closer, feeling her body yield to his anxious embrace as he ran the last few steps to the entrance of Eagle Mountain Hospital. The doors slid apart, and a warm flood of air welcomed him as he charged across the yawning space toward the doors to the emergency room. As if her body knew they had reached safety, Morgan relaxed into his arms; her head lolled against his shoulder, her breath sweet against his neck.

"My daughter's an epileptic and she's having a seizure. Get Dr. Fennell," he ordered, barely glancing at the nurse who appeared before him.

"Certainly," the nurse said, keying in the page on the phone hanging on the wall at the head of a bank of four unoccupied stretchers. Neill laid Morgan on the nearest one.

He couldn't take his eyes off his daughter and her endearing face, her high cheekbones hinting of beauty to come, so like her mother's. Her auburn hair clinging to her cheeks reminded him of the many times he'd sat with her in the early morning before school, forcing the mass of curls into what Morgan called a bun.

"Dr. Fennell's on his way," the nurse said, her voice soothing as she moved to the other side of the stretcher. "Your daughter's lovely, Dr. Brandon."

Neill anxiously watched Morgan, waiting for her eyes to flutter open. "Yes, she is lovely." A gift life had given him—his taste of redemption.

Dr. Fennell strode into the room, his lab coat flapping around him. "Neill, what's going on?"

Neill explained to Mike what had happened and how long the seizure had lasted, all the while vaguely aware of the nurse standing across the stretcher from him as she checked Morgan's vital signs. Although he'd trained himself to remain in control, to be calm, the struggle to steady his breathing and to keep his hands from trembling where they held Morgan's was difficult. His medical training told him his response was normal, but normal no longer mattered. All he wanted was to gather Morgan in his arms and promise her it would never happen again—a promise he couldn't guarantee he could keep. No one could. But it didn't stop the impulsive need to protect and care for her in whatever way possible. Her illness had made him understand why doctors didn't treat their own family members, except in dire emergencies. Emotions could so easily cloud judgment.

He answered the doctor's questions as clearly as possible as he struggled to figure out what could have caused this sudden recurrence. "No, Morgan hasn't had a seizure in over two years," he said in response to Dr. Fennell's final question.

"I'll get an MRI ordered, check her blood work and, to be on the safe side, I'll admit her for a few days. We'll know more after that. Do you have her medical record from Boston?"

Those months of testing five years ago had been the worst of his life. As a doctor, he knew the ominous possibilities related to seizures, and it was almost a relief to get the diagnosis of epilepsy. She had a good chance of outgrowing her condition, or so he'd believed until now. "Yes. I'll get it for you. It's at the house."

"Great. In the meantime, I'll make arrangements for her admission and talk to you once we've got the MRI results."

What had gone wrong? Had the move been too much for Morgan? In his eagerness to move back home and take over his uncle Nicolas's medical practice, he hadn't considered that it might trigger a seizure in his daughter. How could he have overlooked the possibility?

With his ex-wife's parents both deceased, he'd hoped that the move would give Morgan a sense of family and a community that provided a safe environment. With his mother's support and encouragement, he'd bought a house, a house he'd admired when he was growing up in Eden Harbor. To make Morgan's transition easier, he'd painted her bedroom her favorite shade of pink, partly in appreciation of her upbeat approach to the move and partly just to see her smile. His daughter had maintained her sunny disposition and her enthusiasm throughout the move, much to his relief. But had Morgan been more stressed about the move than he'd realized? Willing his daughter to open her eyes, he squeezed her hand.

He heard Mike Fennell offer instructions to the nurse, and a part of his mind registered the fact that they seemed perfectly typical of what should be ordered. Even under the stress of the situation, he couldn't stop himself from paying close attention to every detail. He had been that way all his life—a trait that had driven his ex-wife to distraction.

That reminded him; he'd call Lilly as soon as Morgan was settled in her room. Although his ex-wife lived in Houston, she'd probably be there on the earliest possible flight.

The nurse gently placed a warm blanket around Morgan's body.

As she tucked the blanket around Morgan's shoulders, her hand brushed his. His gaze moved to her in response. Her wide, hazel-green eyes held a strange uncertainty under the harsh fluorescent lighting. As they stood across from each other, her expression went from one of warmth and concern to one of wariness.

"Neill, I'm sorry this happened," the nurse said.

Noting the beautiful mane of sun-streaked hair, the way her uniform fit her curves, he struggled to remember who she might be. Something about her was so familiar.... Her gaze was so intent. Had he met her before? He'd met so many people in the two weeks since he'd moved back, faces he couldn't always put a name to. But he hadn't been back for years, and so many of the people were only vaguely recognizable. "Forgive me, you look really familiar...."

The tentative smile faded from her lips and her expression changed. An emotion he couldn't identify flickered on her face and then disappeared. She turned her back to him, her attention focused on the patient chart.

"Daddy!" Morgan cried out, her voice fearful. "Daddy, what happened? Where am I?"

Forgetting the woman standing across the stretcher from him, he gathered his daughter in his arms. "You're in the hospital, sweetie. How do you feel?"

SHERRI LAWSON STEADIED her hands on the edge of the surgical cart, overwhelmed by the hurt tightening her chest, forcing her to turn her back on the man holding his daughter in his arms. She couldn't believe it. Neill hadn't shown even a flicker of recognition. Did he really not recognize her? Had twelve years changed her that much?

It was true that he'd been out of her life for all those years, but surely he couldn't forget her so easily. She touched her highlighted hair as the heat of embarrassment climbed her cheeks. Granted, she'd lost over thirty pounds, had eye surgery to correct her vision and wore makeup now. She'd even gotten her teeth whitened and managed to find a hairdresser who did a beautiful job of coloring and layering her hair. But still...

Relax and stop jumping to conclusions.

She took a deep, calming breath. He might not have recognized her because of his concern for his daughter. She'd seen the haunted look in his eyes when he'd first come into the emergency room. Was she being unreasonable to think he *should* have recognized her?

Or was she just making excuses for him the way she did during those long, dreary months after he'd gone off to medical school in Boston, leaving her to fend for herself?

And if she were to speak up, how could she explain who she was to the man who'd once been the love of her life—without being totally humiliated? And if he apologized for not recognizing her, would anything change other than the red blotches on her cheeks?

A long-buried ache rose through her chest at the mortifying truth. Of all the responses she'd imagined from him, this was not one of them.

But what had she expected? Had she harbored the notion that he might one day see her again, rush into her arms and tell her how much he'd missed her? Plead for her forgiveness and offer to marry her?

He'd married a doctor from his medical class and had a child with her. That was how much he'd missed her! Meanwhile, she was acting like a lovesick schoolgirl, an *angry* lovesick schoolgirl.

One part of her wanted to jump into his arms—the other part wanted to punch his lights out. And then there was the part of her that wanted Neill Brandon the teenager she remembered so well....

When she had learned that Neill was returning to Eden Harbor to take over his uncle's medical practice, she'd decided to avoid any contact with him if possible. She'd accepted that she'd probably run into him at some point between his arrival and her departure—when she left for her new job in Portsmouth. Yet, she could hardly have imagined that their first encounter would be such a disaster.

It was just her rotten luck that because of a nursing shortage in Emergency, she'd taken this extra shift today. Now all she could do was wait for this embarrassing scene to end.

The sooner she got Morgan Brandon moved to her inpatient room, the better. This was one scene she didn't intend to repeat. Ignoring the man and his daughter, she contacted Admitting to learn that Dr. Fennell had made arrangements and the room was ready. "Dr. Brandon, if you like, I'll take Morgan to her room while you complete the paperwork in Admitting."

"Thanks so much." He moved around the stretcher, his arm brushing hers, sending tiny shock waves reverberating over her skin. She stepped away from him.

"Sorry, I didn't mean to startle you."

"You didn't," she said, fighting to control the sudden awareness snapping through her.

How could she still feel anything for Neill? Hadn't those lonely months and years accomplished anything? Those desperate weeks when she'd had to face the fact that Neill Brandon wasn't coming home had exposed her to a kind of fear she'd never experienced before.

Forcing back the memories, she studied the drip chamber on the intravenous as if her life depended on it—anything to keep her eyes from his. Yet she couldn't block out his words, spoken so gently to his daughter, words filled with love. Hearing them, she remembered another child.

A child who had lived only fifty-two hours.

Unable to bear it any longer, she made another quick note and closed the chart. "I'm going to transfer your daughter now."

"Morgan, you're going to be okay. I'll see you in a few minutes," he said.

His voice drew her like a moth to a flame to the man who had once held her heart. Not fair. Totally not fair.

She felt the urge to touch him, to be in contact with him, his skin on hers. Nothing had changed. Years after he'd dumped her, he'd returned to her life and the fantasies were beginning all over again.

What is the matter with me?

Is this what having no man in your life did to you?

Not if I can help it. Time to take back control.

And she knew just where to start. Her grip on the stretcher was strong and uncompromising as she unlocked the brakes, tucked Morgan's chart under the corner of the mattress and moved toward the door.

Hitting the door pad, she waited impatiently for it to swing open, and then strode out into the corridor, pushing the stretcher ahead of her.

Look on the bright side. At least the dreaded first contact with him is over.

She turned the corner and headed toward the elevator. And wasn't it just as well that he *hadn't* recognized her? No need for awkward "how have you been?" chatter. No going back over the past twelve years and dredging up old memories that still held the power to inflict pain. But most of all, no empty excuses required.

She was free to go ahead with her plans, confident in the belief that the worst was over. She could look forward to her job in Portsmouth and her new life.

CHAPTER TWO

As Sherri approached the outpatient clinic nurses' station the next morning, her mind was made up: from now on she'd refuse any shifts outside the clinics she normally worked. Now all she had to do was finish her shift in the outpatient clinic and then she was off for a couple of days.

She was going to Portsmouth to look for a place to live and to meet with the members of the nursing department she'd be working with in her new job. During the interview a few weeks ago, she'd discovered that she and the nursing coordinator shared the same approach to risk management, a key function in modern hospitals. She might even go to Bangor tomorrow and buy something special for the trip. Just thinking about her new job and the potential it held for a career in nursing management excited her.

Seeing Neill with his daughter, being aware of how focused he was on his life now, had made one thing clear. Neill Brandon had moved on; he had made decisions in life to meet his own personal goals. And so should she. When she'd told her friend Gayle Sawyer about meeting Neill, Gayle had been shocked to learn he hadn't recognized her.

Gayle's take on the situation was that the sooner she resolved her feelings around Neill, the easier it would be for her to move on with her life. In Gayle's mind, there were unfinished issues between them. What Gayle didn't seem to get was that Sherri had moved on. She wasn't interested in resuscitating an old relationship. Neill's presence in her life would be fleeting and of no real importance in the end.

After work yesterday, Sherri had dropped into her mother's house before going home to her condo. Colleen had been preoccupied with the fact that her son, Ed, was about to be paroled and what that would mean in their lives. With her mother's attention on Sherri's older brother, it wasn't difficult to talk about seeing Neill again. Her mother had been curious about the incident, but Sherri had convinced her that everything had gone well, that they had been perfectly civil with each other. Nothing more.

Her mother didn't know that Neill was her baby's father. Even back then, her mother's attention had been on Ed, who'd just been jailed for drug smuggling. Sherri didn't want to give her mother any more reason to worry.

Sherri's husband, Sam, had died five years ago. She'd let her mother assume that her baby had been Sam's. He'd been in love with Sherri for years, and when she'd met him again in Bangor, they'd started dating. When she could no longer hide the fact that she was pregnant, she'd confided in him what had happened. He proposed to her that night. Feeling she had no other option, she'd accepted.

Sam wanted to be a father very much, and was delighted to have her son carry the Crawford name. She was so grateful for everything he had done for her, and it seemed the right thing to do under the circumstances. He'd supported her by telling everyone that the baby was his. He'd even gone along with fabricating a story about the date she'd conceived. But all of the small lies and minor fabrications had been unnecessary in the end when her son died only hours after he'd been born.

Sam's parents and his brother Charlie still lived in Eden Harbor, and she saw them at church on the Sundays she wasn't working. Charlie and his wife, Freda, included her in their children's birthday celebrations and the Crawford family always invited her for Christmas. She would forever be thankful that Sam was the kind of man he was, despite his problems with alcohol, and that his family treated her like a daughter.

Neill's arrival in Eden Harbor had complicated her life, but it was nothing she couldn't manage. She'd decided six months ago to leave Eden Harbor, long before she'd heard that Neill was moving back. She was not leaving because she didn't like living there; she loved it. But she needed to expand her horizons, find a more challenging nursing job and meet new people. The social scene in Eden Harbor consisted of married couples and twenty-year-olds. Obviously, she didn't fit into either category.

As Sherri approached the desk, Gayle Sawyer glanced up, her mass of black curls bouncing around her high cheekbones. Any other day Sherri would've arrived early for her shift so that she and Gayle could start the day off with a quiet chat. Although Gayle had only arrived in Eden Harbor a year ago, they'd developed an instant rapport that had led to a very close friendship. There were few secrets in Sherri's life that she hadn't shared with Gayle, including her relationship with Neill.

"Sorry I'm late, but I got caught in the traffic on Higgins Road. There are days when I wonder why I bought a condo so far from the center of town, but I love waking up to the sound of the ocean." Her condo building was designed as a series of semidetached units that wrapped around the edge of a hill with a view of the ocean.

"They're finally doing those road repairs they've been talking about. None too soon," Gayle said, her smile anxious. "I've got some bad news."

Resting her arms on the raised counter in front of Gayle, she waited, fearful that Gayle's teenage son, Adam, was in trouble again. "What happened?"

"Dr. Brandon is working the clinic this morning."

"Neill's here today? His daughter's a patient on Pediatrics. What's he doing here?" Sherri had a sudden urge to check her makeup; instead she controlled her rush of anxiety by tidying the already-neat pile of charts on the desk.

"He's covering for Dr. Keith, who's been called away on a family emergency."

"They all seem to be having family emergencies," Sherri said. "What's next, I wonder?"

"You'll have an overwhelming urge to leave work early?" Gayle's eyebrows twitched.

"Not a chance. Neill's return to Eden Harbor is just fine as far as I'm concerned."

"Sherri, it's me, remember? What if someone starts gossiping about you and Neill? People have long memories, especially when it comes to a new doctor in town. Rumors can ruin lives."

Sherri suddenly remembered that her medical chart was in his uncle's office—now Neill's office—with her past health history, including what had happened in Bangor. Neill knew about the pregnancy, and if he read her chart, he'd learn how their son had had no chance of survival. The struggle she'd had to keep her sanity, and how that struggle had ended. What she didn't want him to discover was what had happened after that. She was entitled to her privacy when it came to the man who had no right to know what she'd been through. "He won't find out. I'm out of here in a couple of weeks, and I'm taking my chart with me."

"I hope you're right."

"You worry too much," Sherri cautioned, although she worried enough for everyone, including herself. But where had all that worrying gotten her? She still lived in the town she'd grown up in. She hadn't traveled anywhere in her entire life. Another reason for getting out of Eden Harbor.

Neill's uncle, Dr. Nicolas Brandon, had been her family doctor all her life. Now it was Neill's practice. And now people had reason to gossip about the newly divorced doctor and his past relationship with one of the nurses. Keeping her secret for twelve years had been tough, and all that effort would not be in vain if she had anything to do with it. She deserved to be able to move on with her life without becoming the subject of unfair gossip.

How had she forgotten about her chart? Did she have time to drop by his office and pick it up? She could request it because she was moving—a simple explanation. She glanced at the clock.

Gayle followed her glance. "Dr. Brandon hasn't arrived yet, but he did call to say he'd be here in a few minutes."

Too late. She'd go to his office after her shift. "He's probably on Pediatrics visiting with his daughter."

Gayle nodded, a smile teasing the corners of her mouth. "The building is buzzing with the news that Dr. Brandon's ex-wife is going to be here very soon. She's a doctor, and she owns a medical supply company in

Houston. It seems that even though they're divorced, Neill and Lilly get along very well. Not your typical divorce in my experience."

The last person Sherri wanted to talk about this morning was Neill, and her second least favorite topic was his ex-wife. "Neill's going through a difficult time right now. I hope his daughter is feeling better."

"I do, too. Anything else you're hoping for?" Gayle asked sweetly.

"After yesterday, I'd hoped to avoid seeing Neill again, but if I have to, I will." She tapped the counter emphatically.

"I just want you to know I'm here for you if you need me, that's all." Gayle's smile was sympathetic as she answered the phone.

There were lots of people in the small town of Eden Harbor who were curious about the new doctor—especially those who remembered him as a teenager growing up in the town. And of course everyone was interested in his personal life. Only Gayle knew the whole story about how her relationship with Neill had ended. Sherri intended to see that it stayed that way. After yesterday, there was no doubt that the past was over.

Gayle made a quick note as she hung up the phone. "We've got a busy morning ahead," she said, glancing past Sherri toward the main doors leading from the hospital.

"All the more reason to keep personal issues out of the conversation," Sherri muttered. She'd worked through all the hurt and pain that loving Neill had created in her life. She would never let him hurt her again.

With determination bolstering her self-confidence, she turned as the doors connecting the clinic with the main hospital slid open and Neill strode in.

His hair was still a deep auburn that kept threatening to curl if allowed to grow too long. He carried his six-foot frame with a clear sense of authority. His presence dominated the space, and the air seemed to pulse with expectation. Facing him across the expanse of corridor, she prayed her bravery of a few minutes ago would hold.

He walked up to her, his smile warm and inclusive. "Sherri Lawson, I want to apologize for not recognizing you yesterday in the emergency room. It's just that you look…well, you look so different."

His frank appreciation sent a fluttering sensation down the length of her body. This was a man who knew his impact on women. She'd experienced that impact firsthand and had lived with the consequences. Yet, did he really believe that he could walk in here, offer her a quick apology and everything would be fine between them? "It's been…a while since we've seen each other," she said stiffly.

He was standing so close she caught a whiff of his cologne. She was acutely aware of how dark his eyelashes were against his perfectly clear skin. "And I was completely preoccupied with Morgan's emergency. But my concerns for Morgan aside, I'm so pleased to see you here in Eden Harbor. The last I'd heard you were working in Bangor."

"I've been back in Eden Harbor for three years now."

His gaze registered surprise. "That long?"

So much for wondering if he ever thought about her. She was dismayed to feel heat rising up her neck again.

There was an awkward pause caused by her inability to come up with a response that would politely put this topic to rest. Engaging in conversation with Neill could lead to complications she didn't need in her life. "You were focused on your daughter's health. I'm not surprised that you didn't recognize me. But it doesn't matter."

The lie set her on edge. His lack of interest *did* bother her. With him standing so close, forcing her to face him, she cared deeply that he made her feel somehow…less of a person. It hurt to admit that he could so easily forget her, someone he'd claimed to love twelve years ago.

Or was she looking for his approval? Did she want him to admire all the changes she'd made in her appearance? No. Definitely not. "It's only right that you should concentrate on your daughter."

"I'm relieved to hear you say that. I really didn't mean to upset you, especially when we'll be working in the same hospital."

Not for long, she thought. She'd rather work in a garbage dump than share workspace with a man whose only response to her after all these years was to worry if he'd upset her. To block any further discussion between them, she changed topics. "Have you met Gayle Sawyer? She's new to the clinics."

Neill's face was alight with enthusiasm as he moved around the desk. "It's nice to meet you, Gayle."

"Thank you. I understand you're doing Dr. Keith's clinic today," Gayle said.

"I am. Will you page me when my ex-wife arrives? I told her I'd be here instead of in our daughter's room. Lilly was supposed to meet me in Morgan's room an hour ago." He glanced at his watch.

Sherri wished she could leave, go anywhere that didn't include Neill and his ex. Still, she was a little curious to know what the former Mrs. Neill Brandon was like.

Just then the doors opened and a statuesque blonde

walked into the clinic, her chocolate-brown business suit a perfect backdrop to her flawless makeup and hair.

Neill walked toward her and they hugged. With their arms still linked, they came to the desk, stopping beside Sherri.

The woman was breathtakingly gorgeous, the kind of woman men desired.

Neill had obviously set his sights on the prettiest girl in his medical class, and he'd won her…at least for a time.

Was Neill's disinterest that fall day she'd called him, seeking reassurance that he loved her and their baby, due to his infatuation with Lilly? Or worse, had he been dating Lilly when Sherri had called to tell him she was pregnant?

She remembered that call—his shock, his distracted response, followed by his bumbling suggestion that she come to Boston. What was even more humiliating was she'd seriously considered going. If she'd found Neill with another woman… What a fool she would've made of herself. In the end, of course, it hadn't mattered.

"I'd like you to meet Dr. Lilly Russell, Morgan's mom."

Lilly smiled. Sherri smiled back. "It's so nice to meet you," Sherri said, and in the oddest way, she meant it. Somehow, she sensed that Lilly was someone who'd be a good friend, someone who would be kind to others. "How's Morgan?" she asked.

"She's doing much better. And I understand you're the nurse who was so caring and concerned about our daughter." Lilly smiled at Neill before returning her gaze to Sherri. "Thank you for everything. I wish I could have been here, but having you with Morgan and hearing Neill sing your praises was so reassuring."

How could he be such a hypocrite? He had shown

no interest in their little boy, but he could praise her nursing abilities to his ex-wife. "It was a pleasure. Your daughter is a wonderful little girl."

"She is. I've been concerned about how she'll make out with the move here. So I've decided to stay for a few days to be with her. Neill got me a room at the Way-farer's Inn on Waterside Street."

"You'll like it there."

"I'm sure I will. I'm so pleased to meet some of Neill's coworkers. For months he's hardly talked about anything other than practicing medicine here," Lilly said with genuine friendliness as she smiled at each of them in turn.

Sherri had to admit she could see what had attracted Neill to this woman. Besides being beautiful, she was outgoing, friendly and at ease with people. "We're all pleased to have Neill back with us."

Now who's being a hypocrite?

"Are both of you from here?" Lilly asked.

"Sherri went to school with Neill, but I'm new here," Gayle offered, leaning her elbows on the desk.

"Neill, you didn't tell me you were surrounded by beautiful women," Lilly teased.

Well, what do you know? Lilly didn't have the faintest clue that she and Neill had been friends for years and had dated in high school. It was nice to know just how much he'd thought of their relationship.

Once again, she was so thankful that Sam Crawford had been there for her, for her unborn child. Sam had been a wonderful man and a good husband who would have made a great dad.

NEILL COULD HAVE kicked himself for his stupidity as he watched his wife charm the two women. Seeing Sherri that morning, he'd wondered what she believed about him. Probably she saw him as a complete jerk, or worse, for not acknowledging her or giving her any indication what she'd meant to him.

In his defense, he hadn't expected to find her working in the emergency room of Eagle Mountain Hospital, not to mention being the clinic nurse this morning, at least until Mike Fennell had told him. He'd been having coffee with Mike an hour before, discussing Morgan's condition, when Mike had said something about Sherri being the nurse in Emergency yesterday.

As he stood there listening to the banter between the women, he focused his attention on Sherri, his heart hammering in his chest at the realization that she was easily the most attractive woman he'd met in a very long time. With her wide hazel-green eyes and her sun-streaked hair framing her face, she was beautiful. So different from what he remembered—the light brown hair, the large-framed glasses and a careless disregard for a few extra pounds. He'd actually found Sherri's lack of concern over her weight a relief as his mother had always been obsessed with her weight and the refrigerator reflected her rigid diet concerns. The worst possible scenario for a teenage boy who was always starving.

But he was delighted to see that Sherri had blossomed from the teenager he'd known into a woman whose body language suggested a very self-assured and confident person who knew what she wanted from life. He tried not to stare. He didn't need to add another mistake to his first one of not recognizing her.

"Well, it's been lovely to meet you both. I'm going up to see Morgan, but I'm sure we'll run into each other over the next few days." Lilly turned to Neill, her smile bright. "You'll be along when you're finished here?"

"Of course. You're all she talked about this morning at breakfast," Neill said, relieved that Lilly was there for a few days. Morgan missed her mother.

Experience had taught him that Lilly, as much as she loved their daughter, would stick around until she was assured that Morgan was being competently cared for. Once she was satisfied, she'd return to her medical supply business in Houston. Lilly had purchased the company with proceeds from her parents' estate, and she had insisted Neill move to Houston with her. That was the first major disagreement they'd had. He couldn't see himself as chief operating officer of a company any more than he could imagine living in Houston. They'd compromised; he'd stayed in Boston but had agreed to be on the board of directors.

Lilly had left Boston, leaving their daughter behind with promises of returning every other weekend and holidays and taking Morgan to Houston for her school break, most of which never happened. Parenting was not one of Lilly's strengths. Maybe it wasn't his, either, if the move had caused Morgan's seizure.

"And we have to get to work," he said, glancing from Gayle to Sherri.

"Hope your daughter is able to go home soon," Sherri said, her smile open and friendly. "Let me know if you need anything while you're here."

"Thank you, I will."

Lilly touched Neill's arm as he walked her to the connecting doors between the clinic and the hospital. "When you're finished with your clinic, we need to talk about Morgan. I'm worried about her."

"Me, too. Wait for me, will you?" he asked, feeling the weight of Lilly's concerned expression, one he knew only too well. Lilly didn't like problems, especially those that were unsolvable. When they'd first met, he'd been drawn to her take-charge approach, as had many of his classmates. They'd been dating for two months when she'd asked him to marry her. Flattered and in love, or so he had believed, he'd said yes.

Lilly Russell was a natural leader, exciting to be around back then. Now, her determination to lead, to take control, grated against his need to go slow, to be more thoughtful and circumspect about life.

But they'd continued to disregard their differences until the day they'd been forced to accept that the love and excitement had gone from their relationship. There didn't seem to be any point in blaming each other. They had their own careers. Though they still shared a friendship and a love for Morgan, loving each other had become a distant memory.

As Lilly walked through the doors, Neill turned his attention to the pile of charts on the counter. "Where do we start?"

"Follow me," Sherri said, picking up the charts.

He matched her stride as they moved down the corridor. "Sherri, it's great to see you again. I've taken over my uncle's practice," he said lamely, anxious to smooth over the obvious lack of rapport between them.

"Yes, your uncle was an excellent physician."

Was that skepticism he heard in her voice over his ability to step into his uncle's shoes? "Yeah, and now he and Aunt Mildred are enjoying retirement in Sarasota."

Sherri made no response as they moved down the corridor. Patients were waiting in each of the exam rooms. Sherri called out to several as they passed, and the warmth and compassion with which she treated each of them didn't surprise Neill. She had a gift for making people feel appreciated.

Especially the skinny kid with the doting parents whose only ambition had been to go to med school. During the months they'd dated in high school, he'd loved her most for the way she'd made him feel valued. Appreciated.

He smiled to himself as he watched her. This was her life now, and her devotion to her job was evident.

Still, being near her again reminded him of how close they'd been during their last year of school. He'd gone off to university homesick for her and the idyllic world they'd shared.

He hadn't heard from her after the short, really awkward phone call about two months after he'd moved to Boston. She'd told him she was expecting his baby, and he'd behaved so stupidly and so hurtfully, he'd been ashamed. But when he had called back to talk to her, she hadn't answered the phone. And every time he'd tried after that day, she'd refused to speak to him. She was in her first year of the nursing program in Bangor, part of the dream they'd shared, a dream about working together as doctor and nurse. When he'd left for Boston, he'd wanted her to go with him, but she hadn't made it into the nursing program she'd applied to in Boston.

After her brief call about the baby, he hadn't heard from her again, although he kept trying. Then one day when he'd called, her roommate had answered and told him Sherri had quit nursing, that she had left no forwarding phone number. He'd called her parents' house to be told she'd married Sam Crawford, a man two years ahead of them in high school and a guy Sherri had dated in tenth grade.

Wanting to congratulate her on her marriage, he'd gotten her number from her mother. When the message he'd left wasn't returned, he didn't try again. Was his pride hurt? Probably. And he'd let his busy life take over, a life he was so sure he wanted back then.

His mother had told him about the death of their baby, and then about Sam's death in a boating accident. He'd tried to phone Sherri when he heard about the baby, but she wouldn't take his call. When her husband had died, he'd tried again with no response from her. He'd tried to write her a letter, but his words about being taken by surprise, needing time to absorb what she was telling him, seemed so immature and selfish he'd torn it up. Walking beside her now, remembering the past, his neck glowed hot with embarrassment.

Back then he'd told himself he'd done everything he could to reach out to her, but he recognized what a total lie that was. He could have done so much more. Having Morgan in his life, he knew a joy he'd never known before. Yet he'd denied the same joy to Sherri by not supporting her during the pregnancy.

Being back in familiar surroundings made him remember what they'd once had between them, how he'd missed her during those early years. And now those old feelings were back. "Sherri, can we talk?"

"About what?" she asked. Her hazel eyes flared green.

He motioned toward the medical dictation room.

Once inside, he stood next to the counter. "Look, I don't know how to say this, and I'll probably get it wrong." His smile, meant to be encouraging, faltered against the stiff set of her lips. "We meant so much to each other, yet everything's changed between us... I want you to know how sorry I am."

"About what?"

He could only imagine her devastation at the loss of their child. "The...baby."

"It's a little late for that, don't you think?" Her tone was hard, uncompromising.

"Yes, it probably is," he replied, aware of the emotional distance between them. "And Sam. I'm sorry. I liked him. He... His father gave me my first job in his hardware store," he said, fumbling his words.

"Sam was a good person, a good husband."

"You didn't take his name?"

Her sadness evident, she murmured, "No. He wanted me to. I should have. His parents weren't comfortable with my decision, but they didn't say anything."

A mix of emotions, some he couldn't identify, cascaded through him. The sudden urge to touch her nearly overwhelmed him. "Look, this isn't easy for either of us, but we'll be working together," he continued, determined to say what needed to be said.

"You mean you don't want anything to interfere with our professional relationship." She stood just inside the door of the tiny room, her arms crossed. "I agree completely."

Her words sounded so cold, so impersonal, making him suddenly aware that he hadn't said what he'd meant at all. "That's part of it." He sought her eyes, needing her encouragement to continue. "I want us to meet somewhere, not here, but somewhere we can catch up, reestablish contact."

"Why?" she demanded, her eyes harboring suspicion. "What would you and I have to discuss at this point in our lives?"

"I...I didn't recognize you yesterday. I didn't mean to imply that I don't remember you. I do." Feeling suddenly very awkward, he jammed his hands into the pockets of his lab coat. "You surprised me," he blurted out.

"How?"

"I wasn't expecting to see you here."

"You thought I'd never come back here because of what happened," she said, her gaze aimed directly at him.

"Maybe…" Why did he feel so tongue-tied around her? He never used to be.

"It's been a long time, hasn't it?" she asked, her voice clear and untroubled.

"That's my point. I want us to—"

"Neill, please don't say any more. You and I have a clinic to do. Let's leave it at that."

Her voice conveyed strength, but her eyes swam with emotion. Seeing her anguish, he leaned toward her. With their bodies nearly touching in the narrow room, their heat mingling, need flared in him. He wanted to take her in his arms, awaken those old feelings. "Do you remember that night at Reef Point Lighthouse—"

"DON'T!"

His body was so close, so touchable. Sherri closed her eyes to block out the image of him, of that night— his body pressed to hers, the excitement and their happiness.

"Seeing you again has brought it all back for me," he murmured.

Did he remember that night the way she did? Their lovemaking, the raw need driven by the knowledge that very soon they'd go their separate ways to different places, all the while vowing to love each other forever.

What that night had cost her would live forever in her memory—the night she'd conceived. In the excitement of their graduation party, they hadn't used protection. When her pregnancy test had come back positive, she'd been so eager to share her news with Neill, believing he would be excited at the prospect of a child. It would be difficult to raise a baby while Neill did his medical degree and she'd have to drop out of nursing school when the baby was born, but she had faith in them, in their love. They could do it...together.

She'd called, prepared to tell him. He'd been so full of stories about his career, his hopes and dreams, none of which fit with the arrival of a baby. When she'd finally cranked up her courage to tell him, he'd acted like she was kidding him. He'd wanted to know what she wanted him to do about a baby, as if their baby was some sort of undesirable nuisance. She'd been so upset, she'd hung up the phone, convinced that she would never be able to get him to understand that she loved him and their baby.

Maybe she should've tried harder for her baby's sake. Should have called him back, given him another chance. But he'd become so involved in university life in Boston that she'd felt she no longer fit in his world. She didn't want his pity, didn't want him to feel obligated to do the right thing. Or worse, pretend he cared.

As she met his gaze, confusion and doubt stilled her heart. "It was graduation night, and we were dancing under the moon."

"And you never looked more beautiful."

Don't let yourself remember. Don't. It's not worth it. He's not worth it.

She took a deep breath, willing herself to speak calmly. "We have to get back to work."

His fidgeted with his tie, ran his hands through his hair. Mesmerized, her eyes followed his hands as she recalled the excitement of his touch.

"Sherri, I'd like to see you sometime. Socially, I mean. Dinner perhaps?"

How could he possibly think he could make up for the past and what they'd lost by inviting her out to dinner?

Yet his voice, his openness as he looked at her and his uneasy smile—they were all so familiar. She waited to see if he'd rub the back of his neck after running his hands through his hair.

When he did, a rush of feeling—long held hostage by her fear—flooded to the surface. It was as if he'd never been gone. She stepped back in shock and disbelief.

How could he still have this effect on her?

She had to stop herself from reaching for him, for everything his love had once offered her. "Dinner? That's hardly necessary," she said over the blood pounding in her ears. She leaned against the wall for support, hoping he didn't notice her apprehension.

When would she ever be free of these feelings? It had been twelve long years since she'd seen him…since he'd seen her. And still he held the power to make her want him.

"A date for coffee then. We can go anywhere you'd like. We could escape to Portland," he said, his voice flowing around her.

Searching for an easy exit, she glanced around. Several patients stood outside the room, their curiosity directed at the two of them. All she needed was for people to start talking about her and Neill—talk that could lead to questions whose answers could hurt her and her family. "Dr. Brandon, this isn't the time or place," she cautioned.

"I'm only asking for a chance to talk things out," he countered.

Why should she agree to meet him in Portland or anywhere else? What difference would it make?

"What's the point? We're professionals. We can keep our private lives to ourselves, can't we? I can."

"Sherri, you have to admit we never really ended our relationship. I went off to medical school, and you went into nursing. Then we—"

"Yes, we both made choices. We've both gotten what we wanted."

"On the professional front, but what about personally?"

"My personal life suits me just fine. Yours does, too, I assume."

He shook his head as his gaze swept the floor and then rose to meet hers. "Would you just consider going to lunch—or dinner or coffee, whatever—with me? For old times' sake?"

"What would that accomplish? We're not friends. And, as close as we once were, our past relationship is hardly a subject for conversation now."

He fisted his hands and shoved them into his lab coat pockets. "I'm not asking you to change anything, only to have a meal with me. We don't have to talk about the past if you don't want to. Let's just get together like old friends."

The despondent look in his eyes stopped her anger in its tracks. She hadn't expected him to give a damn about what was going on in her life or care whether or not they ever spent any time together. She'd expected him to behave like a big-city doctor, to treat her like he would any other nurse working with him. Instead the old Neill shone in his eyes as he continued to watch her carefully.

She couldn't help wondering if he'd missed her. Had *he* wondered why she hadn't called him again? Why hadn't he come looking for her to offer his support, if not his love?

What had hurt the most that day she'd called him had been his preoccupation with his career, as if that was all that mattered to him. Prior to that phone call, she hadn't considered the possibility that his life in Boston had changed him—that maybe he'd stopped loving her. Words she hadn't admitted to herself until she'd come to the realization of what her life would be like alone with a baby.

Had he come to regret saying he loved her once he got to medical school and became immersed in his new life in Boston? She hadn't tried to reach him over the years because her life had been tumultuous enough with having to leave nursing, getting married, the pregnancy, followed by the loss of her baby and then losing Sam. What she and Neill had shared was somehow irrelevant in her life during those years. But her mother often mentioned any news involving Neill. It would seem he'd led a life she could only imagine. During their brief love affair in high school, they'd made plans, but none as big as what Neill had planned with Lilly.

Although their plans back then had fueled their love for each other, they were only kids, filled with hope and driven by dreams. Today was their reality. They no longer shared anything worth believing in.

And now she wanted to be free to explore life outside Eden Harbor. For years she'd looked after the needs of those she loved, her patients included. She owed it to herself to put her past to rest and move on to her future.

In a matter of weeks she'd be in Portsmouth, a move she now saw as essential. In the meantime, she'd consider meeting with Neill on her own time when his nearness didn't cloud her judgment. "Let's not decide today."

A long sigh emanated from him as he reached for a chart. "If you don't want to go, just say so."

"We're in no rush, are we?"

"I'm offering you an invitation to dinner, not to the rest of our lives," he said, frowning.

So she'd annoyed him. So what? Maybe that was how he behaved in Boston, ordering what he wanted and expecting others to comply. She needed to end this conversation before one of the patients started asking questions. "Fine. I'll get back to you about dinner. Or lunch. Whatever."

His smile brightened. He leaned closer, his gaze meeting hers, his breath warm on her cheek. For a fraction of a second, she feared he was going to kiss her.

Edging away, she pressed her back against the wall.

"Now we have something to look forward to," he said, his tone charming and intimate.

Wrong pronoun! *She* wasn't looking forward to dinner with him. He must never learn that even now he could influence her so easily. She eased closer to the door. "Then let's get back to work. There are patients waiting."

Determined to maintain her distance from the one man who, it seemed, could turn her life upside down and back again, she walked out of the dictation room to the waiting patients.

Someday before she left Eden Harbor for good, when she wasn't feeling so mixed up, she'd have dinner with him and find the closure she needed. Nothing more.

HE'D NEARLY KISSED her—the second worst mistake he could've made. One dumb move after another...

He followed her out into the corridor, berating himself for doing everything wrong. Suddenly he focused on another possibility. Was there another man in her life? Had she not wanted to go out with him because she was seeing someone?

An even greater concern was the fact that she hadn't shown any interest in their past, not even when he'd given her an opening. It had to be on her mind as much as it was on his.

As they proceeded to see the patients in the clinic, her lack of communication, except when it involved a patient, made it very difficult for him to concentrate on his work. Feeling dissatisfied and completely out of his element, he finished his clinic and took the elevator to Morgan's room.

Whatever Lilly had to say would be thought-out and logical, because that was how Lilly dealt with problems. Thinking of her opened the door on his insecurities about his failed marriage.

Why hadn't he been able to be the husband Lilly needed? His parents had made marriage look so easy, so natural. He'd assumed his would be like that, as well. He'd given what he had to the relationship, only to discover that they made better friends than lovers, better business partners than life partners.

Entering the room and seeing Morgan enjoying her mother's company, he pushed aside all other concerns. "How's it going, sweetie?" he asked, hugging his daughter tight. Morgan hugged him back; the scent of her strawberry shampoo filled his nostrils.

"Good. Mommy says she's going to bring in a pizza for dinner tonight. Can you stay and have pizza with us?" she asked, her eyes intent on his face as she squirmed out of his arms.

Lilly's arrival had obviously lifted Morgan's spirits, for which he was grateful. "Absolutely."

"Mommy says she's staying for a few days, that you and her have things to talk about," Morgan said, hope brimming in her eyes.

Neill gave Lilly a questioning look.

Neill knew that Morgan wanted her parents back together, and he couldn't blame her. From Morgan's perspective, there hadn't been a problem. Her parents hadn't fought about anything; there were no big differences of opinion expressed in her presence, no passionate arguments. Just two people who should never have married one another.

But explaining the complicated dynamics of a relationship to a child who missed her mother and who needed them both was out of the question. "We do have things to talk about, sweetie. But it's much more important that you and Mommy have a great visit together."

"Maybe tomorrow when you're discharged, you can come and stay at the inn with me. It's a lovely spot, and we can rent a sailboat and go out on the bay," Lilly said, her smile encouraging as she tucked her daughter's hand in hers.

"Can you come, Daddy?"

"Your dad's pretty busy these days. He has so much to do now that you've moved to Eden Harbor," Lilly said, smoothing Morgan's auburn curls off her face, a face now clouded with sadness and disappointment.

"I want Daddy to come with us. We could have a fun day together. I'll help make the lunch. Mom, you and I can go shopping for a dessert to take with us." Morgan swung her pleading eyes from one parent to the other. "Gram says there are eagles off Cranberry Point, and I have to see them," she said.

Neill wanted to say yes with every part of his being, if only to make up for refusing her the chance for a sleepover. But the last time he and Lilly had gone on an outing with Morgan back in Boston, she'd been very upset and tearful when her mother didn't stay the night.

As much as he wanted to indulge his daughter, he couldn't risk getting her hopes up over something that would never be. With a leaden heart, he met Morgan's eager face. "I can't go tomorrow, sweetie. It wouldn't be right."

"What do you mean?" Morgan asked, her eyes wide, her lips beginning their all too familiar quiver.

Lilly edged closer to Morgan, her arm slipping around her daughter's shoulders. "Morgan, your daddy and I are divorced, which means that we have separate lives."

"That doesn't mean you can't go on a picnic, does it?" Her glance flew to her father's face. "Daddy, why can't you come just this once?"

Seeing the plea in her eyes, he wavered. What would it hurt to spend a few hours as a family to make life a little better for Morgan? But he had a day full of appointments tomorrow. "Tell you what I'll do. You and Mommy go out on the sailboat tomorrow, enjoy your day together, and I'll have dinner with you tomorrow evening."

"At our house?" Morgan bargained.

"At our house," he answered, hoping he hadn't simply added to the problem.

Lilly kissed her daughter's cheek and hugged her close. "I'm going to walk out with your dad and arrange for the pizza and then I'll be back, okay?"

"Yeah, Mom." Morgan turned to her father, her smile of joy twisting Neill's heart. "See you later, alligator."

"In a while, crocodile," he answered, playing the old word game he'd taught her as soon as she could talk. At times like this he wondered if he and Lilly should have tried harder to fix their marriage—for Morgan's sake.

Outside the room, Lilly said, "Neill, you shouldn't be so unyielding with Morgan. She only wants to spend time with the two of us together. After all, she's had a lot to deal with, considering the move and the changes in her life. She's given up her friends and all her activities to come here to Eden Harbor. I understand your need for change in *your* life, but have you thought about the impact on her?"

"I've thought of nothing else." Morgan had been a happy little girl in Boston; her only complaint was she wanted more attention from her dad. He'd assumed she'd do well with the move. He'd planned for them to lead an idyllic life in the community that had provided him with such a happy childhood. She'd have new friends and the love and attention of his mother. They'd have more time together, since he wouldn't be teaching medical students.

"Well, we certainly don't want a repeat of this," Lilly admonished.

"Morgan cannot be allowed to believe we're getting back together. That would be cruel. We have to remain firm on this or she'll continue to work on each of us," he responded, frustrated by Lilly's inability to understand that offering false hope to their daughter would only delay her acceptance of their divorce.

He glanced back at the door to make sure Morgan hadn't followed them out into the corridor. "She's constantly searching for ways to get us together. She brings you into our conversations whenever she can. She's always remarking on how you do something versus how I do it. What you tell her on the phone becomes her motto for the day."

"She obviously misses me."

"And she misses the life she had when we were married. And it's left to me to explain why that can't be."

She touched his arm. "I realize how hard this must be on you—to be the one who constantly has to remind her of the truth."

"I hate it." He ran his hands through his hair in frustration.

"Okay. Let me see what I can do. I'll talk to her again when we're out on the boat tomorrow."

"It would help if you'd see her more often. Whenever you cancel a visit, she goes into a funk."

"I'll do better. I promise."

"Lilly, I've heard this all before. Why can't you see what you're doing to our daughter? Why don't you at least try not to promise her something, then break that promise?" he asked, his voice rising.

She gave him a faintly disapproving stare.

Why did he bother trying to reason with her? Lilly would never change. Her parents had spoiled their only child to the point where she had no understanding of anyone else's needs.

But was he any different?

CHAPTER THREE

"ANOTHER WEEK OVER," Sherri said to Gayle on their way out the staff door to the back parking lot of the hospital.

"Yeah. TGIF. Tomorrow I'll go back to worrying about paying my bills. Tonight's my time-out," Gayle offered ruefully, hitching her huge black-and-silver purse over her shoulder.

They were going to a birthday party at the pub for Peggy Anderson, the phlebotomist at the clinic, and Sherri fully intended to put this particular week well behind her. She would not give Neill Brandon one thought. Not for a minute would she allow the past two days to ruin her evening. "I'll go home, get changed and pick up my gift. I'll meet you at your place in about an hour. We can walk to Rigby's from there."

"You got it."

She drove home, fed her cat, got ready and drove back along Higgins Road, pleased to see that the repairs had been completed. When she and Gayle walked into Rigby's, they were surrounded by blaring karaoke music and the smell of barbecued spareribs. Immediately drawn into the crowd of people who'd shown up for Peggy's party, Sherri felt better than she had all day.

Gayle led them through the crowd to the bar. "Where's Henry?" she asked the new guy behind the bar after ordering an apple martini for each of them.

"He's sick, got the flu or something. I mean, like he's

really sick. There've been a couple of people in the past couple of days who've come down with this flu." The bartender shook his head.

"Sorry to hear that," Gayle called over the din of voices and music.

Leaning toward Sherri as they stood against the bar waiting for their drinks, she returned to the conversation they'd begun on the walk over to the pub. "This may come under the heading of 'unsolicited advice,' but since you're not asking I'll tell you anyway. You should go out with Neill just to settle it once and for all," she said.

"Easy for you to say. How would you feel if you were me?"

"I'd want to get past it, move on, enjoy life, get to that new job in Portsmouth. But what I'd really want would be to show him just how good my life is now, how little his behavior influenced me. Would that be true?"

Would it? No. He could still turn her knees to Jell-O. All the more reason to escape to Portsmouth. "The truth really doesn't matter and neither does the past," she said emphatically, more to convince herself than Gayle.

Sherri accepted the drink offered by the smiling young man behind the bar and took a huge gulp designed to blur the image of Neill. "Didn't we agree to have a good time tonight and forget about what may or may not happen in the future?"

"We did." Gayle smiled at someone across the room. "I'm going to make the rounds, see who's here." She pointed to a group of people standing near the fireplace along the back wall. "I'll start over there. I see that new guy from Respiratory Technology. He's hot." She held up her gift. "Meet you at Peggy's table."

"Go for it," Sherri said, spotting Ned Tompkins, a

high school classmate on the stage at the back of the room singing karaoke. His voice wasn't half-bad. She leaned against the bar and listened.

As she watched, her cousin Nate Garrison slid his arm around her. "What's a beautiful woman like you doing in a place like this?" He winked.

"Old line, but I love you anyway." She stood on her tiptoes and kissed his cheek.

"Love me enough to tell me how you're doing these past few days?" He eased his cane against the bar stool and hugged her.

"You mean with work?"

"That, too."

Her cousin's inquisitiveness reminded her that he had been a very competent police officer until being shot in Boston some years before. That hadn't dulled his protective instinct when it came to her and her sister, Linda, as well as his own sister, Anna, and her two boys. One of the things she loved most about Nate was that he'd been there for her family when Ed went to prison. But as much as she loved him, she wanted to be free of any discussion involving Neill Brandon.

In his overprotective way, Nate had warned her that he intended to take a very personal interest in what happened when Neill arrived in town. "Can we skip past Neill and move on to something more interesting?"

"I ran into him the other day at the grocery store. And I decided to have a chat with him."

"Nate! Tell me I wasn't the topic of your chat."

"It gets better. I let him know that I wouldn't stand by and see you hurt again."

"You did not! Tell me you didn't!"

He nodded sheepishly.

She was *so* relieved she'd never told Nate about Neill

being the father of her child. If he reacted this way to an old boyfriend being back in town, how would he have reacted had he known the truth? "Having you don your white knight armor is not what I need right now, Nate. You've got to stay out of it."

"Oh, so there *is* something between the two of you?"

"No! I just want people to forget about Neill and me. There's nothing going on, and there won't ever be. I have my life and he has his."

"And you're okay?"

The concern in his eyes told her where he stood. Nate had been her defender since they were kids. "Listen, I've got everything under control. I'm happy, see?" She flashed him a huge smile. "You've got to mind your business on this one."

"You *are* my business." He tweaked her nose and smiled down at her. "But I'll leave it alone for now. Are you ready to party?"

"Absolutely."

"So am I."

They sipped their drinks and listened to the music until two women showed up at Nate's elbow. Although he'd never married, Nate collected women with an ease that astounded her, and his cane seemed to add to his appeal where women were concerned. Too bad that kind of talent didn't run in the Garrison genes. She'd love to have a man or two dangling off her arm, if only to erase Neill from her mind.

Snap out of it. This is a party, not a wake.

Leaving Nate to his female admirers, she chatted with several people who worked at the hospital, finally wedging herself into the crowd around Peggy. "Happy birthday." She handed Peggy her brightly wrapped gift.

"Thanks, Sherri." They shared a jostled hug. "This is

such a great party. Makes me feel so good. It's so nice to have such wonderful friends."

"Enjoy every minute of it."

"How did it go with Neill today?"

Was there no other topic for tonight? "Fine, just fine."

"Wonderful." Like Gayle, Peggy had expressed a keen interest in Neill's return to Eden Harbor.

Maybe in a community as small as this, it was only natural that he was the subject on everyone's lips—but it was driving her nuts.

After making her way back to the bar, she found herself standing with a group of people, and their topic of conversation was the fact that Neill had bought the old Gibbon property on the edge of town. Tightening her grip on her martini glass, she moved on.

Alone at the bar again, she was feeling downright depressed about her predicament when Ned Tompkins appeared at her elbow and asked her to dance. She wasn't crazy about either Ned or dancing, but she accepted, mostly to fend off any more interest in Neill and her. As they moved around the dance floor, Ned began talking about a possible class reunion now that Neill was back. She was about as interested in a reunion as she was in the invitation hinted at by the movement of Ned's hands sliding down her back.

Even after they'd stopped dancing and she'd made her excuses, Ned continued to stare at her from his perch at the other end of the bar. Ned had tried to date her when she'd first moved back from Bangor, but she wasn't interested and had let him down as gently as possible. Not because she didn't like him, she simply wasn't interested in a relationship. Feeling isolated, she glanced around to see that Gayle was happily chatting with some of their coworkers. She decided to go outside for a few minutes.

She caught Gayle's eye and pointed toward the door. Gayle broke away from her group and came over. "Are you okay?" she asked.

"I need a little fresh air."

"This isn't about Neill, is it?"

"No, of course not."

"Want me to come with you?"

"No. I'll be back in a few minutes."

She went down the front steps and out into the cool night air. The full moon reminded her of another full moon years before when she and Neill were the only two inhabitants in the world they'd created. Their months together had been so sweet, so exciting; she'd believed they'd go on forever.

A lump formed in her throat. Tears hugged her lids. *No.* She couldn't start crying. It had to be the alcohol making her teary. She swallowed and jammed her fingers into her palms.

Drawing the night air into her lungs, she began to feel her old resolve return.

Concentrate on your life and what you want out of it. You have plans—focus on that.

Lifting the hair off her neck to cool her overheated skin, she took a few steps toward the street.

Rigby's Pub had been part of downtown Eden Harbor for over a century and it boasted a beautiful view of the harbor. Tonight the view was undeniably spectacular. Moonlight danced off the water at the foot of the street, creating a black velvet sheen over the surface. Stars bathed the heavens in ethereal light.

Eden Harbor was one of the most beautiful places on earth and would always remain a part of her life, regardless of where her plans might lead her. Out here, under the night sky, she felt more in control. She was about to enter a whole new phase of her life, making tonight's scene in the bar a distant memory. Once again, she began to feel excited about her future in Portsmouth.

She was staring out over the water when a voice broke into her thoughts.

AFTER HIS CONVERSATION with Lilly, Neill had gone home to his new house, now so empty without Morgan. All the while, guilt dug into him, guilt about bringing Morgan here, guilt about letting her down when his marriage failed and now, suddenly, guilt and a sense of foreboding about the future.

During his successful career in Boston, he'd practiced medicine and taught on a part-time basis at the medical school. It had worked reasonably well until his uncle Nicolas, intending to retire, had asked him to come home. His uncle had been very persuasive, and Neill had been ready for a change in his life. Despite his success in Boston, he'd discovered that he'd missed the close connection with people that a smaller community offered. The truth was he'd returned to Eden Harbor to make a difference, to be the kind of doctor people here needed. Yet today he had to admit that he'd also returned to fill a need…to find what was missing from his life.

Tonight he was feeling a strange sense of unease as he roamed around the house, checking Morgan's room, unpacking a couple of boxes of books in his office, all in an attempt to fight a sense of restlessness and longing. Despite having had pizza with Lilly and Morgan, he was still hungry for something to help fill the strange emptiness. He opened the fridge, scanning each shelf for anything he didn't have to prepare, or maybe something sweet. There was nothing but milk and a loaf of bread.

How had that happened? No wonder Morgan wanted to spend her time at his mother's house. He needed to pay more attention to the everyday things. He had promised Morgan that she would have a good life here. He knew how nice it had been to grow up in this community. All he had to do was provide Morgan with a pleasant home environment. With that, along with his mother's loving support, Morgan would have a great life.

Maybe what he needed was to go downtown and walk around a bit. Friday night had always been the night to go into town and have a beer at one of the local bars. Grabbing his jacket from where he'd tossed it on the sofa, he left the house and strode down the road. Falling into an easy stride and invigorated by the ocean-cooled air, he began to feel more upbeat and positive.

If he was honest about it, a lot of what he was feeling had to do with seeing Sherri again. He hadn't expected to feel the way he did—gripped by an urgent need to reconnect with her. Did his feelings have more to do with his physical response to her than anything else? Or was he hoping to redeem the past somehow?

Sherri had been his best friend in high school until they'd started dating in twelfth grade. And then everything had changed. *He'd* changed. Because of Sherri, he'd become more focused, so much more in charge of his life and what he wanted from it. She'd inspired him to see a life filled with possibilities.

After she'd broken the news of her pregnancy, and he'd behaved so badly, they never spoke to each other again. Simple as that. He'd been hurt at first, and then worried, and then he'd found reason to move on—too damned self-absorbed to see that she needed him to be there for her.

But why was he thinking about Sherri? He had a daughter who needed his help in adjusting to her new life, a daughter who was ill. And if these seizures continued, he'd have to take her to Boston for reevaluation. If her condition had changed, he'd move back to Boston so she could have access to the best neuroscientists, putting an end to any concerns or interests he might have in Eden Harbor. There was no other choice.

So why did he want to have dinner with Sherri when his own future held such uncertainty? Had he invited Sherri out to dinner in an attempt to rekindle their relationship? His body flooded with warmth at the thought. But Sherri would never forgive him if he left her again, and he might have to—if Morgan had any more problems.

Beneath it all, he had to confess to a deeper problem, one that had slammed into him during those first minutes of Morgan's seizure. Despite years of medical experience, he feared being needed the way his daughter needed him. As much as he wanted to be there for her, he was afraid he wasn't good at it, that somehow in the end he would fail her, the one person in the world he loved without condition.

With his anxious thoughts ricocheting around his mind, he hadn't realized how fast he'd been walking. Suddenly he was down by the harbor, standing in front of a pub he hadn't been inside for years. As he stared up at the pirate ship facade, he saw Sherri standing on the steps, her chin raised, her gaze fixed on some point out in the harbor. She looked so completely lost he wanted to go to her.

With the moon high overhead, and Sherri there alone, he couldn't resist the opportunity. He moved toward the entrance to the pub but hesitated on the bottom step. "I didn't expect to see you here tonight."

She glanced down at him, a look of surprise on her face. "There's a birthday party going on inside." She nodded to the door behind her.

"And you're invited, but you needed a breath of air." He thought she'd never looked more beautiful than she did tonight, with the light playing off her hair, creating an aura around her face. As if drawn by some invisible force, he moved up the steps toward her.

She gripped the railing, her smile tentative. "Yes."

"I suppose the place is packed as usual."

She shrugged. "Yes." Her discomfort was evident in the way she refused to meet his gaze. "What are you doing here?"

He couldn't admit to having come to town to walk off his troubles. As he stood there looking up at her, he suddenly wanted to go into Rigby's and have something to eat, to spend time around people without any responsibility for them.

He wanted to have fun. "I suppose there are people in there I'd know."

"Yeah. Lots of them," she replied before she started down the steps toward him. Just as she reached him, she moved to the other railing and continued past him. "Good night."

Was she simply going to walk past him as if he didn't exist? He hadn't expected to see her tonight, but now that he had, he didn't intend to let her walk away. He crossed the stone steps, placing his hands on the railing in front of her. "Wait."

NEILL WAS SO close she could touch him, but all the touching in the world would change nothing. "What is it?" she asked, focusing all her attention on the harbor spreading out to the horizon in the moonlight, the gentle bob of boats tugging at their moorings, anything to avoid looking at him.

"I was hoping you might go back inside with me."

"And give everyone with a pulse reason to believe that you and I are back together?"

The moonlight heightened the expression of surprise on his face. "I hadn't considered the possibility."

In other words, nothing's changed.

He moved to the step below her, his face level with hers, the full force of his appeal threatening her self-control. "Sherri, I don't expect you to understand why I did what I did back then. But you have to admit that today has been a difficult day for both of us. Could we put aside our differences and have a drink and a bite to eat?"

She glanced up at the door to Rigby's and back at him. "I can't go back inside there with you."

"Can I ask why?"

"Because we don't have anything in common other than our work, and I won't be the subject of idle gossip. You're the lucky one, you realize."

"How's that?"

"You didn't have to face being alone while you worked out what to do about a baby the father wasn't interested in."

"That's not fair!" He scrubbed his face, ducked his head, started to say something and then stopped.

The look of sheer agony on his face had her gripping the railing to keep from reaching for him. "I'm sorry. That was cruel of me. I...I don't want to talk about this, about us. You see, until you arrived here I had my life under control. I was at peace with my past and ready to move on. With you here it's all come back. And I don't like how it makes me feel."

"Can we go somewhere and talk about this? We can't work together with so much unspoken between us. I've hurt you. I'm back, and clearly I'm not welcome in your life. I understand that."

He didn't really understand anything, but she'd already said more than she'd intended.

"Would you be willing to go up the hill to Marco's? You used to love having their meatloaf and Caesar salad with garlic toast."

"Now what made you remember that of all things?" she asked, unable to keep a smile from forming on her face. She loved Marco's Restaurant and always had. It was one of her favorite places, as much for the exuberance of Marco Speranza as for the food.

"How about it? A quick meal, no strings attached."

What could she say that wouldn't sound hurtful and mean-spirited? Neill was a good man and a great doctor, but it ended there. She supposed she could agree to go to the restaurant with him. But why should she? She wasn't hungry. She didn't need anything more to drink. "I can't."

"You won't reconsider?" he asked, stepping back away from her.

Didn't he get it? He hadn't had to give up anything or change anything in his life twelve years ago. He'd simply taken her phone call and gone back to his world of being a medical student, while her life floundered against the certain knowledge that she had a child on the way.

"I don't know what we'd have to say to each other that wouldn't leave us sitting through an awkward silence. It's been a busy week, and I need to get home. You have to appreciate just how difficult this is for me."

"I do."

He spoke so softly it felt more like a breath on her cheek than a spoken word. She would have been better off walking away than letting the feelings flushing through her hold sway. But with the moon on his hair and his eyes on her, she was beyond being able to stop any of it. "Oh, Neill, how did we get to this place? What happened to us?"

Confused, angry, hurt and now mortified that she'd asked the very question that had haunted her all those lonely nights, she gasped for air. Tears began their bitter sting against her lashes. She couldn't stand there any longer, knowing that if she did, she would succumb to his request to go to the restaurant with him.

Afraid her knees might not work, and clutching her purse to her side, she summoned her courage and began to move. She went around him down the steps and started walking back to Gayle's place.

"Sherri!" Neill called, his voice filled with urgency. "Wait!"

"Don't!" she said, tossing a warning glance over her shoulder.

She raced up the hill away from the pub, searching the night air for any sound of his feet treading the cobblestones behind her. Resisting the urge to look back, she increased her speed. When she finally reached Gayle's driveway, out of breath, her face soaked in tears, she got in her car and drove home.

ON SUNDAY MORNING, all Neill could think about was Sherri and the self-loathing that had kept him company as he'd walked back to his house on Friday night, his appetite gone and his thoughts weighed down by the idea that he had only made things worse between them.

Sherri had made it clear just how hurt and angry she still was. His only defense was that twelve years ago he was a different person—uncertain, yet driven by those uncertainties to succeed regardless of the cost. And now more than at any other time in his career, he knew the real cost of his behavior toward Sherri and their baby.

Deep down, he knew the real reason he hadn't gone to her in Bangor, and it had nothing to do with her not answering the phone. He hadn't known what to do. He couldn't have told his parents, and he hadn't known where to turn for advice. Even worse, he was ashamed at the relief he'd felt when she hadn't returned his calls.

Earlier this morning, he'd driven Morgan over to her grandmother's on his way to the hospital to check on two of his patients. He planned to return to his mother's house for lunch, and he wanted Morgan to spend time with Lilly before the meal. He'd agreed to the meeting at her place rather than at his new home because having Lilly at his house the other night had been a mistake. Just as he'd feared, at the end of the evening, Morgan had wanted her mother to stay rather than go back to the Wayfarer's Inn.

If there had ever been any doubt about whether or not he should have ended his marriage, it had been erased over the past couple of days that Lilly had been in Eden Harbor. When she'd arrived at the hospital, she'd been solicitous and supportive of Morgan and appreciative of his efforts to be a good parent, but he was coming to realize that Lilly was at her best when words were all that was required. It was a different story when actions were needed to back up the words.

When Lilly had come over for dinner, she had chatted to Morgan in between taking long calls from her office in Houston. After the third call and the tiny frown line that had formed between Morgan's eyes, he had asked Lilly to turn off her cell phone until they'd finished dinner. As she had often done in the past, she ignored his request. Lilly was driven by the needs of her business. But it also showed him how Lilly's priorities had shifted since their divorce. There was a time when she wouldn't have let anything interrupt her opportunity to spend quality time with their daughter.

What worried him most about Lilly's behavior was that she didn't seem to be aware of her impact on Morgan, despite sharing her concern over their daughter's seizure. When Morgan had pressed her about when she'd see her mother again, Lilly had been enthusiastic about having Morgan fly to Houston. She'd given no specific date, which had left an anxious expression on Morgan's face. And of course, after Lilly had left to go back to the inn, Morgan had been tearful and resentful that she didn't have a family like her newest best friend at school, Tara Williams. He'd done what he could to reassure Morgan that he and Lilly loved her, but he was beginning to worry about how well his daughter was coping. Maybe it would all be better once Lilly was back in Houston.

His shoulders tense, his eyes dry from another sleepless night, he opened the window of the car and breathed in the sea air as he turned up the street leading to his mother's house. He hoped that the rest of Lilly's visit went better for Morgan.

When he got out of the car, Morgan met him, squealing in delight. "Hi, Dad!" She giggled.

"What are you up to?" he asked. He lifted his daughter up in a quick bear hug before taking her hand in his and starting up the walk.

"Gram let me invite Tara over for lunch with us so that she could meet my mom."

"That's wonderful," he said, his spirits lifting at the sight of his daughter looking so happy. "What are we having for lunch?"

"Gram says she's making chicken fingers and French fries for Tara and me, and you guys are getting quiche. Yuck!"

"Where's Tara?"

"She's inside, talking to Mommy. They're in the living room looking at old pictures of me at Camp Wasi. Mom says I was the best swimmer that summer," Morgan said proudly.

"We'd better get in there before Tara discovers the photos of you and me clinging to the Ferris wheel for dear life."

"We weren't clinging! You maybe, but not me," Morgan said.

He opened the door leading into his mother's kitchen, and the familiar feeling he'd experienced the first day he'd moved back home assailed him. It was as if he'd never left—the same white curtains, the same green floor tiles, the same everything, including the scent of citrus and cilantro that his mother had favored for as long as he could remember.

"Hi, Mom."

She put the hot dish on the top of the stove before turning to him. "I hear you all had dinner last night. Morgan told me all about it this morning in between games of Scrabble with Lilly."

His mother's worried frown told him she wanted to

talk about Lilly, but now was not the time. "Anything I can do to help out?"

"Tara and I set the table and filled the water glasses," Morgan volunteered, an impish expression on her face. She seemed so normal, as if there wasn't any problem, and Neill caught himself wishing it were true. Yet he couldn't seem to stop watching her, wondering—as he had years before—if she was about to have another seizure, and he hated himself for seeing his daughter that way.

"We're about ready to eat," his mother said, taking a cookie sheet of chicken pieces and fries from the oven.

Just then Lilly appeared in the kitchen with her arm around Tara's shoulders. They were laughing at something, eliciting a quick glance of resentment from Morgan.

Neill hugged Morgan to his side. "Okay, kiddo, let's eat. By the way, you did a great job setting the table," he said. She hugged him back with such ferocity Neill realized he'd been right in his assessment. Morgan wanted all her mother's attention, and he could hardly blame her. Lilly had announced last evening that she would be returning to Houston later today.

Putting aside his worried thoughts as they all took their places at the table, he settled next to Morgan, focusing all his attention on her. "So, rumor has it that you not only set a great table—you're also becoming quite a cook."

"Yep." Morgan's eyes did a quick check of her mother. "I make mac and cheese from the box." She ducked her head and giggled.

"Then we're lucky to have two cooks in the house. Did you help do the cooking today?"

Morgan nodded vigorously. "I put the chicken fingers on the cookie sheet, I'll have you know," she said, her voice brimming with enthusiasm.

"So, we have you and your gram to thank for such a nice lunch."

"That you do," Donna said, her round face beaming with pleasure.

"It's so nice to be here all together," Lilly responded, her eyes meeting Morgan's.

They ate and chatted, Morgan teasing her grandmother about her lack of internet skills and how she was going to get her dad to buy her grandmother a cell phone that she could text on. Lilly left the room twice to take a call, while everyone else huddled together, laughing over another one of Tara's silly jokes. When everyone was finished, the attention turned to Lilly as she announced that it was time for her to leave for the airport.

Knowing Morgan would be upset when her mother drove away, Neill followed Morgan and Lilly out to the car. Morgan hugged her mom fiercely, her shoulders drooping as Lilly let go of her, opened the car door, got in and snapped on her seat belt. Offering a wave and a kiss to Morgan, she eased the car away from the curb and drove down the street. Morgan shielded the light from her eyes, waving until Lilly's car turned the corner and disappeared. With a too-bright smile, Morgan grabbed her father's hand and pulled him back toward the house. "Want to play Scrabble with us?"

"Sure. But can I win just this once?" he asked, relieved that Morgan had taken her mother's departure in stride. This was the first time there hadn't been tears. Could he dare hope that being in Eden Harbor and spending time with his mother was part of the reason?

"Dad, I'm not going to let you win. You have to earn

your win," she said, pointing her finger at him as they approached the door.

They settled in front of the game table with the board. A mere twenty minutes later, his daughter had won easily. "Dad! You need a dictionary!" Morgan's laugh rang out in the room as his mother and Tara clapped.

"Enough. I'm a beaten man," he teased, tousling her auburn curls. With that he got up to leave. "Are you staying here with your grandmother, or are you coming home with me?"

"Dad, can Tara come with me?"

"Why not? You guys can help me put the trampoline up in the backyard."

Morgan wrinkled her nose. "Dad! That's work!"

"That's right," he said, shepherding the two girls out the back door toward the car.

His mother followed him, a look of concern on her face. "Can I talk to you?"

"Sure, Mom." To the girls he said, "Get in the car, and fasten your seat belts. I'll be right there."

"What's up?" he asked, almost certain his mother wanted to talk about Lilly.

"I'm worried about Morgan. That seizure the other day…"

Relieved, he agreed, "Me, too, but all we can do is be supportive. She knows what to watch for, and she's a good kid."

"Do you think she's happy here?"

"She seems to be. School is going well. She and Tara have struck up a friendship. Morgan talks about her a lot."

"What happens if she has another seizure?"

"I'll take her back to Boston to be reevaluated. I won't have a choice."

"Would you move back if she needed to be near a bigger center?" she asked with a look of loneliness so profound it frightened him.

His father had passed away four years earlier, and he'd known how lonely his mother had been living without him. She played bridge and had a large circle of friends, which helped. Yet, until that moment, seeing the look in her eyes, he'd had no idea how much his mother needed Morgan, her only grandchild, in her life.

"Mom, we're here to stay. Morgan is fine. Her seizures are under control. We want to be here with you, and I'm glad to be back," he reassured her.

His mother's arms came around him, and she pressed her head to his chest. "I'll help you any way I can. Your happiness means everything to me." She stepped back as if embarrassed and smoothed her gray bob. "You go and have a good day. I'm going to play bridge this evening, but if you need me…"

She left the sentence unfinished, but he knew she would be there at a moment's notice. It had been that way all his life, and even more so when his father was alive. Because he was an only child, and they'd been married almost fifteen years when he was born, they doted on him. Thriving on all the attention, he'd let them. "Thanks, Mom."

Sherri used to tease him about how spoiled he was, how his allowance was too much, how little he had to do at home, while she always had after-school chores. But all the spoiling hadn't done him any harm, and he appreciated his mother's help.

As he stood with his mother, he realized how fortunate he was to be among people he knew and cared about and who cared about him. It was something he'd missed living in Boston, where he had none of his old friends or relatives to complete his life.

His cell phone rang. Caller ID showed the hospital. That puzzled him, since he wasn't on call, and the two patients he'd been in to see that morning were stable. "Hello."

"Hi, Neill. It's Bill Hayes, and we have a problem. I need you in here as soon as you can make it. The emergency room is full of people exhibiting symptoms suggesting food poisoning or a serious flu outbreak. We're not sure which. I've called everyone in to help."

"I'll be right there." He ended the call. "Mom, I've got to go. Can Morgan—"

"Of course."

He explained to his daughter and Tara that he had to go the hospital, eliciting long groans from them as they piled out of the car and followed him back into the house. "I'll call you, Mom, as soon as I can. You may have to go to the house and get Morgan's school clothes for tomorrow."

"Don't worry. We'll be fine. Won't we, girls?" his mother said, smiling wide.

"I owe you, Mom," he said, realizing once again how lucky he was.

"No, you don't. Now go and do your job. We'll be here."

His mind on what lay ahead, he drove down the driveway, up Orange Street and onto Tidewater Avenue toward the hospital.

CHAPTER FOUR

SHERRI HAD SPENT the weekend doing housework, cleaning rooms that were already immaculate, anything to keep from thinking about Neill. When'd she fallen into bed on Sunday night, she'd dreamed of him, each dream ending with her in his arms.

On Monday morning, she went into her shift at the clinic to discover that the hospital was turning away visitors. All the doctors on staff were working to stop the spread of a flu that had hit the town over the weekend.

Public service messages on local television and radio encouraged people to seek medical attention if they developed flu symptoms. The inpatient beds of Eagle Mountain Hospital were filled to capacity.

For the next three weeks while the flu spread through the town, she worked twelve-hour shifts, going home, sleeping a few hours and coming back to work for another twelve hours. Everyone at the hospital was working overtime, and no one complained because of the number of very ill people they had to care for around the clock.

Given the situation, she could no longer avoid Neill. They worked side by side for long hours during which he proved just how capable a doctor he was. Sharing the same need to do their best in a difficult situation, they'd slipped right back into the easy rapport they'd had all those years before when they'd been in high school. Sherri had never been happier or more content despite her constant state of exhaustion. She'd had to call Portsmouth and delay her arrival at her new job. The hospital simply couldn't spare her.

Finally, the situation had returned to normal and she was back to working full-time in the clinic. They'd had a busy day today, but Sherri had found a couple of hours to sit down in her office and start wading through the pile of paperwork she'd left undone. She rubbed her forehead, trying to ease the headache that had plagued her all morning.

She probably needed something to eat, but she was expected at a meeting to review the results of how the flu situation had been managed by the hospital and its staff. She couldn't skip it as she was taking the nurse who would replace her when she went to Portsmouth at the end of the month. She wanted to familiarize her replacement with how an emergency situation was handled and introduce her to the members of hospital management who would be at the meeting. One thing was certain, Neill would be given a lot of credit for the success of the plan they'd implemented to manage the flu outbreak.

In fact, she had to admit that Neill's knowledge and devotion to his work since his arrival at Eagle Mountain Hospital had allowed all the staff to be more involved with patient care and treatment. Neill never hesitated to confer with staff or to explain how he came to a diagnosis. The rest of the medical staff loved every minute of the time he spent with them; he treated them like members of the team.

For her part, she was just relieved that he hadn't mentioned anything about that night in front of Rigby's or the fact that they hadn't gone out to dinner. Maybe he was as relieved as she was. A niggling sense of disappointment clicked through her as she considered the possibility.

She was answering her emails when Neill appeared at the door, looking a little less tired than the last time she'd seen him. She hit the send button on her last email, glancing at him as he strode into her office. "How's it going?" she asked, shutting off her computer.

"I've just come from a meeting of the internal medicine group, and we've been discussing the clinics."

"That sounds interesting. Anything new?"

"Well, yes and no. Have you had time to consider my proposal on reorganizing the clinics?" he asked, settling into the chair across from her.

"Not yet. I've had other priorities."

"Yes, I realize that, but the number of no-shows at the diabetic clinic is worrisome. We talked about this at the meeting and concluded that we need to get more of these people in here for follow-up and education."

"One of the major problems is that many of those people work all day and find it hard to keep an appointment during working hours."

"Plus, I suspect they don't want to change their eating habits."

"Which only increases the issues around weight reduction and elevated blood sugars."

"It's a vicious circle." He rubbed his jaw in thought. "Could we consider an evening diabetic clinic?"

In the past they'd been unable to schedule an evening clinic. The doctor responsible for the clinic could rarely work evenings because of family responsibilities. "You'd be willing to run it?"

"Sure. Mom is really enjoying looking after Morgan, and she says that if I need to do an evening clinic, she'll look after her. Could we get nursing and dietitian support?"

How long had she wanted to do this? There had always been little interest by anyone but her. There seemed to be an overall sense that people with diabetes didn't require more than an assessment, with little consideration given to supporting them while they made long-term lifestyle changes. Basically, they were given a diet and appropriate medications, then sent back out into the community to fend for themselves. The trouble was, they needed a lot more than that. Most of the patients couldn't leave work to attend the daytime clinics, and without an evening clinic they missed out on further help and evaluation as they tried to keep their diabetes under control.

But with Neill advocating for improvements, there was an opportunity to change these people's lives and their family's lives, as well. "I'm sure administration will approve the nursing hours, and Melanie Waller would work with the patients on their diet. Until I find someone to do the evening nursing hours, I'll be there."

"That's fantastic! With your involvement we'll be able to make this into a really effective program," he said, his pleasure shining in his eyes.

Before she left for Portsmouth, she'd find a nurse with a special interest in diabetes to look after the evening clinic, someone who felt the same way she did about the support needed for these people. "I'll set up a meeting with Melanie, you and me, and we can decide which evening of the week and how many people we can reasonably see during the clinic."

"Great." He tapped the desk, his brow furrowed, as if he wanted to say more.

He glanced up, his eyes searching her face. She

waited for him to share his thoughts with her the way they'd once done so easily.

Stop thinking that way. You're not a teenager. Neill is not your boyfriend.

"Was there something else?"

His eyes met hers, and a tentative smile softened the lines around his mouth. "No." He shook his head. "I'm looking forward to working on the plan for the new clinic."

THE ORGANIZATIONAL MEETING went without a hitch, and a week later they were holding their first evening diabetic clinic. Sherri was delighted to be able to get this up and running before she moved to Portsmouth. Twelve people registered for it and all twelve showed up, which meant a busy evening.

Sherri was putting a final nursing note on Alice Higgins's chart when Neill came around the corner of the nurses' station with two cups of coffee in his hands. "Here, drink this. You look like you could use a little caffeine."

She did feel tired, even irritable at times. She had for weeks. "Not coffee at this hour." She checked her watch. "It's almost ten o'clock."

"I thought you were a night owl." He glanced at the pile of paperwork next to her. "You still have charting to complete. You need a little caffeine—it's the best defense against falling asleep on the job. Take it from someone who knows," he teased, putting the cup on the desk and sitting down in the chair beside her. "I put cream in it, just the way you like it."

"Thanks," she said, pleasure spiking through her at the concern he showed for her, the camaraderie that had grown between them in the past hectic weeks.

Sitting so near him, the heat of his body mingling with hers, she wanted to close her eyes and imagine what it would be like if they'd moved back together to work as a team. The number of shifts they would have worked together, the hours they would have spent in his office where she would have worked as his nurse.

Firmly shifting her thoughts back to reality, she forced a smile to her dry lips. "Yeah, I'm a night owl who needs food. I'm starving. Come to think of it, I'm always starving."

"Sorry to be the bearer of bad news, but other than a few stale crackers and a bottle of orange juice, the kitchenette is empty. I'm going to talk to Melanie about restocking the cupboards with food appropriate to the diabetic diet. What do you think?"

"That's a great idea." She looked directly into his eyes and knew that his interest in the success of the clinic and the well-being of its patients was real. "Maybe we should consider holding meal-planning and cooking classes, as well."

"I like that idea," he said, his voice warm, his smile pulling her into his space in that same old way of his.

"I've always believed we'd do a better job with our patients if we could show them how to prepare healthy meals," she said, her eyes seeking his, despite her determination not to give in to his appeal.

"Has anyone told you lately how much you're appreciated around here?" he asked, his familiar quirky smile lighting his face.

Sighing, she put her pen down and leaned back in her chair, tiredness claiming her limbs. "Not recently."

He put his hand over hers, where they rested in her lap. "You are so important to this clinic, your patients—" He hesitated. "You're a fantastic nurse. I…we are so lucky to have you here."

Lost in the moment, his words flowed around her, easing her loneliness. He was so sweet, so much like the Neill Brandon she remembered.

For a fleeting interval, she allowed herself to imagine what it would be like if they could erase their past and step back into the life they'd known as teenagers.

The gentle squeeze of his fingers on hers suspended her thoughts, slowed her pulse. She desperately wanted to lean her head on his shoulders and feel his arms around her. It had to be the tiredness that had plagued her all evening that made her feel this way. Suddenly her head swam and her stomach rolled as nausea swept over her. She pulled her fingers from his, and the sick feeling grew worse. "I need something to eat. I feel really faint."

"Do you need to lie down?" he asked, his tone worried.

"No. I…don't think so." She clutched the edge of the counter for support.

"Your color's not good. Put your head down between your knees," he ordered, his voice gentle but firm.

She lowered her head, but she still felt awful.

"Have you been nauseated like this before?" he asked, his hand on her back as he leaned closer, his other hand reaching to check her pulse.

"No," she said over another wave of nausea that made her gag.

He took her hand and pulled her to her feet, wrapping his arm around her as he ushered her toward an exam room. "Okay, it's time we checked you out."

"I'm fine," she protested.

"No, you're not." His firm grip allowed no argument as he led her to one of the clinic exam rooms.

She climbed up on the stretcher and laid down, the cool pillow beneath her head a welcome comfort.

"I'm going to check your blood pressure, and then we'll get a stat blood test done on you."

"Please don't do that. I just need to eat something."

"Maybe so, but better safe than sorry." His eyebrows twitched in concentration, his attention focused on taking her blood pressure. He unfurled the cuff and the air slid out.

"Your blood pressure's low, your color's not good and your pulse is way too fast." He touched her forehead, his hand cool against her skin, his glance analytical and professional.

She had to get out of there. The last thing she needed in her life was for Neill to be involved in her medical care. Facing him at work was one thing; having him near her in an intimate way as her family physician was out of the question. She had to leave before he offered to drive her home. She couldn't have him come home with her, a poignant reminder of what might have been. Determined to escape, she swung her legs down and sat up. "I feel much better. I'm going to go home and get something to eat. I'll be fine," she said emphatically.

"You're not going anywhere," he said, his gaze searching her face. "I want to check your throat." His tone was serious as he reached for the light on the wall and a tongue depressor.

"All I need is something to eat. I'm hungry," she protested after he checked her throat.

"You're feeling fatigued, right?"

"Yes, for a while now, but I've been so busy with the clinic."

"Have you lost weight recently?"

"Maybe a little."

"Let's see." He took her hands and eased her to her feet. "Hop on the scale."

Not with him watching. "What's my weight got to do with it?"

"If you've lost weight, it might help me determine what's going on with you."

"I don't see how," she said grumpily.

"Humor me." He led her to the scale in the corner of the exam room. "Here, get on. I won't look. Just tell me if you've lost weight."

Grudgingly, she climbed on the scale and adjusted the weights. Down three pounds. "Yeah, I've lost a little more."

"More? How much more?"

She held up three fingers.

"How much in total?"

"Nine over the past two months, but I've been trying to lose weight," she said defensively.

"Are you thirsty more often than before?"

"Yeah, I am. But it's dry in here, and I'm in this building more than I'm home," she said, making her way back to the examination table as a wave of dizziness assailed her. She grabbed the soft edge of the table, shifted her feet up onto the stool, turned and sat down as the room whirled before her eyes.

"Lie back," he said as he expertly gathered the blood-testing equipment, tightened a tourniquet around her arm and inserted the needle into the engorged vein. When he finished, he released the tourniquet and carefully put the blood samples in a webbed plastic box. He took the diabetic testing unit off the shelf next to the exam table. "Hold out your finger."

"You don't think I have diabetes."

"Let's see," he said, his tone offering her no choice but to comply with his request.

She watched as if in a dream, her mind racing over the possibilities, apprehension flooding her thoughts.

He checked the meter. His jaw tightened. "Your blood sugar is 432."

She was stunned. It had to be a mistake.

"Wait right here," he ordered, leaving the room only to return with a glass of water. "Here, drink this."

She sipped the water, feeling the coolness of it all the way down to her stomach. It felt so good. She didn't realize how thirsty she was until Neill returned with another glass filled to the brim. She drank that also.

"Do you have a ketone meter around here?" he asked.

"No. We did have one, but we ran out of strips. The clinic budget is pretty tight. We don't use them very often and they often go past their due date on us. If the doctor wants ketones done, we send the patient to the lab."

Neill observed her closely. "So let's run through this. You've lost weight. Your blood sugar is high. You're hungry, and you're tired most of the time. And now you're dizzy and feeling nauseated. I'm ordering a full workup on you. It may be that your symptoms are due to type one diabetes."

"Type one? No, it can't be. Young people get type one." His words hit hard, and her head swam as her dizziness returned. The glass nearly slipped from her fingers as she clutched the edge of the exam table and steadied her breathing.

There had to be some mistake. Surely she would have had some warning. She was a nurse and knew the symptoms.

Like a kaleidoscope, the past few weeks flashed and mutated before her eyes. She had been so tired and listless, hungry and thirsty, going to the bathroom a lot more than normal. She'd assumed that it was because of the long hours she'd been putting in at work—if she thought about it at all.

Neill had to be wrong. Her mother depended on her. Her cousin Anna, a single mom, needed her to help with the boys. She didn't have time to deal with a serious health issue, and certainly not one as complicated as diabetes. "That can't be. I'm healthy. A little tired, but otherwise fine."

"Didn't you recently have a pretty severe bout of the flu?" he asked.

She knew what he was getting at. Type one diabetes was often preceded by a viral illness. "About a month ago I had flu symptoms, but they only lasted a couple of days…I think." It was hard to remember given how busy she'd been with her job and her plans.

He took her hand, his touch warm as his gentle smile entwined itself around her heart. "Let's do the workup and be sure."

"You're not thinking of admitting me to the hospital, are you?" she asked, aghast at the idea that he'd even consider such a thing and equally determined to stop him. "All the necessary blood work can be done from my doctor's office."

He turned his high-powered gaze on her in that inquisitive way of his. "Normally, I'd agree. Do you live alone?"

"Yes," she said, feeling that she'd exposed her private life to him, shown him that she had no one special in her life. It was true, but it was also none of his business.

"Then I'd like to admit you to hospital while I do the workup. I want to know you're safe."

"Safe?" she asked, shocked at his words.

"Sherri, you nearly passed out sitting at your desk. I'm concerned that you could be in ketoacidosis. You had no idea your blood sugar was so high, and we don't know how long this has been going on. I need to see your full blood chemistry. As you know there's always a danger of a coma in these circumstances."

"Neill." Rarely had she spoken his first name aloud since he'd returned to Eden Harbor, yet it left her lips with such ease. "All that's wrong is I'm exhausted and I'm starving. Once I have a good meal, I'm certain I'll be fine."

"Listen to your doctor," he said, a teasing but kind note in his voice. "I'm not prepared to take chances with you. I'll admit you, and it will only take a couple of days to sort out what's happening."

"No, thank you. I'm not going to be admitted."

His startled glance transformed into a frown of disapproval. "Why? I'm on call tonight, and it won't be a problem to admit you. We'll get the testing done, and you could go home as early as tomorrow afternoon."

"It might be that simple for you, but not me," she argued.

"I don't understand."

She wasn't about to tell him that she was leaving Eden Harbor in a couple of weeks. Her life was private, removed from his. As nice as he'd been the past few weeks, there was no future here for her, and it was not open to discussion, especially not with him. But her most important reason rested in her medical chart. When she'd returned to Eden Harbor from Bangor, she'd brought her chart to Dr. Nicolas Brandon, her family doctor, and he'd placed all relevant test and procedure results, including the report from her obstetrician and her psychologist, in her file.

"You don't have to worry about me. It's my health, and if there's a problem, I'll deal with it. Besides, I'm not alone. Mom's just a couple of streets away from my house. If you think I need someone with me until the tests are completed, she'll stay."

Neill stood perfectly still, barely breathing, his eyes on her, his expression one of disquiet. "As your friend and coworker, I'm recommending that you be admitted, but I can't force you to do anything." He rubbed his jaw, turned away and made a notation on her blood requisition.

For a brief moment, she wished she could explain, but what would she say? She had no intention of being admitted under his care. Having him around her workplace was bad enough. Having him in a position to invade her life in other areas was out of the question. Besides, she had agreed to the blood tests he wanted. If he was right, she'd do any follow-up once she moved to Portsmouth.

"I am well aware that if I have diabetes—and that's a big if—I'll need to make changes in my life. But for now, I'm going home to have something to eat."

When he turned around to face her, the intensity mixed with concern in his eyes made her wish she could allow him to care for her. A wave of longing, an overpowering need to be cared for and the rush of memories his voice evoked nearly swept her into his arms. Thankfully, they remained separate, apart, staring at each other.

Awareness rippled through her as he took her hands in his. His eyes moved over her face, searching, the moment stretching out between them. "Sherri, please don't take chances with your health."

She couldn't listen. His words were so imbued with caring.

Then, as if awakening from a dream, Neill let go of her hands and stepped back. "I'll do whatever I can to help you," he said, his tone making his disappointment evident.

"Thanks," she said, suddenly anxious about the wedge of distrust yawning between them. She might not be interested in a relationship with him, but she trusted him and wanted him to trust her. "I have to get home now, but I will make a doctor's appointment."

He made one final entry in his cell phone before giving her his patented under-the-brows look. "You were a patient of Dr. Nicolas Brandon's."

"Yes," she said, anxiety climbing her shoulders.

"That makes you my patient now."

How could she have forgotten that? She would enter the doors of his practice for only one purpose—to retrieve her health record and take it with her to Portsmouth. She'd have to move quickly before he had reason to open her file and learn how devastated she'd been when Patrick died. Her agony over her son's death described in a clinical note made a mockery of what she'd survived, and she couldn't bear the idea that he would read about her pain and loss in a medical file. He had no right to any information about what those days after losing Patrick had been like.

The sound of his pager buzzing reverberated in the room. He checked the number before picking up the phone.

With his attention drawn to the person on the other end of the line, Sherri saw her opportunity to leave gracefully, without any further questions from Neill.

She had to get home to the peace and safety of her

condo and the comforting presence of her cat. She had beef stew she could warm up for her late-night meal. Yet, feeling too weak to move, she stared at her hands as she tried to grasp what her life would be like if Neill had made the correct diagnosis.

Her mind refused to go there. He had to be wrong— that was all there was to it.

She forced herself to move off the exam table and went to the door. A sudden sense of sadness assailed her. Was this all there was to their relationship? Two colleagues, one of whom could be seriously ill?

Whether it was the vulnerable state she'd found herself in or the late hour, she couldn't help remembering how close they'd once been, no secrets between them, nothing to get in the way of their feelings for each other.

A lifetime ago they would have worked together on her diagnosis, shared the impact of her illness. Now, her only thought was to put as much distance between them as she possibly could. Yet a part of her, once so in tune with him, couldn't simply walk out. Anxiety making her hands tremble, she turned back to face him. "I hope your night on call isn't too hectic," she offered.

For a split second their eyes met, and his loneliness rolled over her like a wave. Once more, she searched his face for any sign of what they'd once had, knowing all the while the futility of it.

His pager pealed again, and he took it out of his pocket without breaking the connection between them. "Thank you."

After he glanced at the pager number, he frowned and grabbed the phone. Watching him as he talked to the emergency department, a memory surfaced.

Twelve years ago, when she'd started nursing school while still clinging to the hope that she might not be pregnant, she let herself believe that one day they'd be working in the same hospital, maybe in the same area of medicine. She'd always assumed that working together would be part of their future, but never like this.

And never once had she considered that she might become ill or face an uncertain future. Nursing had kept her going through all those years when she was grieving her son, her husband and the family life that might have been hers.

Whatever her relationship with Neill was now, it would never be what it had been back when they believed that anything they wished for was possible. The past was truly over, and now all that was left was an uneasy friendship.

She picked up a meter and some strips and slipped them in her pocket as she turned to leave the room.

Feelings of loss and confusion propelled her down the clinic corridor to the nurses' locker room and then home. When she got there her cat, Perkins, was waiting just inside the door, his back arched, waiting for a pat. She scooped him up. The feel of his solid body and warm fur was her only hedge against the loneliness shrouding her mind.

She headed for the kitchen to get something to eat. She slumped into a chair as she tried to process what had happened at the clinic. She couldn't have diabetes. She reached into her uniform pocket and took out the meter. Quickly, she tested her blood sugar.

540! And she hadn't had anything to eat. She had no choice but to call Neill and go back to the hospital.

She started to cry.

NEILL RUBBED HIS neck wearily. It had been a busy evening so far, and it wasn't midnight yet. A long night stretched out before him, and he needed a cup of coffee, a good old jolt of caffeine. He was just about to leave the emergency department for the cafeteria when the door ahead of him sprang open and Sherri stood there, tears glistening on her face.

"Sherri, what is it?"

Sherri clasped her shaking hands together. "My blood sugar is 540."

"Follow me," he said, leading her to one of the examination rooms down the corridor. Without a word she climbed up on the exam table and looked at him; her expression mirrored his anxiety. He rechecked her blood sugar to find it was still 540.

"I haven't eaten. I'm so thirsty."

"Sherri, I want to admit you overnight. Please don't argue. I'll get your admission arranged and your insulin ordered and request more blood work. You can't go home. That's final."

"What about my cat?"

"Give me your keys and I'll feed your cat after I get you admitted."

"It's okay," she said in resignation. "Mom will take care of Perkins."

"Call her now and tell her where you are. You need to be treated before you have a dangerous health incident. You know that, don't you?"

She nodded. Seeing the uncertainty in her eyes, he fought to keep himself from taking her in his arms and telling her she'd be all right. That he'd look after her for as long as she'd allow it. Instead he said, "Then let's get you upstairs."

Haltingly, she took the arm he offered as they crossed the room and walked toward the elevator. The pressure of her fingers gave him hope that he'd made the first step in proving he would be there for her.

THE NEXT MORNING after breakfast, Neill arrived in her room. She braced herself for what she realized probably had to be bad news. She sat up straighter in the bed, feeling at once afraid and yet somehow relieved. She had no intention of having him oversee her treatment, as she would be in Portsmouth soon, and her nursing classmate there had already lined up an appointment with an endocrinologist. Her friend had also told her about the diabetic clinic they had at the Portsmouth hospital, and she planned to attend the clinic if what Neill had to say proved she had diabetes.

He opened a file and took a deep breath before meeting her gaze. In that split second the air crackled between them with unspoken emotion, confirming her worst fears. "Sherri, the symptoms you described to me and these lab results suggest you have type one diabetes. You need to start on insulin right away."

His voice was so gentle as he said the words that the air was knocked from her lungs. For the rest of her life she would remember this moment, no matter where she went or what she did. The diagnosis meant she'd have to test her blood sugar levels and learn to give herself insulin based on the results. She'd have to alter her eating habits and start an exercise plan. After that, her mind froze. What else it could mean remained to be seen.

"May I see those numbers?" she asked, trying to appear brave and in control, her shaking hand demonstrating that she was failing miserably.

He passed the paper to her, but she couldn't read the numbers through her tears. Without a word she passed it back to him, being extra careful not to meet his eyes.

"Sherri, I'm sorry."

She raised a warning hand and shook her head.

"This is difficult for you. It would be for anybody, but you do have friends and family who love you and will be there for you."

His words seemed unreal, uttered to placate rather than reassure—the response of a professional uninvolved in her life. And for the second time in as many minutes she didn't want to understand what her mind was telling her. She had diabetes and Neill was being the consummate professional.

Yet a professional approach was much better. She didn't think she'd be able to hold back her tears if he'd said anything personal. Or worse, if he'd tried to take her in his arms, she would have lost all semblance of control. And she had vowed never to lose control around him ever again.

She braced her hands on the mattress. "Yes. Mom will take this pretty hard, but I sort of warned her."

He pulled a chair beside the bed. "Sherri, if there's anything I can do…anything at all." His face was so close to hers, his eyes so clear, so aware of her.

She forced her eyes away from his and tugged the sheet up around her neck, her body flooding with heat and longing and desperation. "Thank you. I assume you'll set up the testing protocol you want me to follow and order the type of insulin you want me to take."

She closed her eyes to blank out the feelings of loss, forcing her mind to remember how he'd hurt her. She could defend herself against the attraction rushing through her, even against the thought of how different this moment would be if they were husband and wife, but his concern was threatening to slip past the protective wall she'd so meticulously built around her.

"Is there anything else I can do?"

"No. Nothing."

"Sherri, I want to help you through this. I let you down once, but I won't this time, I'm sorry—"

She held up her hands to block his words. "*Sorry* is such an easy word to say when the damage is done, and we've both moved on."

Was he really feeling guilty about what he'd done? She'd convinced herself that he hadn't felt guilty at all. Seeing him now, she couldn't help but wonder if he might have changed.

His eyes darkened. "And sorry seems to be about all I get to say to you these days."

"Not my fault." She couldn't resist saying it, anything to vent some of the anger burning in her stomach.

"I understand completely."

You understand nothing.

"This is not the time to discuss anything other than what I have to do next."

"Sherri, please let me help you."

"Why?"

He rubbed his face. "Because I can't go on like this. When we met that day in the clinic, when I asked you to have dinner with me, I was really asking for a chance to talk to you."

"Why?" she repeated.

"Because I hurt you, and I need for you to tell me everything, good or bad."

He didn't understand what he was asking of her, but she was too distraught and too tired to care any more about him or his life. Worried, she turned on him. "You left me to face raising our child on my own without a thought to how I'd do that. When I most needed your love and care and attention, I was left to face the questions of a small town where everyone knew me. I was forced to leave my career behind while you went on with yours."

He moved toward her. "But you wouldn't take my calls. And when I called your mom, she didn't seem to know anything about what was going on with you other than you were in Bangor doing your nursing program. I didn't know who else to call who might be able to reach you. Finally I just gave up. I realize that was wrong, and I should have gone to Bangor," he said calmly as he watched her.

"And why should I have taken your calls? You couldn't be bothered to come home when I told you about the baby. I needed you to help me figure out what we should do."

I wanted you to marry me. To make our love legitimate along with our baby.

"The fact that you didn't want our baby, that you would deny your son a chance to be raised with a father whose name he'd have was the act of a coward." She never thought she'd say those words out loud, but now that she had, she couldn't take them back.

"I was young and ambitious and stupid. And I made a terrible mistake. Haven't you ever made a mistake you wished you could change?"

Not recognizing the seriousness of Sam's alcohol addiction came to mind, but that was none of Neill's business. Besides, she hadn't abandoned Sam when she'd discovered the truth about his drinking. "We all make mistakes, just not ones as big as yours. You chose not to be a father, while I had no choice but to cope in whatever way I could. If our baby had lived, how do you think he would have reacted now? Would you have come back here to Eden Harbor? Would you have finally taken responsibility for your son?"

Neill covered his face with his hands. "I didn't know our baby was a boy."

"And you weren't interested in finding out, were you?" she asked, gritting her teeth, fighting to keep her anger under control.

He met her angry stare, his voice low with longing. "Sherri, please don't do this. I can't make up for the past and will have to live with that and what I did for the rest of my life."

The look in his eyes cut to her heart. "Neill, I wish you had come home to me. I wish I'd had the courage to insist that you meet me in Bangor. But I didn't dare insist on seeing you because deep inside I believed I wasn't pretty enough. I wasn't smart enough. I wasn't anything like the woman you'd want to marry. As much as you claimed to love me, I simply couldn't trust that love. And when you didn't immediately say you were on your way to me, I took that to mean you were never really in love with me."

"How could you ever believe something like that? I loved you. I wanted you in Boston with me, part of my life, but you wouldn't leave and come with me after graduation. Besides, when you called about the baby, why didn't you insist that I come home then?"

"I told you I was expecting our baby. Why wasn't that enough for you to tell me you'd meet me in Bangor?" She felt her voice begin to shake and was mortified that he might see her tears.

She'd vowed twelve years ago that he'd never see her cry, and somehow she had to hang on to her pride. Her pride was all she had left when it came to Neill. And now his pleading eyes threatened everything. The urge to collapse into his arms, forgive him and try to put the past behind her had her teetering on the edge of capitulation.

"I want to forgive you someday, to be able to look at you and realize that what we once had was worth all the pain. But what you did altered my life forever. My dreams of a life with you were lost when you rejected our son."

"Oh, God!" He ran his hands through his hair, and despite the emotional situation she couldn't help noticing the few gray hairs near his temples. "I would do anything to make it up to you." He reached for her.

She couldn't let him touch her, to feel his skin on hers, to face the reality that she wanted to forgive him, needed to forgive him. And it was only in that moment of dire pain and awash in memories that she could admit to herself that she needed to forgive him to set her heart free. "Don't. Please don't touch me."

"I'm...sorry—"

"Don't say that word! You carried on with your life while I was nearly destroyed."

No. He had no right to her secrets—ever.

He had no right to hurt her or to help her.

All that was left for her was to escape from him, from Eden Harbor, and find a new life where she might have a chance, once and for all, to drive him out. "This is all wrong," she said as gently as she could.

"What is?"

"You came here to discuss my diabetes. I need time to get used to the idea that I have a chronic illness."

"Sherri—"

"If you don't mind, I'd like you to leave while I get dressed. I want to go home."

He closed the file, got up from the chair and walked out of the room.

SHERRI WAS STILL in shock when she left the hospital later that day. When she told her mother her diagnosis, Colleen had immediately offered to stay with her for a couple of nights, just to be certain everything went okay as she started her insulin and got accustomed to testing her blood sugar.

She was taking her mom out for lunch to tell her more about the new job in Portsmouth and as a thank-you for staying with her. She'd hoped she could convince her to accompany her to Portsmouth while she hunted for a place to live, but Colleen seldom left Eden Harbor.

She found her mother's need to remain in a community whose condemnation she'd feared all these years really strange. After Ed's first arrest on drug trafficking charges, Colleen had never seemed the same. She went to her job at Leonard's Grocery as if nothing was wrong. But the quiet sobbing coming from her mother's bedroom late at night had kept Linda and Sherri awake worrying about her. The brave face her mother offered to the world had proved futile against the final humiliation when Eddie was arrested a second time in her driveway.

Determined to forget the past and move on with her life, Sherri had awakened with a plan to retrieve her patient record from Neill's office. She'd called to see if Ethel, the longtime secretary who worked in the office, would be in by ten o'clock and found out she would. What she planned to do wasn't very professional, but in her mind she had no choice.

Parking her car in the parking lot, she took a deep breath to calm her nerves. This was it. Now or never. Blocking the anxious thoughts reeling through her mind, she hurried upstairs. Ethel's smile was warm as Sherri entered. Suddenly Sherri realized that Ethel would almost certainly mention to Neill that she'd taken her chart.

She couldn't let him know the details of her problems in Bangor—the fact that she'd wanted to die and nearly had. She hadn't told anyone else. There was no way she was going to let Neill see any reference to that time in her chart, no matter what she had to do.

"Ethel, how are you?"

"I'm fine. Waiting for Dr. Brandon to come through the door. His ex-wife left a message for him. Don't know why she called here when he's always got his cell phone with him. Honestly! What is the world coming to when a good doctor like him is chained to a caterwauling piece of plastic?"

Sherri had to smile. Ethel Stairs had been a fixture in Dr. Nicolas Brandon's office for years, and everyone knew just how much she cared for him and his patients even though she often scolded him about his long hours. Neill was probably in the throes of learning how Ethel operated the office, including her need to be kept informed about everything that was going on. But cell phones had clearly usurped her position as the central monitoring device for all the doctor's activities, and the woman didn't like that change.

Ethel scanned her morning appointments, her bobbed hair sleek and perfectly groomed. "What can I do for you? You don't have an appointment."

"I know, but I need my chart to check something… the dates of past immunizations." Why hadn't she been prepared for that question? She needed to focus on what she was doing. If Neill should arrive… She couldn't let her mind go there.

Ethel tapped her fingers, their bright red tips in sharp

contrast to the blond wood of the desktop. "Immuniza-tions? Are you going out of the country?"

Ethel's suspicious expression made Sherri's palms sweat. If Ethel caught on to what she was up to... "No. I just wanted to be sure I was up to date. The flu out-break reminded me that I haven't checked—"

"Oh. You're worried, and I don't blame you. So let me find your chart. Dr. Nicolas kept excellent records." She got up and went to the filing cabinet to look for it, pulling open the appropriate drawer. "It'll only take me a minute," she said, just as the phone rang.

Ethel's indecision over whether to pick up the ring-ing phone or pull the chart made for a perfect oppor-tunity. "Go ahead and answer it," Sherri said. "I can find my chart."

The indecision gone from her expression, Ethel moved back to the desk. "You find what you're look-ing for, honey, and I'll see who this is."

Sherri quickly found her chart, the obstetrician's re-port describing her hospitalization after the loss of her son and the psychological assessment done on her, and suddenly her hands were shaking. She couldn't let Neill see the report from the psychiatrist, this humiliating proof of how completely devastated she'd been when Patrick had died. She rubbed her left wrist with her right hand. This was her past, her life, and Neill had no right to sit in his office and read it at his leisure, which he would certainly do when he made his physician's notes about her diabetes.

She lifted the file out of its file folder and shoved it deep into her handbag before gently closing the file drawer. Ethel was having a very animated conversation with someone on the phone, giving Sherri the break she needed. Holding up a scrap of paper, pretending she'd noted down her immunization dates, she waved and ducked out of the office.

She made it to the bank of elevators, her hands trembling as she hugged her purse close to her side. When the doors opened, Neill stood there, a somber expression on his face.

"Here you are." His eyebrows arched quizzically. "I was looking for you. I called your house. When you didn't answer, I called your mom's house. She said you were meeting her for lunch at the Sage Bistro. What are you doing here?"

Now what? She couldn't lie, but telling him the truth was out of the question. Feeling her chest tighten, she forced her legs to move toward the elevator.

His arm blocked her path. "Wait. Where are you going?"

CHAPTER FIVE

SHERRI WAS THE last person Neill had expected in his office today, even though she'd been on his mind. With her standing in front of him, he had the perfect opportunity to insist that she stay and see him in his office before he began returning calls. He wanted to reassure her that he'd get her in to see the best endocrinologist in Bangor as soon as possible.

"You're just the person I need to talk to," he said.

Her expression was a mixture of trepidation and defiance. Had something happened to bring her to his office this morning? He looked closer and noticed the sheen of perspiration on her forehead. "Are you feeling okay?"

"Neill, I'm sorry, but it'll have to wait. I've got an urgent…" She clutched the strap of her purse. "I have to go."

"Your mother will wait for you at the bistro."

She stepped onto the elevator and turned to press the button, her gaze fixed on the floor indicator light above the doors. "Yes, and I'm late."

He blocked the door. "I assume you've started on your insulin."

She licked her lips. "Yes."

There was something suspicious about the way she refused to meet his eyes. "Come back to my office with me." He beckoned her to get off the elevator and come with him down the corridor.

She hesitated before stepping off the elevator. "Can't we do this later?" She brushed her hair off her face, exposing her damp forehead.

He moved closer. "Sherri, you're perspiring."

She stepped back and squinted as she searched the corridor. "It's hot in here, that's all."

"It's not, and you know it. What's going on?"

She hugged her purse, her lips forming a tight line. "I—I really have to go."

With that, she strode down the corridor toward the red exit light indicating the door to the stairs. Without breaking stride, she yanked open the door and charged through it. The door slapped closed behind her.

"What the hell?" he muttered.

Sherri was upset about something, and whatever it was, he hoped Ethel would know. He walked toward his office, passing several other doctors' offices along the way.

He stopped. Maybe she'd been on this floor to see someone other than him, a doctor she didn't want him to know about. There were two family physicians' offices and a gynecologist. Had she decided to change family doctors? He hadn't thought about it before, but maybe she was uncomfortable with him being her physician. The relationship between them was difficult given their past, and she might have decided to find some other doctor to care for her while she adapted to having diabetes. He was still mulling it over when he arrived at Ethel's desk.

"Ethel, did Sherri Lawson come in here?"

Ethel glanced up, a neat frown between her dark eyes, her black-framed glasses perched on her forehead. "Yes, she did. She was here a little while ago, and I have to say that she's certainly improved her appearance.

That new hairstyle, and without glasses she looks years younger. And of course she's lost weight—"

"What did she want?"

Ethel put her pen down and pursed her lips. "She seemed anxious. She was looking for her immunization record." She glanced around her desk, her frown deepening. "I was about to get it for her when the phone rang," she said, her eyes darting from the filing cabinet to her desk.

"Why would she want her immunization record?"

Ethel shrugged. "Don't know, other than she seemed worried about the flu."

So she hadn't been looking for a new family doctor, a fact that made him unreasonably relieved. Still... Neill shook his head in disbelief. "That doesn't make any sense at all."

"Maybe not, but that's all I know about it. In the meantime..." Ethel leaned forward and grabbed a sheaf of pink message slips. "Dr. Brandon, you had a call from your ex-wife, one from the medical director at the hospital and another from a Dr. Reynolds at the Children's Hospital in Boston."

"Thanks. I'll return the calls in my office," he said, distracted by the call from the Children's Hospital and what it might mean.

He'd put a call in to Dr. Reynolds the day after Morgan's seizure. He and Lilly had chatted with him to reaffirm that he didn't see a need for Morgan to return to his pediatric neurological unit unless she had another seizure. His pulse picking up speed, he dialed the number, which was instantly answered by Dr. Reynolds.

"Hi, Neill. Thanks for getting back to me. Lilly called me, concerned about Morgan, and I thought I should check in with you and see what's going on."

"I'm surprised Lilly would have called you. She was here with Morgan a few weeks ago, and she saw how well Morgan was doing after her seizure. There's been no change in Morgan's condition since then."

"I'm glad to hear that, but Lilly did sound very concerned. She wanted to know if Morgan should be reassessed."

Neill's stomach twisted in anger. Lilly had given up any claim for custody, had basically been an absentee parent, and suddenly she was directing Morgan's care without discussing it with him. "Dr. Reynolds, I'm not sure you're aware of this, but Lilly and I are divorced and I have full custody—with Lilly's full agreement, I might add. I'm a little concerned that she would see fit to call you without talking to me first."

He was more than concerned. He was infuriated at Lilly's interference. She wouldn't have witnessed any symptoms that should have raised concern. And if she had seen anything, she owed it to him and their daughter to discuss it with him first. "In fact, Morgan is settling in well. She lives with me here in Eden Harbor. Her grandmother and her teacher are aware of the situation and if there'd been a problem, I would've been informed about it."

"That's a relief. Then you'll call me should you need me."

"I will. You can count on it." The minute he was off the phone, he called Lilly. When she answered, he wasted no time. "I just spoke with Dr. Reynolds. Why did you call him?"

"I was worried."

"Worried enough to call him, but not to stay here a little longer with your child? You know she's doing well. You had no right to go behind my back—"

"Oh, for heaven's sake, Neill. I wasn't going behind your back. I just wanted to make sure our daughter was okay. Why are you suddenly so hostile?"

Whenever Lilly turned a situation back on him, it was her way of trying to escape any blame. Lilly was always blameless, no matter what the issue. He'd learned that early on in their marriage but had been too infatuated to call her on it. Today, however, he'd had enough of her tactics. "I am not hostile. But I'm not going to tolerate this kind of behavior from you. From now on, when you want to know about our daughter, you call me. Is that understood?"

"What's gotten into you, Neill? There's no need for this," she said, her tone of disapproval unmistakable.

Lilly's disapproval didn't matter to him, and it had been that way for a while, he realized suddenly. "This call is to remind you that I am Morgan's legal guardian and I will handle any issues around her health. Understood?"

"Neill, I'm sorry. I didn't mean to upset you—"

"Then don't do it again." He hung up, knowing that he'd been rude. Yet, for the duration of that brief call, he'd felt the old frustration that had haunted his marriage. Lilly had done exactly what she wanted and left him to deal with the aftermath of her one-sided decisions. Bringing his emotions under control, he gazed around his office, at the old paintings of sailing vessels bequeathed to him by his uncle Nicolas, at the brass bookends his mother had given him his first day in the office and the photos of Morgan lined up along the credenza. All reminders that he had a new life and that the frustrations experienced during his marriage were no longer meaningful.

What mattered now was that he had to find Sherri.

AFTER A RUSHED trip back to her condo to drop off her chart, Sherri made it to the Sage Bistro in time to meet her mother. At sixty-three, Colleen Lawson was still a very attractive woman. In addition to her outgoing personality and her impeccable grooming, Colleen was kind to everyone. She truly cared about the people in her life.

Sherri's dad had died twenty years ago, leaving Colleen to single-handedly manage a large, rambling house on the edge of town—a source of concern for Sherri. But after her narrow escape from Neill's office that morning, Sherri wasn't worrying about her mother at the moment.

She'd managed to evade Neill's questions today, but there was no way she could go back to his office and face his scrutiny when he discovered her chart was missing. As for her diabetes, she was managing just fine.

Feeling the warmth of her mother's smile from across the restaurant, she made her way to the table, settling into the seat across from Colleen, which looked out onto the back courtyard of the restaurant. "I hope you haven't been waiting long," she said.

"No, not at all. I'm early as usual, and it gave me a few moments to talk to Joann Saunders about her mother. The dear woman is being placed in a nursing home out on Cranberry Point."

Needing a few minutes to catch her breath and sort through her thoughts, Sherri picked up the menu and started leafing through it. "Joann was always so good to my friends and me back when we were in grade school. I remember when I got my first allowance I went straight to her grocery store and bought a bag of potato chips."

Colleen chuckled. "How well I remember, and you still love potato chips."

"I do. I know it's a bad habit, but they're easy to eat on the run."

"I wish you'd slow down a little. With all those shifts you're doing at the hospital and your diabetes… I don't mean to be bossy. It's a mother's job to worry about her children." She touched Sherri's hand. "I'm so glad to see you. I've been waiting for a chance to tell you about my new idea."

Grateful to have something to talk about other than her health, Sherri put her napkin on her lap, and focused on her mother. "What's your idea?"

"I'm wondering if I shouldn't consider turning my house into a bed-and-breakfast. I mean it's so large, and it has those big front rooms, the library and the five large bedrooms upstairs. And now with Linda making plans to buy her own house, mine will be empty."

Linda and her two sons, Tom and Michael, had lived with her mother for the past five years after being abandoned by Linda's husband—a man who was allergic to responsibility.

As she listened to Colleen's enthusiasm over her plans for the house, Sherri felt a little less guilty about moving away. If her mother was busy, she wouldn't miss her as much. "I think you'd make a great B&B owner and hostess, and with a little planning it should be fun. You wouldn't have any trouble finding guests, of that much I'm sure."

Her mother laughed in delight. "Thank you for saying that, and for being so supportive. There are a few of my friends who think this isn't such a great idea, but they don't know how lonely it's been without your dad all these years."

"I understand, Mom. I miss Dad, too."

Colleen smiled in understanding. "Tom and Michael would be able to help me with the yard work, and one of the women down the street has offered to clean for me. And I know how to make a great breakfast. Honey, I am seriously considering this."

Sherri touched her mother's fingers. "It sounds like you've got it all thought out. Is there anything I can do to help? Paint a room, maybe? I love to paint."

"It's strange. I've thought about doing this so many times, and each time I talked myself out of it. But I finally faced up to the fact that if I'm ever going to do it, I have to get started now."

"Mom, that's part of the reason I accepted this job in Portsmouth. I need a change, and I need to see what's out there for me. I'm not getting any younger."

"Hey, don't talk like that! That's something *I* should be saying, not you!" her mother teased.

"You're right. But some days I do feel a little old."

"Whenever you feel that way, go out somewhere, go shopping, go for a walk or a jog. The feeling will pass."

"But look at you, ready to take on a whole new challenge."

Her mother sighed, her face wreathed in an expression of delight. "And there are lots of good things ahead in your life, too. I'm glad Neill was there for you. Learning about your diabetes after you moved to Portsmouth would've been so much harder."

"Yeah, it was a busy time for everyone at the hospital. Dr. Brandon was very helpful."

"*Dr.* Brandon? Don't tell me the two of you aren't back on a first-name basis."

"*Neill* was very helpful."

Her mother had fretted for weeks after the announcement that Neill was coming back to Eden Harbor. "I told you, we're fine," Sherri added.

"He's divorced, isn't he? And Portsmouth isn't all that far away."

"Don't go there, Mom. Neill and I will never be anything but friends. He has his life, and I have mine."

"I'm sorry to hear that. I'd hoped someday…" Colleen shrugged. "I wanted so much for the two of you to be together. You were so perfect for each other."

"I know you did, but it didn't work out. And I'm okay with that. Really. In fact, I wanted to tell you about my new job in Portsmouth."

Her mother frowned. "Tell me what about it?"

"For the first time in months I'm really excited about the future. My new nursing position is in risk management—it's the sort of job I've wanted for a very long time." She lowered her voice. "I have to get away from here."

"Sherri, are you doing this because of Neill?"

"Of course not. This is about me and my life," she said, trying to keep her voice even.

"I know, honey. You deserve to be happy, and I didn't mean to imply anything about you and Neill." She brightened. "Sam was a good man and you were happy together, except when the baby passed away," her mother said, her voice suddenly filled with emotion.

"Sam was a very good husband. I still miss him."

"I'm sure you do, but you can't change the past no matter how hard you try." Her mother sighed. "It's just… I still can't help wondering what your life would've been like had you and Neill stayed together. I remember how happy you both were. He adored you. I've never really understood why you broke up, and a mother can't help being curious. Do you think the two of you might date now that you're both free?"

The last person on earth she wanted to talk about was Neill, and she especially didn't want to talk about how their relationship had ended. She'd told her mother that she and Neill had drifted apart because of their course loads and the miles that separated them. Whether her mother believed her she didn't know. Obviously, she still hoped there was a future for them. After being nearly caught stealing her chart from Neill's office and worrying about all the stuff she had to do in the coming days, she was starting to get a headache. "Mom, can we let the subject of Neill rest until we've eaten?"

Her mother's expression was apologetic. "Absolutely. Let's order. Do you want a glass of wine?"

"No, thanks." Sherri touched her forehead and rubbed the back of her neck. She felt hot all of a sudden.

Colleen watched her carefully. "Did you check your blood sugar?"

"Yes, it's fine. I'm just a little tired from everything that's going on. It's been a busy few weeks." She didn't want her mother to worry about her, but she didn't feel well. "I hope I'm not coming down with the flu," she added, reaching for her water glass.

"Sherri, I'm getting our waitress over here right now so we can order," her mother said, scanning the restaurant and waving the young woman over. "You need to eat."

Sherri sighed deeply. "You're probably right."

The waitress came by then and took their order.

After she left, Colleen studied Sherri with concern. "I'm not sure you should be thinking of moving under the circumstances. Why don't you contact the hospital in Portsmouth and tell them you need another couple of weeks?"

Sherri reached across the table and took her mother's hand. "Mom, every new diabetic goes through an adjustment period, and this is mine. Please don't worry about me."

"You should come and live with me for a while, at least until you have everything straightened out where your health is concerned."

"Please don't worry, Mom," she said again. "I've got everything under control." It wasn't the whole truth, but she didn't want to worry her mother any more than she had to. Besides, diabetes was perfectly manageable, and she was an experienced nurse.

Their meal arrived, a pleasant interruption from her mother's questions. They ate and talked, and Sherri began to feel a little better. By the end of the meal, they'd made plans for Sherri to go with her mother when she discussed the changes to be made to the house with a contractor. They were just about to leave when her mother smiled at someone on the other side of the restaurant.

"Well, what do you know? I haven't seen you since you came back. Welcome home, Neill." Her mother rose, her arms extended. "Give an old girl a hug," she said.

"You'll never be old," Neill said as he wrapped his arms around Colleen.

She leaned away from him and smiled up into his eyes. "Are you here to have lunch with us?" Colleen asked.

"No, I'm here to see your daughter." Neill towered over Sherri, annoyance simmering in his eyes.

This was not a good sign. Neill Brandon was like a

hound on the scent when he got his back up about something. And it was clear he was upset with her. How was she going to get out of this mess? Had he discovered that she'd taken her chart? If he had, surely he wouldn't bring it up here in the restaurant. She glanced at her mother, who stood smiling at Neill as if she'd just been reunited with her long-lost best friend.

Why did Neill have such a devastating effect on women? There was no age limit on his charm, obviously. She considered excusing herself, going to the ladies' room and leaving from there. But that would just cause her mother and Neill to go looking for her, and how embarrassing would that be? She glanced around to see that most of the patrons in the restaurant were watching him. And then she felt Neill's eyes on her. Glancing up, she recognized the inevitable truth. He would not let her leave there without him.

Facing him, she stood up. At least that way, he was less intimidating. "You wanted to see me?"

"Yes, but after you and your mother are done with your lunch."

"Oh, we're done," Colleen said, her eyes darting from Neill to Sherri and back again, her expression hopeful. "You two run along. I'll pay the bill and head back to the house." She hugged Sherri, kissing her cheek. "Call me later, will you?" she whispered, practically forcing her into Neill's arms.

"Mom, don't go. Weren't we going to talk some more about your plans?" she asked. "And I wanted to tell you more about mine."

"Later, dear." Her mother waved as she headed toward the cashier.

As her mother moved through the restaurant, Sherri

turned to Neill. "What did you need to see me about that was so urgent?"

"You're coming with me," he said, his tone allowing no argument.

"What for?" she demanded. He may be a doctor, but he'd given up the right to make demands of her a long time ago.

"I want to see you in my office."

She couldn't go there just yet. She needed time to come up with an excuse, some reason why she'd taken her chart from his office without telling anyone. "I can't go with you. I have an appointment," she said, but it wasn't for another two hours. She intended to go straight home and go through the contents of her patient record before going to her hair appointment.

His gaze was locked on her. "When will you be available?"

"Tomorrow morning. I promise."

He checked his schedule on his cell phone. "Okay. My office. Eight o'clock sharp."

She could not let him see what was in her chart. It was her life, her loss and her secret. "You got it."

He looked as if he didn't believe her, and she really didn't care. Somehow, she had to put her chart back in his office before tomorrow morning, but how could she do that? How would she remove the information about her psychologist's report without Neill noticing that it was missing? She watched him leave, determined to put a stop to anyone ever finding out about her life in Bangor. All she had to do was hide the relevant documents and get a copy of her chart in preparation for moving to Portsmouth.

She watched as he left the restaurant. She had no intention of letting him follow her and discover she wasn't going to an appointment. Once she saw his car pull out of the parking lot, she headed out of the bistro.

When she got home, she turned off her phone, spread the file out on the kitchen table and began going through it. After an hour of careful reading, it was clear that Dr. Nicolas Brandon hadn't made any comment about her breakdown or her attempted suicide in his physician notes. The only mention was in a letter written by her doctor in Bangor in which he'd detailed her diagnosis and her eventual recovery from her breakdown. With a deep-seated feeling of relief, she removed the letter and hid it in the back of her underwear drawer.

Now all she had to do was find a way to put the chart back in the filing cabinet in Neill's office tomorrow morning—without anyone seeing her do it. But if Neill told Ethel about her appointment the next morning and if Ethel pulled the charts for tomorrow's office hours before she left today… And she would.

Ethel was extremely organized.

Darn! She had to get back to Neill's office and return the chart this afternoon before Ethel left.

CHAPTER SIX

WHEN SHE ARRIVED at Neill's office, the chart tucked into her bag, Ethel was typing on the computer, her fingers flying over the keys. She stopped and glanced up at Sherri. "Twice in a day. We've got to stop meeting like this," Ethel said in a droll tone.

Sherri smiled nervously, her fingers twitching on the outer edge of her bag. "Yeah, I have an appointment tomorrow at eight with Dr. Brandon, and I'm a little worried."

Ethel squinted up at her, started to say something and then pressed her brightly painted lips into a thin red line. "Is there something I can do for you?"

"Is Dr. Brandon in?"

"No, he's left for home. What can I do for you?"

Sherri eyed the desk but didn't see the usual pile of files for tomorrow's office hours. Maybe Ethel hadn't pulled them yet. She could only hope. "I was wondering if you have my blood results yet," she fibbed.

"Sherri, you know I can't disclose that sort of information. That's up to Dr. Brandon."

She swallowed over the panic rising in her throat. It was essential that she convince Ethel to go somewhere, to leave her desk and the file cabinet for a few minutes until she could manage to slip her chart into its proper place. But what would make this woman get up and leave the room? "I'm really worried. Could you check and see if they're on his desk? I won't ask for anything other than that. Please, I'm really worried."

Make that more like terrified.

Ethel shot Sherri an irritated look, got up, went into Neill's office and closed the door carefully behind her, but not before firing another glance at her.

Thank you.

Sherri scrambled behind the desk and pulled open the file cabinet, searching for the slot where her chart belonged. But the files had shifted... K...L...Last-man...

Finally! She yanked the file from her bag, shoved it into the slot and slid the cabinet closed.

"What are you doing?" Neill's deep baritone voice cut through her thoughts with laser precision.

NEILL THOUGHT HE'D seen Sherri in his patient file cabinet, but he couldn't be sure. All he knew was that she was standing behind the desk, looking guilty, and Ethel was nowhere in sight. "Sherri, I asked you a question."

Sherri's face was paper-white, and her fingers were trembling against the top of her satchel.

"Are you not feeling well?" He wanted to go to her, to lead her gently to a chair before she collapsed, but her eyes warned him off.

"I'm fine. I came to see—" She swallowed and glanced around. "I came to see Ethel."

Just then, the door to his office opened, and Ethel walked out. Her eyes went from him to Sherri and back to him before she spoke. "Dr. Brandon, I didn't expect to see you again today." She closed the door behind her before going to her desk and giving Sherri a warning glance. "Did you forget something?"

What were these women up to? They both looked

guilty of something. "I left my pager in the office." He turned his attention to Sherri, raising an eyebrow in question.

"I came here—" She looked at Ethel before moving around the desk toward him. "To ask Ethel for a favor, and I shouldn't have. I'm sorry."

Her expression was uncertain as she looked into his eyes. Beautiful eyes that forced him to remember a long-ago time when standing like this with Sherri was the prelude to a kiss, to a touch or a hug that would create a moment of intimacy between them that he'd never experienced with anyone else. A lifetime ago he would have placed his hands on her shoulders as his fingers worked their way up along her neck and into her hair.

"What sort of favor?" he asked, forcing his arms to stay at his sides.

"She's worried," Ethel interjected as she sat down at her desk and began typing furiously.

"Are you?"

"Of course. I wanted to see…" Her voice trailed off, and her eyes moved from his face to his chest, reminding him that he still had her lab results folded up in the pocket of his shirt.

"Can I help?"

She sighed. "No. Not really. It's okay."

"You're sure?"

"Yes," she said, her voice rushed as she checked the large black wristwatch protruding from the sleeve of her jacket. "I have to go now."

For some reason, Sherri was being very evasive. He wanted to know why but it would have to wait. He was due back at the hospital.

CHAPTER SEVEN

NEILL HAD SPENT part of the night awake, trying to figure out what was going on with Sherri. He'd let her walk out of his office aware that something was amiss. But if he had insisted on knowing, she would have told him it was none of his business.

And it wasn't, he supposed.

He got up and headed downstairs. After a hot shower and a pot of coffee to clear his head, he called her house, but she didn't answer. She had to know who was calling and didn't want to hear from him. He couldn't blame her for that. He needed to back off and give her some space and hope that she'd come to him if she needed his help.

After his office hours, when she hadn't appeared, he called the hospital but Sherri wasn't at work. He called her house again, and there was no answer. Finally, he called Colleen, who told him that she had gone to her uncle Matthew's house in Peppermill Cove about five miles south of Eden Harbor. Neill remembered Matthew Hugill, a retired train engineer and a man he had always admired.

He dropped by his mom's house and asked her to pick up Morgan from school. Thankfully, she didn't ask why he wouldn't be available because he didn't want to tell her and he didn't want to lie to her. His mother had made it clear that he needed to focus on Morgan, and he was doing that. Yet, during his long hours of restless soul-searching, it had hit him. He still loved Sherri. He had always loved Sherri. What had most attracted him to Lilly were the qualities that reminded him of Sherri. By marrying Lilly, had he settled for an approximation of Sherri? He took Fox Run Road down along the coast to Peppermill Cove, rehearsing what he wanted to say and how he wanted to say it. Of course he'd first have to convince Sherri to listen to him, and that would be the most difficult part.

As he pulled into her uncle's driveway, he spotted Sherri and Matthew down along the cliff face below the house. They were seated in bright yellow Adirondack chairs overlooking the green-blue ocean. He called and waved to them, and when they turned in unison he saw the frown forming on Sherri's face. She wasn't pleased to see him, and he'd expected that. What he hadn't expected was the wrecking ball of fear forming in his stomach.

Matthew Hugill gave him a desultory wave as they walked together up the lawn. The breeze whipped Sherri's hair into a halo around her head. When they reached him, her uncle got straight to the point. "Sherri's told me about your conversation, and she also told me things I hadn't known and have promised to keep to myself. I will, however, tell you that you will never hurt her like that again, if I have anything to say about it. You're damned lucky to have known her, let alone have her in your life under any circumstances."

Neill recoiled in shock. "I didn't— I mean, you're right," he said, looking to Sherri for support. She was staring at him, her expression calm, her hands holding her hair off her face.

Matthew put his arm around Sherri. "Do you want to talk to him, or shall I ask him to leave?"

Sherri hugged him close and buried her face in his neck. "He's here." She shrugged as she eased away from her uncle. "It's okay. And thank you for listening."

He kissed her forehead. "Anytime. You're the daughter Sarah and I never had. She's probably watching from heaven right now and sees how happy I am to have you here."

"I hope so."

Matthew hesitated for a moment, never once looking at Neill. "Then I'll leave you two to yourselves. If you need me…" he said, his sharp glance toward Neill finishing his sentence. With that, Matthew followed the path to his house, his shoulders straight, his stride strong.

"When I decided not to tell my immediate family about you being our baby's father, I had to have someone to go to for advice. Uncle Matthew helped me see that I had made my decision based on what I believed to be best for me and for my baby."

"Sorry" was on his lips once again, but he knew she didn't want to hear it, and he sure as hell didn't want to go through the sadness he felt in saying it. "I'm glad you were able to talk to him."

"Do you mean that?" she asked, looking straight into his eyes for the first time since he'd arrived.

"I do. I'd like to see us get past what happened before, and if talking to your uncle, or anyone else for that matter, will help with that, I'm all for it."

"Don't. You make it sound as if I had an illness."

"No. That wasn't my intention at all."

"Why did you come here?"

"Because I spent a sleepless night thinking about everything you said. I came here to ask you if we could go somewhere and talk this out."

She fidgeted with the ties on her blue hooded jacket. "We could sit down there." She nodded toward the chair she'd been sitting in.

He didn't feel comfortable staying there, mostly because he suspected that her uncle was waiting, ready to intervene at the first sign of trouble. "It's pretty breezy out. Would you like to go somewhere warm and have a coffee with me? We could go to Dunkin' Donuts."

She shook her head. "Too many people around."

"Why don't we go to the library, to the old reading room in the basement? It's still there, isn't it?"

"Yes. The kids are in school, so it should be quiet and fairly private. The library will work." Sherri stopped. "No, Cindy Atkinson is still the librarian. You must remember her and the interest she took in all of us?"

"Who could forget her? Okay, that's out. Where else would you like to go?"

"What about the park? We could drive up to the first lookout."

A sharp pain in his chest heralded the memory of the day they'd gone for a hike and seen an American bald eagle swoop over their heads and land on a pine tree towering above them. "I haven't been up to Acadia Park since I left home. I'd like that very much."

They both went to their cars, and as he followed her down the highway leading back along Fox Run Road, a feeling of hope and a sense of optimism surrounded him. He would find a way to work this out with Sherri because of what she meant to him, and she needed him now even if she didn't realize it. He'd screwed up before, but he would make it up to her. He would look after her and help her cope with her diabetes. She would have the best care possible. He would see to it. It wouldn't make amends for what he'd done, but it might allow them a chance to reconnect in a meaningful way.

Sherri watched him in her rearview mirror. She didn't know which was worse, the fear that he would want to involve himself in her life or the fear that he wouldn't. Everything had seemed so simple a few weeks ago when she'd first heard he was returning to Eden Harbor. She'd made her plans and had worked out how she'd deal with being around him at the hospital until she left for Portsmouth. She'd had no illusions about how hard it would be to face him. What she hadn't expected was the rush of emotion that had overcome her when she'd first seen him, or the old feelings that had haunted her every time she'd seen him since.

She couldn't wait for Friday when she'd be leaving for Portsmouth. She still hadn't packed anything. Her plan was to keep her condo for another month while she found a place in her new city. Meanwhile, talking things out with Neill might make her feel better—if she managed to remain calm. It would give them both a chance to close this chapter of their lives. Uncle Matthew had suggested that, and it made perfect sense.

They arrived at the first rest stop on the long drive up the mountain, a rest stop displaying a breathtaking view of the Gulf of Maine. Pulling over, Sherri got out and made her way to the lookout point.

"My uncle has been so good to our family," she said, her anxiousness causing her words to run together.

Neill gazed out over the panorama of evergreens and the wide expanse of water stretching out toward the horizon. "He's a good man," he said, his hands buried in his pockets.

It was so much easier to start this conversation when

his attention was on the view below. "So, let's talk. We both need to get past this point of feeling…uncomfortable with each other, don't you think? Why don't you start?" she asked, feeling ridiculously pleased that she was coming across as someone in charge. A woman with a future away from here.

"I owe you an explanation for what I did, the mistakes I made."

She maintained her quiet, in-control tone. "But why now? If you're worried I'm going to drag your name through the dirt, don't be."

"I wouldn't blame you if you did," he said ruefully.

Feeling tiny pinpricks of unease at the way his smile reached inside her to that place that had never seemed to heal, she took a deep breath. "The things I said to you yesterday and the way I've been behaving since you came back here…it's because seeing you again has brought back the old anger." Suddenly aware that she was hungry, she pulled a packet of cheese out of her pocket and broke it open. Swallowing it in one bite, she made her way to a table in the shade of a covered picnic area a few feet away.

He followed her, his shoes making a crunching sound on the gravel. "Have you gotten a chance to talk to Melanie Waller about your diet?"

"Not yet."

"You should treat yourself the way you would any other patient. You need to go over your diet with Melanie."

"Is that what we're doing here? Going over my treatment plan?"

He shook his head. "I need to explain what I did. I realize that nothing I say will change anything, and I don't blame you for being upset—"

"I don't want to blame anyone for anything, Neill. You and I have a history, that's all." Talking with her uncle was a good thing, and he was right. It was time for her to listen to Neill, especially if it would end this feeling of remorse that kept tugging at her.

He sat down across from her. "When I left you and went away to university, I was so lonely I couldn't sleep. The courses were new and hard. I had to keep my marks up for my scholarship and for my uncle Nicolas. And, of course, my parents, who were writing me weekly with all sorts of advice, sending care packages and that sort of thing. They meant well, but I was feeling so much pressure."

She thought of Neill's early calls, his voice tight with tension, their shared loneliness. "Go on."

"Your calls were the best part of my week. I missed you so much and wanted you to come to Boston with me. I was well aware of all your arguments about money, and how you needed to be able to earn a living if we were to get married. But alone in my dorm room, I couldn't understand why that was so important to you."

She'd needed to prove herself because of the shame. She was ashamed of her brother Ed's behavior, of how people gave her pitying looks when she walked by them in the grocery store. "But we had no money!"

"Yes. But our lack of money didn't change how lonely I was."

She'd had to face people who were just waiting to hear about another screwup in the family. "But that still doesn't explain why you rejected me when I called about our baby."

"All I remember about that phone call is being so distracted, so lonely, so fearful that I'd flunk out and disappoint everyone that I simply couldn't get my head

around the idea that there would be a baby to care for."
He rubbed his face with the palms of his hands, his
breathing fast and shallow. "You will never know how
hard it's been for me…what a fool I was. And you didn't
put any pressure on me to take responsibility. That's
not an excuse, not at all. But after my failed attempts
to reach you, I sank back into the demands of school,
and somehow it all seemed like a dream, part of someone else's life, not mine."

Why hadn't she stood up for herself and insisted that
he help her? At least help out financially? Why hadn't
she insisted that he do what was right for their son?

Slowly she began to see her life differently. She had
never stood up for herself. She'd been the one in the
family who was expected to prove the community of
Eden Harbor wrong.

Her dad had married a woman his family hadn't
approved of, a woman who had no money, no education and none of the social graces expected of the wife
of Edwin Lawson, son of Carl Lawson, entrepreneur
and one of the wealthiest men in the state of Maine. So
when her brother got into trouble and her sister's marriage failed, the community had felt vindicated in their
opinion of Colleen Hugill Lawson.

For her entire life, Sherri had been the one who everyone looked to when it came to acceptable behavior
within her family, and she'd let Eden Harbor decide the
standard she had to keep.

When was she ever going to stand up for herself?
When would her expectations of others equal her expectations of herself? Surely she deserved other people's
thoughtfulness and consideration as much as anyone
else. "Our baby may have felt like part of a dream for

you, but not for me. It was my life that was altered permanently, but you know that."

"Why didn't you tell people that I was the baby's father?"

"Because I was mortified that I would end up having a baby by myself. My pride wouldn't let me admit to what you'd done to me. If people knew about you, I'd end up feeling I'd done something wrong. And Mom had been through so much that I didn't want to add any more stress to her life. She needed one of her children to be successful."

His lips twisted into a wry grin. "After you called that day, I failed a chemistry test, but I couldn't have cared less. I needed to talk to you, to ask for a chance to make amends, to come up with a plan. It was such a shock for me to get a call out of the blue that we were expecting a baby, that I was expected to be a father. We'd only had sex once. When I finally got my head around the idea, I couldn't find you. Why didn't you take any of my phone calls?"

"When I made that call I never imagined that you would not come home right away. I never imagined that I would be facing the situation alone. Never," she said, the old anger writhing inside her, only this time the heat had dissipated just a little.

"Why didn't you take my calls?"

"Because once I'd made the call, I began to think that maybe you didn't really want me and the baby. You had a whole new circle of friends, and when you didn't immediately say you were coming home, I had to consider that I'd made a mistake in believing in you."

He shook his head as if trying to clear his vision. "You didn't make a mistake! Why didn't you give me a second chance?"

"Because I was alone and afraid," she said, fighting to remain calm. "I can't believe that you're making this out to be my fault—that somehow I did something wrong. You're the one who abandoned our baby, not me!"

"How do you know what I would have done?" he asked quietly. Outside the enclosure a chickadee sang its cheerful song, making Sherri wish she had the emotional strength to get up and leave.

Instead she studied her hands. "Actions speak louder than words. It's highly unlikely that you could have helped when you wouldn't even take the time to come to see me," she said, caught up in the need to defend herself against his suggestion that he would have acted differently if she'd given him a second chance.

Silence invaded the space with a vengeance as they both sat staring at each other. Somewhere off in the distance, a gull screamed. A squirrel rushed along the railing beside them as they sat so physically close to each other, yet emotionally so far apart.

"So you won't concede that you could have handled it differently?" he asked.

"Handled it differently? This wasn't a project or an exam or some random object. It was our son," she almost yelled at him. She took a deep breath and forced herself to calm down. "I managed the best way I knew how. If it hadn't been for Sam showing up in my life when I needed him most, I would have been faced with raising our child on my own. That's what I can't forgive you for. That you claimed to love me but you wouldn't come to Bangor and be with me."

"Why didn't you come to Boston and pound some sense into me? Wasn't our child worth you taking the chance on confronting me?"

"Confronting you? Begging you to reconsider your response to my phone call? How dare you try to blame me for your behavior," she said, her voice rising in volume again.

But she wanted to do more than shout. All the hurt and anger she'd pent up for twelve years burst forth. She stood up and glared down at him. "You chose to leave me on my own with our baby. Then when your marriage didn't suit you, you divorced your wife. Your life has been all about making choices that suited your selfish needs and nothing more. You're terminally spoiled, and there's no cure for that."

"Sherri! What do you want me to do to make up for what I've done?"

"Nothing! I don't want you to do anything but stay out of my life. It's too late for you to make amends. When I lost the baby, I had a nervous breakdown. I tried to kill myself! When Sam died, I thought my life was over. You cannot ever make up for any of that because you weren't around when I needed you."

Oh, God! She'd never meant to say any of those things. Now he knew her secret.

She glanced at him to see his head resting on his hands, his shoulders heaving. "Sherri, I'm so sorry. I had no idea. What a mess."

"I was so lucky to have Sam in my life. He loved me, and he loved my son. He wanted to be a good dad. Sam stood by me through it all. You wouldn't have been welcome. Sam despised you."

The air stilled. Neill remained where he was, and then ever so slowly he raised his head, his eyes swimming in tears, two tracks of moisture shimmering on his cheeks. "You're right. It's too late for my sorrow. It's way too late. I will not bother you again. I'll reconsider my decision to move back here. I'll move somewhere else. I have no right to expose you to any more hurt."

She couldn't look at him and know that her angry words had made him cry. He'd never cried in all the years she'd known him. Yet now, when it was all too late, he had shown her that he, too, could feel the kind of pain she'd felt.

"You don't have to move away. You belong back here in Eden Harbor. I'm the one who doesn't. I've made my plans. I'll be out of here soon."

Wanting to escape the whole painful mess, she headed to her car. Behind her, she heard his footfalls on the gravel. "Wait! What do you mean?" He grabbed her arm, the pressure of his fingers slowing her. "Where are you going?"

She turned and looked up into his face, at the pain she saw in his eyes, and steeled herself against the onslaught of emotions she'd fought so hard to bury. "I'm leaving Eden Harbor. It has nothing to do with you. I made my decision to leave before I knew you were coming back."

"Don't go. Please."

She stood perfectly still, her whole body wanting him, his touch, his caring, to once again experience how it would feel to be in his arms, to be part of his life, to resuscitate the dreams they'd once shared. She focused intently on the elegant balsam fir reaching toward the sky before them. "I want a life where I can start over, find out who I really am. Maybe find someone who will stand by me through whatever happens. That's all I've ever wanted. Love doesn't count—if in the end you feel alone."

He let go of her arm. His eyes, dark with emotion, remained on hers. "I wish you'd stay in Eden Harbor, but I have no right to expect you to consider my feelings. Regardless of how badly I've handled things in the past, if you should ever need me for anything, anything at all, you only have to ask."

Feeling his presence like an irresistible force, she had one thought left that mattered. "All my life I've felt I had to live up to others' expectations, to somehow prove that I could do whatever others wanted of me. In a way, that's what happened during that phone call. As desperate as I was to have you say you wanted our son, I heard the dismay in your voice, the shock.

"What if you thought I'd gotten pregnant just so you'd marry me? In that split second, I convinced myself that if you hesitated, it meant you didn't want to marry me. I wanted to prove to you that I wasn't the kind of person who would trap you into marriage, or do the unthinkable and ask you for money."

"I would never think that under any circumstances, and I'm so sorry you even considered such an idea. You know what? I felt so damned lucky when you and Sam broke up after eleventh grade and you agreed to go on a date with me."

He smiled that old smile of his that made her heart shudder. A flood of raw need stormed through her, tearing away her veneer of feigned indifference. She wanted him with every part of her being, with every breath she dragged into her lungs.

She'd made a terrible mistake in talking to him without being sure how she felt about him and without steeling herself against the unwavering appeal he exerted over her.

Despite everything that had gone wrong between them, everything she'd had to survive to hold herself together, to make a life for herself, she wanted to tell him how much she'd missed him, how much she'd hoped that they could somehow overcome their past. She was the worst kind of fool for all those thoughts, and yet they were the truth.

"You don't have to prove yourself to me, Sherri. Never. You were everything I ever wanted in my life, and I made one hell of a mess of it all. Please, don't ever feel that you have to live up to my expectations."

"Thank you," she said, her throat swollen with unshed tears.

"As for people's expectations, I came back here to live up to my family's expectations. I went to medical school partly because it pleased my parents so much. But I also did it for me, for us. I wanted the good life that being a respected physician offered. I still do, only it's different now."

"Maybe it's time we lived up to our own expectations. I plan to," she said.

"Where are you going?"

"I have a job waiting for me at Portsmouth General."

"I…" He rubbed his hand over his head. "I was hoping we might have a chance."

She couldn't let her thoughts go there, let the pain reclaim her one last time. "And there was a time when I wouldn't have considered leaving Eden Harbor, but that time has passed."

"I have no right to ask this, but would you consider changing your mind?"

"You never give up, do you?"

"I can't. Not until you tell me that you don't feel anything for me. That what we had didn't survive the damage I caused."

CHAPTER EIGHT

SHERRI HAD NO idea how she managed to drive back to town, only that she was suddenly going down Gayle's street, to the quiet little blue house nestled among tall maples and framed by a cedar hedge. So neat and orderly in contrast to her messed-up feelings. One thing she was sure of, the sooner she left for Portsmouth, the better. In spite of Neill's attempts, he hadn't done anything to show her that he'd fundamentally changed, only that he needed to ease his guilt.

Gayle was in the yard when Sherri drove up her driveway. Climbing out of her car, she called out to her friend. "Am I glad you're home! I should have called first, but I couldn't concentrate in my state of mind."

"You're so pale. And your breathing…your eyes… that look on your face. You look as if you've seen something." Gayle's anxious gaze shook Sherri.

"More like someone." Sherri settled onto the step, grateful for the warmth of the sun and Gayle's reassuring presence.

"Neill? Did you see him?"

"I had no intention of seeing him, but he tracked me down at Uncle Matthew's house. I'd gone there to talk to my uncle. I needed his advice."

"What did your uncle say?"

"I practically had to pull him off Neill when he

showed up. I don't know what possessed Mom. She told Neill where I was."

Gayle's eyes were kind. "She's probably like me. Wishing that you'd settle things between you and Neill once and for all."

"What do I have to do to convince you that it *is* settled?"

Shaking her head slowly, Gayle touched her arm. "What did Neill have to say?"

"I wonder if there isn't something wrong with him. He tried to explain why he behaved so badly on the phone that day twelve years ago. He even tried to place the blame on me, that I should have gone to Boston and forced him to acknowledge Patrick. He made a mess of things, and now he thinks that an apology can make up for his callous stupidity."

"And he probably made you feel worse, and maybe a little confused."

Sherri glanced at her friend. "When did you start reading minds?"

"What if he's sincere in wanting to make amends?" Gayle asked, her voice low.

"Being sincere and backing up your sincerity with action are two different things. If he was so sincere about it all, why didn't he come and find me back then? Why didn't he come to see me when he learned Patrick had died? Where was all this famous sincerity back then?"

"I have to admit that for an intelligent man, he acted really stupid. I didn't know you then, but if he'd come to see you before your baby was born, how would you have reacted?"

"You mean after I convinced Sam to let Neill in the door?"

Gayle nodded, her smile sad.

"I would have been furious, devastated by his lack of feeling and the fact that he hadn't been in touch with me sooner." She clenched her fists in anger, anger she didn't want to feel. She was so tired of being angry.

"And what would it have taken for him to prove that he cared, that he'd made a mistake, if he'd shown up at your door after your baby passed away?"

Sherri stopped clenching her fists and stared at Gayle. "He... I was too sick to care who was around me." She looked at her hands. "I had a nervous breakdown and I was under a doctor's care. He couldn't have helped me by then."

"Did you tell him that?"

"How could I? All this time I've managed my life without him. He shows up here and has this idea that we can be friends. I was so upset, so agitated, that I told him about my nervous breakdown. God knows I didn't plan to."

"And what did he say?"

"He cried. I've never seen him cry." She drew in a lungful of air, remembering his words. "He was so sorry, but *sorry* is his favorite word. I'm so sick of all this!"

"Would you like a glass of lemonade? I just made some and was going to have a glass when I saw your car roaring down the street."

"Was I speeding?"

"You don't know?"

Had she been that upset? "I guess not."

"Wait here. I'll be right back."

When Gayle returned, she passed Sherri a glass of the best lemonade Sherri had ever tasted. She took a long drink and let the cool liquid quiet her nerves.

"Sherri, if you don't mind me saying so, you've had so much to deal with these past few weeks, starting with your decision to move to Portsmouth, the flu outbreak and all those extra hours you put in, and then your diabetes. Are you sure that you're not just overreacting to all the pressure? Why don't you give yourself a little more time before you decide that Neill is a lost cause? That moving away is the only answer?"

Sherri had been so relieved that Gayle hadn't pressed her for details of her meeting with Neill, yet she was surprised that Gayle would suggest that stress was the cause of her unwillingness to accept Neill's apology. Of course she was stressed. Who wouldn't be? But she'd been stressed before, and she'd managed just fine. Maybe not always, but still…

"Gayle, my move is about me getting my life together, not a reaction to Neill being here. You know that."

"Yes, and I understand why you feel you need to start a new life, but are you sure that this is the time to do it?"

"Meaning what?"

"Well, you say you're okay about Neill being here, but you can't seem to come to terms with how he's behaving. There seems to be too much history between you to be ignored."

"You're probably right. But after today, Neill and I are done."

"Why would you say that?" Gayle asked.

"We talked and nothing has changed. It's that simple."

"Is it? You still care about him, despite all your protests. It's obvious that you haven't forgiven him for what he did, and that's eating you up inside."

"No, it's not! I had a hard time listening to his excuses for what he did. That's all. You would, too, if you were faced with someone from your past who had hurt you the way Neill hurt me."

A strange look passed over Gayle's face, but it was replaced instantly by a gentle smile. "Yes, you were hurt, and you've had a lot to deal with because of his abandonment, but you can't go on feeling this way. You have to find it in your heart to forgive him. And trust me, you'll feel so much better when you do."

"Forgiveness has nothing to do with it. Neill wants to make amends. He thinks that a quick fix—a polished apology and an endearing smile—will heal the past. I believe he seriously thinks that we might end up friends."

"Or more, possibly?" Gayle asked with a lift of her eyebrows.

"Any romantic relationship I have in the future will be with someone I meet in Portsmouth," she said emphatically, hoping to close the conversation around Neill once and for all.

"Why? Why can't you accept that you could be happy here?"

"Because Eden Harbor is a community of seniors, kids and married couples—not the place for me."

"What can I do to help?"

"Nothing. Right now, I just need to get back home."

"Want to stay for lunch? I can do chicken and vegetables?"

"That would be great, but I promised Mom I'd take her grocery shopping, and I need to get a few things myself."

"Will I see you back at work tomorrow?"

"You will. And thank you for everything." Sherri hugged her friend, feeling for the first time since the morning in the hospital room that she would get her life on track and figure out how to manage her diabetes. "I'm going to sign up for diabetes education classes when I get to Portsmouth."

"Isn't it ironic? You put together the program here, and now you need it yourself."

"It is." Sherri admired Gayle's absolute confidence in the idea that all of life's problems had solutions. It had been one of the reasons they'd become such close friends, and the major reason why she'd confided in her friend about her past. "I'm so glad you moved to Eden Harbor."

"Me, too." Gayle returned her hug.

Sherri headed toward her car, feeling better than she had when she'd arrived on Gayle's doorstep. Gayle hurried down the steps behind her. "Sherri, I'll miss you when you move, and I hate to think that you'll leave here so unsettled about your feelings for Neill. Please think about forgiving him. It would be best for both of you. Besides, it's the only way to start your new life in Portsmouth."

"To tell you the truth, I wish he'd never come back here, and I really don't understand why he did. He has a child whose health is a constant concern. Moving here couldn't have been the best decision for his daughter."

Gayle shrugged. "Just think about what I said. I learned a long time ago how painful not forgiving someone can be. Why not consider forgiving him and setting yourself free of your anger?"

"How do you know I'd be free of my anger if I forgave Neill?"

"Because you will have accepted his part in your past. Besides, if you're leaving here for a new life, what have you got to lose by letting go?"

For a long time, she'd never once considered forgiving Neill. She'd been so grateful to Sam for providing her with his love and support while she recovered from the loss of Patrick. But it wasn't until the day his motorboat had been found drifting in a lake in the Maine woods that she began to see what he'd really meant to her and her life.

She'd been angry at his death because she'd been left alone again. Had she let her anger decide how she would approach her life? She hadn't thought so until now, but if that was the case, she had to face her anger and let it go. Whatever the next phase of her life offered, she didn't want anger to be part of it.

ON THE DRIVE to her mother's house, Sherri thought about what Gayle had said. She still couldn't see how forgiving Neill would make a difference. Regardless of whether or not she forgave him, he was doing well enough in his new life, while she was still facing challenges in hers.

If Sam hadn't been there for her, life would have been so much more painful and difficult. To show her gratitude, she'd thrown herself into planning for Patrick's arrival. She and Sam had agreed that Patrick should have Sam's last name. And Sam had suggested that they never tell Patrick who his biological father was.

But Sherri had recognized the flaw in that argument. Neill might someday come into their lives looking for the child he'd left behind, leaving Patrick with questions. Sam had finally agreed to let Patrick know about Neill, believing that his son would never have reason to search for his birth father. In the end, it hadn't mattered.

When she reached her mother's house, Colleen had

lunch ready. "Mom, this is wonderful. I appreciate it so much. I don't know what I'd do without you."

"Well, you'll find out when you move to Portsmouth."

"Are you really okay with my decision?"

"Of course I am. You've been such a good daughter, moving home after Sam died and making my life so much easier." She turned her back to stir the soup on the stove.

"But…"

Her mother turned around. "But what, dear?"

"You can't fool me. Whenever you don't look at me it means you're not telling me how you really feel, only what you think I want to hear."

A gentle smile relaxed her mother's face. She put the spoon she'd been stirring the soup with on the counter and sighed. "I wish you didn't have to leave Eden Harbor."

"Oh, Mom, it's what I need, and you can come and visit anytime you want," Sherri said, saddened by how guilty her mother's admission made her feel.

"Please don't take this the wrong way, but we're all worried about you leaving, especially now that you have diabetes. You're much better off with your family around to look out for you."

Sherri closed her eyes and concentrated on reining in her feelings. "Isn't there anyone in my life who understands that I have to leave here? My life is passing me by while I spend my time doing what everyone else wants me to do. My needs always come second to what someone else expects from me, and it's not fair. I've done my time as a good wife, parent, daughter, aunt, niece and friend. Oh, and let's not forget ex-girlfriend."

"You saw Neill," Colleen said, her voice heavy with concern.

"Who told you?"

"Matthew. He said that you and he were in the middle of a chat when Neill arrived and insisted on seeing you."

"See, there's another reason why I want out of here. I can't do or say anything without everyone hearing about it. Can't I have a conversation with my uncle—just the two of us—without the whole world weighing in on it?"

"I'm not the whole world. I'm your mother."

"I'm sorry, Mom. It would help if people would give me a little space to sort out my problems."

"Oh, honey, I understand that this has to be a hard time for you. And I'm worried about your happiness—"

"If you're going to talk about Neill…" she warned.

Her mother's glance was apologetic. "Okay. Let's talk about your health, then."

"I have an appointment with an endocrinologist in Portsmouth who will look after my diabetes. My nursing classmate at Portsmouth General gave me the names of the various medical people I'll need when I move. I'm a nurse and I'm well trained to deal with the symptoms. Besides, taking insulin, watching my diet and getting more exercise has made me feel better already." Feeling the need to keep the conversation from veering to a topic she didn't want to discuss, she rambled on about her plans for her new life in Portsmouth, her new job and how much she was looking forward to finding a place to live. Until then, she was going to stay with her friend.

"You've certainly thought of everything," her mother said. "So why do you seem so sad?"

"I'm not sad—"

"I'm your mother, and I know the signs. It's Neill, isn't it?"

Denial almost shaped her response, but, seeing the look in her mother's eyes, she nodded, wishing she could leave and go back to her condo where no one was waiting to pry into her life.

"It must be hard on him, having complete responsibility for Morgan. After all, he's looking after a child who has epilepsy. And I don't care if he is a doctor, it can't be easy—"

"Mom! Stop! Neill's not really as responsible as he lets on. He's no saint, despite what everyone thinks. He hurt me in ways you can only imagine—"

Oh, God. What was she saying? She hadn't told her mother that Neill was Patrick's father, and it had to stay that way.

"What do you mean? You and Neill broke up after he moved to Boston and you went to Bangor. I never understood it. You seemed so perfect for each other."

"We weren't, Mom. Really. It was better that we broke up."

"So why would you say he hurt you? Did you not want to break up with him? Had he found someone else?"

From experience she knew she had to say something or her mother would not let the subject go. "Neill changed when he left here. He wanted a different life than I did. I suppose it took a separation from each other to see our differences."

"If you ever need to talk about it, I'm here for you."

In a desperate plea for understanding, she'd told her uncle Matthew the entire story a few hours ago, and now she wondered if it had been the right thing to do. What if he confided in her mother? He'd been so supportive of her mother after her father had died, and her mother had helped him find a house when he'd decided to move back to Eden Harbor. She had to believe that her uncle wouldn't say anything to anyone. "There's really nothing to tell. We grew apart, that's all."

"Come here. We both need a hug," her mother said, her embrace warm and comforting.

Colleen drew back and smoothed Sherri's hair off her forehead, an old habit that brought back a lifetime of comfort. "Let's have our lunch."

They ate and chatted about Colleen's plans for the B&B and Sherri's plans for after she got settled in Portsmouth. Despite the rocky start to her visit with her mother, she was enjoying her company. She would miss her when she left, but there would be lots of opportunities for her mother to visit, and Sherri would be home for holidays and special events. After all, Eden Harbor was only a two-hour drive from Portsmouth.

ONCE LUNCH WAS over, Sherri decided she needed to get back to her condo. She'd had so little opportunity to be by herself and sort out her feelings around everything that had happened. "I haven't had a chance to get to the grocery store in days, and I need to get a few things done before my next shift at the hospital," she told her mother.

"Oh, I wish you could stay. We could decide on the new paint colors for the house. And Linda wants to see you before you leave for Portsmouth."

"I know. I want to see her and the boys, too."

"I'll organize a family dinner."

"Maybe we can plan a girls' night out next week. Just the three of us."

"Absolutely. I'll check the movies in Portland and see what's playing."

"Keep me posted."

Her mother followed her out to the car. "Why don't you come for supper tomorrow night? I'll go to the library and get a recipe from one of the diabetic cookbooks I've seen there. I'll make us a nice meal, and we can talk some more about your move. How does that sound?"

She would miss seeing her mother every day, or nearly every day. They'd become so close since she'd moved back, and there were times when she wondered if she should leave her.

There was that old guilt again—that need to be the perfect daughter, to always put others first.

"Sounds great. See you later."

WITH SHERRI'S WORDS ringing in his head, Neill made his way back to the hospital. He'd had no idea that Sherri had had a nervous breakdown, and he'd seen nothing in her chart to indicate that she'd had one, either. But given her behavior and the hollow look in her eyes when she'd let it slip out, he had no doubt that it was true. He knew so little about her or her life, and it made him sad.

If there had been the opportunity to go straight home, he would have. But he had several very ill patients at the hospital and he hadn't made his rounds yet. Besides, he needed someone to care for, something to feel good about. He sure didn't feel good about his conversation with Sherri. What a complete jerk he'd been.

He was guilty of abandoning her when she needed him most. And all he had as a defense was that she should have tried harder to force him to face his responsibilities.

Shit. What kind of moron puts the blame on the woman he loves?

With remorse and guilt haunting his every step, he took extra pains to talk to his patients and their families while he was making his rounds. He even considered going to Emergency to see if they needed extra help, anything to ease his sense that he was disconnected from what really mattered.

He was so preoccupied with his thoughts that when he got a call from his mother telling him Morgan was waiting for him to take her to the movies, he apologized for being so forgetful. On the way home, he couldn't help thinking about his son, whose life had been so short.

If he and Sherri had been able to communicate better, how different would their lives be now? Would they have married while waiting for the birth of their son? They'd planned to marry after she finished her nursing degree and got a job. Would she have been willing to move to Boston with him until their baby arrived? How would they have managed financially? They were all questions that proved pointless now.

When he arrived at the house, his mother was waiting. "I was beginning to wonder where you were. I didn't want to call you on your cell phone because it wasn't an emergency."

"Sorry, Mom. I lost track of time."

She nodded sympathetically. "I've got to get going. It's my night to host the bridge party at my house. Dinner's in the oven, and Morgan has finished her homework."

"Thanks, Mom. I'll take over from here." They talked about his schedule for the next couple of days, and he reminded her that he had the evening diabetic clinic on Monday night and would need her then. She agreed immediately.

After his mother left, he went to find Morgan, who was reading in the den. "Mom tells me you've finished your homework."

"Did you know that Tara has a pool?"

"That's sounds like fun. How's it going?" he asked, pulling her into a bear hug as he sat down beside her.

"Great. Dad, where have you been? I thought you'd be home sooner. Did you forget that Tara and I are going to a movie tonight?"

He was about to tell her that he'd been held up at the hospital, but he didn't want to bring his work life home. Seeing how easily Morgan fit into his mother's life and how close the two of them were becoming pleased him greatly. His daughter seemed to be settling into her new life surprisingly well, and he didn't need to burden her with his troubles.

Back in Boston, he hadn't shared much of how he felt with Morgan because he'd been so busy. But after listening to Sherri today, he worried that he wasn't a good parent and that bringing his daughter here had been a mistake as far as their relationship was concerned. "I'm here now."

Morgan closed her book and put it on the shelf next to the sofa. "Dad, Tara told me a story today about someone named Sherri. She said she was your girlfriend when you lived here before. I asked Gram about her, and she told me to ask you."

"Yeah, I went to high school with her before I went to Boston."

"Did you love her?"

His daughter's direct gaze forced the truth from him. "Yes, I did."

Morgan's brows knotted together. "So, why didn't you marry her?"

"I was young and so was she."

"Where does she live?" his daughter asked. "Do I know her?"

"Do you remember the day you were in Emergency?" Morgan nodded.

"She was the nurse who looked after you."

"But I don't remember very much about her. What is she like? Do you want to date her?"

"It might be nice. What would you think about that?"

Morgan's eyes suddenly glistened with tears. "I wish Mommy was here. I miss her."

"I know, sweetie. I know," he said, smoothing her hair as he hugged Morgan close. "Tell you what. Why don't I get dinner out of the oven?"

"Yes! I'm starving. All I had was an apple after school," Morgan said, clinging to him.

"Well, let's see what Grandma made us," he said as Morgan trailed along behind him into the mammoth kitchen. He'd always loved this house, the kitchen especially. He'd done deliveries for Crawford's Hardware store to this house when he was a teenager, and many times he'd delivered building supplies to the old barn at the back of the property.

Morgan helped Neill set the table as they'd done many times before, a comforting routine that eased his worried mind. Watching his daughter move so gracefully across the kitchen, he was amazed at how mature she seemed for a nine-year-old. They ate dinner while Morgan told him about her day, about art class and how much she loved to paint. When they finished, he gathered the dishes and put them in the dishwasher. "Why don't you go upstairs and brush your teeth while I finish up here."

She turned back to him, her expression so like her mother's. "Dad, I really like living here. And Tara is a really good friend."

"I'm glad to hear that," he said, a lump rising in his throat. Was it possible that his worries over his daughter were over, for now at least?

At the bottom of the stairs, Morgan hesitated. "Dad, you're not really going to date her, are you?"

Oh, no. He didn't want to talk about this because he knew from experience that anything relating to his private life always led to Morgan getting upset. Thankfully, his pager put an end to the discussion. He took it off his belt, infinitely relieved that the device had saved him. "I've got to make a call."

"What about the movie? And don't forget I want popcorn with extra butter, and we have to pick up Tara on the way."

He'd never been so relieved in his life to be reminded that Morgan had invited a friend to the movies. "I know. Get your jacket, and we'll stop for Tara, but you two will have to wait in the car while I make a quick stop at the hospital."

"Dad, I'm beginning to worry about you."

"Why?"

"You're getting so forgetful. You forgot we were picking up Tara—I know you did. That's why you have that worried look on. You think you're losing it."

"I do not!"

"Good old Dad. Should I be checking for gray hairs?" she teased.

"Not unless you want me to tell your friends you still sleep with a stuffed dinosaur."

She scrunched up her face and then sighed in capitulation. "Okay, Dad, you win. Last one to the car—"

"Has to take the laundry down to the washer," he finished.

She stopped and looked up into his face, her sweet innocent smile stilling his thoughts. "Dad, when can I meet Sherri?"

"Not right now, unless you want to miss the movie."

"No!" Morgan's face was wreathed in happiness. "Dad, am I going to be an only child?"

Morgan could change topics so rapidly. "Do you worry about being an only child?" he asked while he thought about her question.

"Of course. All kids do. Why don't you give it a little thought, Dad? There's still time for you to have a baby, right?"

"There's still time," he admitted.

"All you have to do is find a woman," she said, her giggles muffled by the jacket she pulled on over her shoulders as she climbed into the backseat of the car. "That shouldn't be too hard."

"Who'd want to put up with the hours I keep at the hospital and at the office?" he asked, hoping to end the discussion.

"There are lots of women, Dad. One of the girls in my class asked me if her mom could meet you. She's not a patient of yours, but she wants to be. That is, if you're taking new patients. Are you, Dad?"

"Maybe. I'm just not sure I want to date any of them."

"Get with it, Dad. This kid in school showed me a picture of her mother, and she's almost as pretty as Mom."

Was Morgan serious? Had she changed her attitude

about wanting her parents to get back together? "What would you think if I started dating someone?"

There was silence in the backseat. "It's not like you'd be marrying her, would it? Mom says you're too busy to be serious about a woman, and she's right," Morgan said, a smug tone in her voice.

CHAPTER NINE

As UPSET AS Sherri had been after her encounter with Neill, she was relieved to be doing her last evening diabetic clinic tonight. Neill was the doctor doing the medical assessments, but she'd handle that. Somehow their best time together always occurred at the hospital.

Four days and counting—four days until my escape from Eden Harbor.

Sherri had been talking to the group about other healthy lifestyle choices that diabetics could make to improve their quality of life, and she was really enjoying the class. Not only was the group listening intently to her, but what she was teaching had a practical application in her own life. She could relate so much better to the others now that she was in the same boat as them. The class would be over in a couple of minutes and she was truly sorry.

"So, we've gone over the benefits of exercise, and the dietitian went over healthy food choices, so that brings us to skin care. Would anyone like to share what they've learned about taking care of their skin in relation to their diabetes?"

Mr. Summerville, one of the older men at the back of the room, spoke up. "I see a podiatrist every month to make sure my feet are in good shape, that I haven't developed a sore spot that could lead to a skin ulcer."

She nodded her head as she listened. Having people

in the class who wanted to participate made it pleasant and rewarding. "And why do you need to do that?" She glanced around the room. "Why do all of us with diabetes need to take care of our skin to prevent pressure spots?"

The room went silent. After a few moments, a man named Larry asked, "Are you saying you're one of us? Do you have diabetes?"

The words had slipped out so easily that she hadn't realized what she'd said. At first she felt self-conscious, but looking around the room at so many familiar faces, she began to see that she could be a role model for them. "Yes, I was diagnosed a few days ago. And I'm just beginning to understand how many changes I will have to make in my daily routine." The entire class was watching her, some with a look of concern, others with sympathy. "I have to tell you that I've developed a whole new appreciation for what each of you is going through...have gone through."

"And it ain't over yet," Marty Butler piped up, making everyone in the room laugh. "Welcome aboard the train to Diabetesville. And let me tell you it's a lot of learning, especially when you first start insulin. Take me, for instance. I can't have a drink of wine without my sugar going through the ceiling."

Her insulin therapy was going well, and her blood sugar was less erratic than the first few times she'd tested it.

"You're so right, Marty. I'm just beginning to really take it all in. Thanks, and I mean it. You are an amazing group of people."

After the class ended, the group converged on the front of the classroom, everyone wanting to add his or her own ideas on how to cope with her situation. Some were anxious to know if she had type one or type two diabetes. At first the questions felt a little invasive, but before long she began to feel part of the group in an entirely different way.

After the class, feeling especially satisfied with the evening's success, she made her way to the nurses' desk and began making notes for the nurse who would be replacing her about where she should begin the next evening class with this group. She was consulting the teaching syllabus when she sensed someone standing behind her.

"Dr. Brandon, hi. Can I do something for you?" she asked, congratulating herself on keeping a professional tone in her voice. They'd been studiously avoiding each other all evening, by mutual consent it would seem.

"I have something I need to discuss with you," he said, his tone equally professional.

She put her pen down and crossed her arms over her chest. "If it's about the other day—" she began.

"No. I just couldn't remember when you said you were leaving for Portsmouth."

"The end of the month."

"That's only a few days from now," he said, visibly concerned.

"Is there a problem?"

He scowled and stuffed his hands into his lab coat pockets. "It's just that we'll have to find a replacement for you for this clinic."

"Don't worry about it. I've already spoken to the outpatient clinics manager and someone has been assigned to take over the nursing part of the program."

"That's great. I also need to talk to you about your own situation and how you're managing."

"That's not necessary," she said impatiently. She

didn't mean to be short with him, but she also didn't want to spend any more time than she had to around Neill, and that included any discussion about her circumstances.

If you're over this man, prove it. Prove you can accept his advice without making it personal.

She glanced at him and softened her tone. "I didn't mean to be rude. It's my turn to say I'm sorry. What did you need to talk to me about?"

"Do you need me to write any prescriptions for you before you leave for Portsmouth? What about insulin or test equipment?" he inquired as he led the way into the exam room, the same exam room where he'd first told her that she might have diabetes. Funny how long ago that seemed now. She listened quietly as he talked about her options, what he wanted to prescribe for her. She watched as he wrote out the prescription for insulin in his careful script.

Despite her resolve to keep this meeting all about her diabetes, she couldn't stop the memories of how they'd once shared every thought, every emotion with each other. How sitting and talking to him had always made her so happy, regardless of the subject.

But most of all, she remembered how easily he had made her want him. And after that night on the beach, the night Patrick had been conceived, she'd never been able to forget how his body felt pressed against hers, how having him make love to her had haunted her through every stage of her marriage to Sam. And she was so ashamed of feeling that way. Sam deserved better than that, a whole lot better. But Sam was gone, and by leaving Eden Harbor and Neill she would soon leave behind her last connection to Patrick.

"There, that should do it. I want you to call me—day

or night—if you have any problems at all." He wrote his contact numbers down on another prescription sheet and handed it to her.

She took the pieces of paper from his hand, and for the first time since she'd seen him that day in the emergency room, she wished that their lives could have been different. But wishing wouldn't make a difference. It was too late for that. "Have you forgotten I'm a nurse? That I've worked for years with people who have diabetes?"

"Being a nurse and being a patient are two different things. Humor me and place my numbers on your fridge…wherever you end up living."

"If you say so," she muttered, hearing the grumpiness in her tone, but she had every right to be grumpy. A few weeks ago Neill hadn't been around. A few weeks ago, diabetes hadn't been part of her life. A few weeks ago, she'd never imagined that she'd be feeling anything but resentment toward the man standing in front of her.

WHEN SHE GOT home, Sherri tested her blood sugar to discover that it was quite low, lower than it should be. She decided to have a sandwich and a glass of milk before going to bed. She would test her sugar level again in an hour, one last time before calling it a night.

As she settled in front of the TV, the thought occurred to her that she'd been having these funny sweats and headaches along with a feeling of malaise a lot longer than she'd admitted to Neill when he'd first examined her. She wasn't certain when they'd started, except that when the flu had run its course in the community and her life had begun to return to normal, she'd felt even worse than before.

Mulling it over, she fell asleep in front of the television only to wake with a start a few hours later. She wasn't sure what had awakened her, but deciding that it was too early to get up and get ready for work, she turned off the TV and climbed into bed.

The next morning when she awoke, she felt a little queasy and put it down to nerves. She was still getting used to giving herself an injection of insulin. She tested her blood sugar and gave herself the required amount of insulin before starting breakfast.

Funny, how many times had she counseled patients on taking their insulin without having any idea how it felt? She had just finished her breakfast when she felt suddenly very ill. After barely making it to the bathroom in time, she remained there, wedged in between the toilet and the tub, waiting for the nausea to pass.

Still not feeling very well, she pulled herself up to a sitting position, the room swinging like a pendulum in front of her eyes as she did so. She felt suddenly very ill again and crouched over the toilet.

Was this the flu? A reaction to insulin? Where was her cell phone?

She couldn't remember. Her vision was blurry, and her head throbbed. Realizing she needed help but unable to trust herself to stand up, she crawled out to the living room. Finding her purse and her cell phone inside, she eased her shaking body down onto the floor as she tried to focus on the keypad.

She had to let Gayle know that she'd be late, but she couldn't seem to remember her work number. In fact, she was having trouble remembering where she needed to go this morning. Maybe her mother... Maybe she should call her mother. She focused her eyes on the screen of her cell phone, trying to find her mother's number in her contact list.

Where was it? Why couldn't she get her eyes to focus? Her chest hurt and she felt so weak all she wanted to do was sleep. Forcing her head off the floor, she tried to organize her thoughts. A sudden wave of nausea overtook her. Her stomach heaving, she forced her fingers to press 911... Everything grew darker with each touch of the keypad.

GAYLE WATCHED ANXIOUSLY as more patients streamed into the outpatient clinic but still no sign of Sherri. They usually had coffee together before the clinic started, but she figured Sherri may have felt she had to eat breakfast at home until she got accustomed to taking her insulin.

Gayle had called her friend's home phone twice already, and each time it rang until it went to voice mail. If Sherri was in the apartment, she would have answered the phone. She dialed her cell phone. She'd never known Sherri not to answer her cell phone. The phone wasn't turned off because it rang at least a half dozen times before it went to voice mail. She left a message.

Concerned, she tried to contain her impatience while she waited. Finally, she couldn't stand it any longer and called Sherri's mother, who answered on the first ring. "Have you talked to Sherri this morning?" Gayle asked, hoping she wouldn't frighten her.

"No, I haven't. I assumed she was at work."

"She's not here," Gayle said, trying to keep the worry out of her voice. "And she's never late for work."

"I'll go over there right now. She seemed fine when I saw her the other day, but she's been under so much stress lately."

And more stress was the last thing Sherri needed; of that much Gayle was certain. "Call me when you've talked to her, will you? In the meantime, I'll keep try-ing her cell phone."

"I will." With that, Colleen hung up, and Gayle was left to wonder what was going on. Meanwhile, she had patients to register and people looking for information. Some were asking when the doctor would be there. She had just completed the last registration, an older woman standing in front of her with a fearful look on her face. "Mrs. Brewster, please have a seat in the waiting room. One of the nurses will call your name when it's your turn to see the doctor."

Mrs. Brewster frowned as if making up her mind whether or not to ask any further questions, when Dr. Brandon burst through the swinging doors, his expres-sion all business as it usually was these days.

She'd been hoping that Sherri and he might work out their differences, but that didn't seem to be hap-pening. Gayle knew better than anyone just how hard it was to love someone again once they'd hurt you as badly as Sherri had been hurt. Some pain was simply impossible to get over.

Yet she really liked Dr. Brandon, and Sherri was her best friend. She wanted them to be happy. And she would miss her friend when she left for Portsmouth. Sherri had been so helpful with her son, Adam, and had made her problems around Adam seem so much more manageable. If she hadn't had to worry about where Adam had disappeared to last night, she would've called Sherri and had a late-evening chat with her as they often had over the past months. She pulled her thoughts back to the present and to Dr. Brandon stand-ing over her with a smile that tipped up one corner of his mouth more than the other. A handsome man with a wonderful smile was the perfect antidote for her worried thoughts. "Good morning."

"Good morning, and how busy will we be today?" he asked, leaning on the counter.

"Really busy. And we're short a nurse at the moment. Have you seen Sherri, by any chance?"

"No." He leaned back and frowned as he glanced around the waiting area. "You called her house?"

"Sherri has never been late for work."

"Well, she's probably on her way here now."

His cell phone rang. He pulled it from his belt and checked the screen, his expression going from one of calm to a look of overwhelming concern as he answered. "Colleen, slow down." His gaze met Gayle's and in that moment, she saw the frantic look of a man afraid for someone he loved. It had to be Sherri's mother he was talking to.

"The ambulance picked her up a few minutes ago? Please don't cry. Do you have someone who can drive you to the hospital?" he asked just as an overhead page advised him to call switchboard. "Can you get Matthew to drive you here? I've got to go, but I'll meet you in Emergency."

"Did something happen to Sherri?"

"Yeah. They're bringing her in by ambulance." He reached over the counter to answer his page.

Wordlessly, Gayle passed him the handset and dialed switchboard for him and then watched in dismay as his expression changed. "They need me in Emergency. You'll have to let the patients know that there will be a delay. I'll call you when I can," he responded.

"Is it Sherri?" Gayle asked, painfully aware of how much she wanted it not to be her best friend. She'd never had anyone in her life like Sherri, someone who was so deeply and quietly available as a friend.

"I assume so. Both ambulances are out, and that was Dr. Fennell."

"Call me, please," she urged.

Through unshed tears, she watched Dr. Brandon race out of the clinic through the doors leading toward the emergency department.

CHAPTER TEN

"SORRY FOR CALLING you away from the clinic, but we're a little backed up here. The first ambulance just arrived and another is on the way. Should be here in a couple of minutes," Dr. Fennell called over his shoulder as he assisted an orderly and a nurse lift an unconscious patient off the ambulance stretcher and onto a trauma gurney.

"The second ambulance just called in to say they have a woman found on the floor unconscious. No sign of head trauma, but they've been unable to revive her. Her blood pressure's dropping and they're dealing with a frantic mother who can't seem to tell them what the cause might be. They started a saline drip," he said over the sudden whoop of a siren.

"Do you have a name?"

"Sherri Lawson. One of the nurses—you know her, right?" Dr. Fennell stopped midway through his examination of his patient, pulling his stethoscope out of his ears. "If you'd rather not be the intake doctor on this, I'll do it. You can take over here for me."

"No, I think I might know what's wrong with Sherri," he said, his heart crushed up against his windpipe, making words almost impossible.

Mike's gaze went from questioning to contemplative. "Anything serious?"

"She's just been diagnosed with type one diabetes, and she only started on insulin a couple of days ago."

Mike looked as if he was about to say something when the doors to the ambulance bay parted and Sherri was wheeled in on a stretcher. Without thinking, Neill strode across the room as the stretcher came to a halt inside the cubicle adjoining the one where Mike was working on his trauma patient.

"White female found unconscious on the floor of her condo. Blood pressure one hundred and five over sixty, pulse ninety-eight, respirations twenty. Oxygen started," the EMT said, swinging the stretcher into the space.

His movements automatic, Neill did a blood glucose test to discover that her blood sugar was alarmingly low. He quickly hung a glucose drip on with the intravenous already running while he listened intently to the EMT's description of the patient's condition, a description that trailed away as the tech watched his movements. In what seemed like hours but was just a few minutes, Sherri's eyes fluttered open. She yanked the temporary airway out of her mouth as she tried to sit up, her eyes wild with fear that quickly turned to relief when she saw Neill's face.

For a few precious seconds, their eyes locked and her hand reached for his. He grasped it, gently rubbing his fingers over the back of her hand. She was here and she was safe, and the urge to never let her out of his sight again nearly overwhelmed him. But he realized that people were watching him, waiting for him to finish his evaluation of his patient. Forcing his thoughts back to his job, his mind clicked over the possibilities and what else needed to be done for Sherri.

Yet the urge to take her in his arms and bury his face in her hair was so powerful it obliterated all other reactions. His relief knew no bounds; the feeling of being open to every nuance of life engulfed him. To ward off the tears gathering just behind his eyelids, he took a long, deep breath, letting the tension locking his shoulders ease away.

"You're in Emergency, Sherri, and you're going to be fine. I'm here, and I'm going to take care of you." He heard himself saying the words. They were the least professional words he could have uttered, but he didn't give a damn. The woman he loved—had loved all his life—was safe. And that was all that mattered—now and in the future.

He issued stat blood work orders, IV infusion rates and monitoring requirements as the staff rushed to meet his orders. And all the while, all he could think about was that she was here with him, that he'd been there for her—that he would be there for her whether she lived here or in Portsmouth. But most of all he would find a way to get her to see how much he still loved her, and that without her his life was boundlessly empty and forlorn.

He had always been a better person when she was around, when she was making him laugh, believing in him, caring for him. And like the completely stupid fool he was and had been, he'd let go of all that. A sob sealed his throat. Embarrassed, he turned away from the curious gaze of the nurse standing on the other side of the stretcher.

Releasing the blood pressure cuff before putting an oxygen monitor on Sherri's finger, the nurse said, "She seems stable, Dr. Brandon," as she assembled the vials and tourniquet needed to draw blood.

"I'll need those results stat," he replied, forcing a normal tone into his words.

"Neill, what happened to me?" Sherri asked so quietly he almost didn't hear her over the thrashing racket his heart was making in his ears.

"When did you last take insulin?" he asked.

"I can't remember." She squinted at the overhead light. "Yes, I do. This morning I took it before breakfast, but before I could eat, I was violently ill. I thought I had the flu, and all I could think about was I had to call Gayle and tell her I wouldn't be in today."

She turned her worried gaze on him. "Did anyone tell Gayle?"

"She knows you're here."

"I feel really foolish. Imagine me, a diabetic clinic nurse, not getting her insulin right."

"We don't know yet whether it was your insulin dosage or something else. Maybe you have the flu. We'll run a full round of tests to see if we can determine exactly what went wrong." He suddenly became aware of how his words seemed to come out in a half squeak.

Way to go, Brandon. Let the whole freakin' world see that you're behaving like a first-year med student.

Her lips quivered as she tried for a smile, and his heart turned over in his chest. "Is Mom here?"

"She's in the waiting room, along with your sister," the nurse said. "There's a gentleman with them, as well."

"I tried to call her, but I couldn't focus well enough to get the number right. I called 911, and that's all I remember."

What he wouldn't give to be able to be with her, to be the one she turned to as she adjusted her life to the demands of her condition. He wanted to be the person she turned to no matter what went on in her life, but he'd abdicated that right years ago. "You rest, and I'll go talk to them."

"Tell Mom not to worry, will you, Neill? She's such a worrier."

"Of course," he said, squeezing her hand in reassurance before heading for the door leading to the waiting area.

When he reached the corridor, Colleen was pacing up and down. She stopped when she saw him. "Oh, God, Neill. Is she all right?"

"She's stable. I'm running tests to determine—"

"I should have moved in with her and stayed while she adjusted to taking her insulin, instead of just being there a couple of nights. I have all the time in the world, and Linda's with me. She can manage the house when I'm not home."

Linda nodded as she held on to her mother's arm. "Mom, we'll look after Sherri."

Colleen shook her head vigorously. "She shouldn't have been alone until she was completely familiar with her insulin and how she reacts to it. It doesn't matter that she's a nurse. She should have had someone with her." Colleen wiped the corner of her eye.

"These things can happen to anyone. Sherri will be fine. You'll see," Linda said, hugging her mother.

Matthew rose from the chair where he'd been sitting and came to stand next to Colleen and Linda. "Thanks, Dr. Brandon…Neill. We're really glad you were here to look out for our girl." He put his arm around Colleen. "When can we see her?"

"You can see her now. She's being moved to a quieter area of the department, the observation area, so that she can rest until we have all the test results back."

"You're lucky you can get her to sit still long enough to be tested," her uncle said, a wry grin on his face.

"Sherri's always been one to play down any health problems."

"No kidding!" Linda interjected. "Remember that time she had appendicitis, and for hours she wouldn't admit that she was even having pain? She was only thirteen at the time."

Colleen smiled for the first time since Neill had arrived. "That's right, Neill. Please make sure she's given a thorough going-over. Sherri hates to admit she has a problem."

"You can count on me," he said, wishing he were part of Sherri's family. Seeing her family and their concern convinced him that he would do whatever it took, however long it took—and whatever conditions she placed on him—to find a way back to the love they had shared. He had to believe that behind all that anger and hurt, she still loved him as much as he loved her.

He would convince her that he meant it when he said he was sorry, and he would go to any lengths to prove how much he loved her.

SHERRI CLOSED HER eyes to ward off the dizzy sensation created by the ceiling lights flashing past above her stretcher as they moved her down the back corridor into the observation area of the emergency department. It was as if she were living in another dimension, removed from what was going on around her.

Was this how it felt when the body was in shock? She glanced up at her IV and down at her arm, waiting for the sense of unreality to pass.

The nurse gently swung her stretcher into the assigned space and clipped the bell cord to the stretcher railing. "There you go, Sherri. Dr. Brandon will be along after your blood results are back. You rest, and we'll check on you periodically," the nurse said, a re-assuring smile on her face.

"Thank you." Sherri closed her eyes, listening to all the familiar hospital sounds, feeling a strange lethargy take hold of her limbs. So much had changed that she was having trouble making sense of it all. She could still see the fear in Neill's eyes as he'd stood over her; she could hear the tremor in his words as he'd struggled to remain calm.

She'd been so wrong about him. So wrong. When she'd first opened her eyes and seen him standing there, seen the naked fear in his eyes, she'd recognized the truth. In those agonizing seconds, there was nothing between them but their love for each other. After seeing the pain in his eyes, she was finally able to admit that he had suffered as well—not in the same way she had, but his pain had altered him in ways she couldn't appreciate.

Finding solace in her discovery, she closed her eyes. In a little while, she heard her mother's breath-less words. "Sherri, honey, are you awake?"

"Yes," she whispered, opening her eyes. Her mother, her sister and her uncle Matthew stood together, look-ing down at her. Her mother's face was splotchy with tears, her cheeks puffy. "Mom, I'm okay. Please don't worry about me."

Her mother gripped her hand, struggling to speak. "You always say that. You never complain. Sometimes I wish you would," she said, a shaky smile on her lips.

"Now, what good would that do?" Sherri squeezed her mother's fingers.

"Don't know," her sister said. "But we love you, and this can't be allowed to happen again. We need to look after you better."

Her mother took a deep breath, her jaw set. "I'll tell you one thing. I'm moving in with you until we get this whole diabetes thing sorted out, even if that means I have to move to Portsmouth."

"You don't have to do that. Tell her, Uncle Matthew. I'm a big girl, and I'm a nurse to boot."

"And what good was all your nursing experience this morning?" her mother argued.

"Mom. I'm fine."

"Why don't you two settle this when Sherri is back home," her uncle said gently.

"That sounds like a great idea, Mom. And besides, you won't have long to wait. I'll be out of here before noon."

"Well, I'm going shopping when I leave here, and I'm stocking your kitchen with all the foods you need, including bottled orange juice and healthy snacks. It's the least I can do for you."

"Mom, you don't—"

"Let me help you just this once," her mother pleaded.

"And me. I want to help out here, too. You're my little sister," Linda said.

"I want to help, too," Matthew chimed in. "We'll all go together to the supermarket and load up."

Sherri looked from one anxious face to another. "You win. You people go and enjoy yourselves in the grocery aisles, and I'll see you later this afternoon when I get off work."

"You're not going to work!" her mother said.

"No, she's not," Neill said as he entered the cubicle, his tone firm.

"Dr. Brandon. It's so good to see you again, and we're all glad you were there for Sherri," Matthew offered, his expression contrite.

Neill moved to the other side of the stretcher, his fingers cool on her wrist as his gaze assessed her. "I am, too. The blood results are back, and I think it's time you and I had a serious talk about your diabetes. No more excuses about you being a nurse and knowing how to manage."

"I agree," her mother said.

"I do, too," Uncle Matthew joined in.

"Are you ganging up on me?" Sherri asked, trying to make light of their concerns, all the while acutely aware of what it meant to have her family here with her. If this had happened in Portsmouth, she would have been on her own to deal with the problem. And this was a minor incident, one easily managed. What if she had to face a serious emergency situation? Would she need to rely on the kindness of strangers, rather than family?

Neill released her wrist. Not knowing where to put his fingers, he wrapped them around the stethoscope dangling from his neck. "The clinic staff, especially Gayle, are all concerned, and they agree that you're not to show your face there until tomorrow at the earliest," Neill said, checking the IV, his gaze following the plastic tubing from the plastic bag down to the IV site on her arm. His fingers left the stethoscope and automatically moved back to her wrist.

He was checking her pulse again, and the thought that he wanted to touch her, wanted to care for her, played along her mind, kicking her pulse higher as she became more conscious of the fact that he hadn't let go.

"You're in good hands." Her uncle exchanged smiles with Neill. "We'll leave you and hit the grocery store."

She turned her attention to her family. "Thanks."

Matthew patted Colleen's shoulder as his face crinkled into a lopsided smile aimed at Sherri. "You're welcome, sweetie. And we'll see you back at your condo. You know your mother. She'll have everything all cleaned and tidied up before you get there—it's her stress management technique."

"We'll look after everything. You have nothing to do but feel better," Linda said, warmth imbuing her words.

"THEY WANT YOU well," Neill said, watching Sherri's family leave before turning back to her. "You're lucky to have people who love you so much."

"I am. I've been thinking about that since I woke up in here. What if I hadn't had someone I could call? Someone who knew me well?"

"Your mother's been very worried. She called me before you got here."

"I'm glad she's here. Those years when I lived in Bangor and didn't have family I could turn to were really difficult." If she had believed she could tell her mother the truth about Patrick's father, how different would her pregnancy have been? But telling her mother would have broken her heart, especially after all her mother had been through. No, she would not have changed that decision.

Neill took a deep breath, his eyes claiming hers. "Funny how we have to leave home to appreciate what home really means."

She gazed up into Neill's eyes before moving to the worry lines bracketing his mouth. "Are you trying to tell me something?"

"I want you to be happy, whatever that means for you or wherever you decide to live. Portsmouth isn't that far away." He reached for her hand again, his fingers sliding to the soft pulse point on the inside of her wrist.

His touch was electric. She wanted to take his hand

but was afraid to break the connection of his touch on her. "After today, I may have to rethink leaving here."

His eyes focused solely on her and he stood perfectly still, his fingers resting on her wrist. "Because?"

"I need my family. I don't want to face any other health scares or emergencies without them."

Neill glanced around the cubicle and out toward the desk area, where staff milled about and phones rang incessantly while the overhead paging system occasionally interrupted the normal flow of sound. "For what it's worth. I don't want you to leave here—ever. You belong in Eden Harbor."

HE'D SAID WHAT he'd been thinking since he'd learned about her moving to Portsmouth. The past few hours had been stressful, not only because of his concern over her recovery, but also because of his profound realization that he had to find a way to convince her to stay. And now that she'd decided to stay on her own without his pleading, he felt like running down the hall shouting the good news.

Instead, his fingers clung to her wrist, his mind racing over the possibilities now that she'd decided not to leave. "I left here believing that my new life would be so much better, so much more rewarding. Like you, I've always wanted my life to mean something, to make a difference. I had to come home to understand that. But you already know that you do make a difference in so many people's lives here in Eden Harbor. If you doubt what I'm saying, think about the clinic patients and the people who come to the diabetic clinic and the difference you've made in their lives…. I'm going on like an idiot."

"No, you're not. I do love caring for the people here. They're my extended family."

He smiled in relief, still holding his fingers to her wrist but not to take her pulse. The only pulse he could feel was his, pounding in his chest. "And you're willing to stay in Eden Harbor?"

"I'm staying, so you can let go of my wrist," she teased.

"Sorry!"

Talk about feeling like a schoolboy.

She slid her hand into his open palm. "Having you here when I needed you has shown me that I should give serious consideration to following my friend's advice."

He didn't dare breathe for fear he'd jinx what he hoped was her confession of how she felt about him. "And what advice was that?"

"That I forgive you for what happened and accept that sometimes there's no closure until forgiveness is offered," she said, her eyes suddenly glistening.

Neill wanted to tell her how much he loved her, but his fear that somehow he'd misunderstood her words held him back. "You can trust me. You can trust your feelings for me, our feelings for each other. Part of why I came back here was to find you again, to rediscover who we were and to see if there might be a chance for us."

Her eyes searched his face, yet her expression remained neutral. "But what if you have to leave here?"

He held her hand in his, playing with her fingers to ease the hammering of his heart. "Why would I do that?"

"What if your medical practice becomes too routine or doesn't offer enough of a challenge? Will you want to go back to Boston?"

"I can't see that ever happening. Besides, I have the life I always wanted."

Or, I would, if you were part of it.

"And if Morgan should become ill again, maybe need the specialty medical services that only a large center can offer. What then?"

"I'd get her the best help possible wherever that was, but I would always return to Eden Harbor."

"Neill, you would never risk Morgan's health for the sake of a small-town practice, no matter what other considerations there might be."

He hesitated, torn between confessing his love for her and fearing that her remaining in Eden Harbor was not about loving him, but about her willingness to forgive him. Nothing more. If she was willing to forgive him, it could mean that she was ready to move away from any relationship with him other than a professional one.

He was suddenly aware of her hand being pulled from his as she sat up. To stop the thoughts he knew had to be racing through her mind, he rushed to reassure her. "But that wouldn't mean that I'd give up my life with you…if we got back together." *Darn!* He hadn't intended to jump so far ahead, but he had to tell her the truth. He loved her, and he would never again let his needs come between them.

"But I don't want to leave here. My decision to move to Portsmouth was because I thought I was missing out on a better career, a more exciting life. But that's not the case anymore. I want to be here, where people love me, where they call me by name when they meet me on the street. Where I can have the emotional and physical support I need. I knew that the moment I heard my mother's voice a little bit ago."

What was she saying? That she would never consider leaving here? Even if he had to? He didn't dare ask her any more about it. He had to trust that once they had time to reconnect, to rediscover their love for each other, that they would find a way to be together no matter what life held in store for them.

Meeting her anxious gaze, he knew one thing for certain. Whatever he had to do to keep her with him, he would do. Her love was all that mattered. The rest would work itself out. "As your doctor, I'd like to prescribe something that will set us on the right pathway."

"What would that be?"

"First, I'm discharging you home to your mother until you get your insulin regulated."

She gripped the railing. "Hey! I'm not a kid!"

He took her by the shoulders and laid her back down gently. "You're not a kid, but your mother and I don't want to worry about you any more than we have to."

"You don't have—"

"No more arguing," he said firmly. "I'm sure the hospital will welcome you back, given how short-staffed they are. On top of that, tomorrow I'm taking you out for a drive under medical supervision."

"What?"

"I'm inviting you on a picnic to Cranberry Point. You and I are going on a date."

"A date? Cranberry Point? I love it there. I've always loved it."

"It's the perfect setting for something I should have done when I first moved back."

"And that would be?"

Kissing her right now was out of the question. There were too many people waiting to make their relationship fodder for the gossip mill.

"Unfortunately, you'll have to wait until your mother gives her okay."

"My mother?"

"Yep. You're going home, and your mother is staying with you overnight. That's the only circumstances under which I'll take you out to the point."

"Not fair. Definitely not fair," she groused, but she was grinning at him. That old grin that told him she was up for any challenge he might toss her way.

He felt good. So impossibly good. The happiest he'd felt in months. Make that years.

"Behave yourself and get some rest. I'll pick you up around eleven."

CHAPTER ELEVEN

THE NEXT MORNING, the kind of morning where the air hung with the scent of lilacs and the sun promised unfettered light, Neill pulled into Sherri's driveway. For the first time since he'd moved home, he felt hopeful. He pulled to a stop as Sherri came out the door of her condo.

He jumped out of his SUV and started up the walk toward her. "You look great," he said. With her blond hair flowing around her shoulders and her blue T-shirt fitting every curve of her body, she made his blood run hot.

"Thanks." Smiling up at him, she passed over the picnic basket. "Mom's contribution to our day."

He took the basket from her as they walked toward the passenger door. "So, how was her grocery shopping trip?"

"Let's just say there isn't a spare inch of shelf space left in my kitchen, and my fridge is positively burdened with veggies."

He opened the door for her, ridiculously happy at the prospect of having her sitting across the console from him. He was tempted to do a jig around the back of the vehicle and had to force himself to walk slowly and deposit the picnic basket in the back before climbing into the driver's seat. He'd promised himself he wouldn't get his hopes up about today, but with Sherri beside him, the intimacy of the two of them alone in his vehicle, his expectations soared.

They drove north out of town toward the interstate and turned left onto the coast road that led down toward the ocean. The conversation was easy and the day inviting. He could tell by her response that she was as happy to be out on a day like today as he was.

"How are you feeling?" he asked.

"Never better, despite Mom's constant worried glances."

The doctor in him wanted to quiz her further for any more symptoms, but he held back. Sherri would bring her concerns to him when and if she needed him. He had to believe that. "I was so relieved to hear you say you weren't moving to Portsmouth."

"Why?"

He could feel her eyes on him and knew that trying to duck the question would simply mean that she'd rephrase it. He gripped the steering wheel tighter. "From the moment I got back here in Eden Harbor and discovered that you were working at the hospital, I wanted a second chance." He glanced over quickly before continuing. "Now I can't imagine Eden Harbor without you," he said, not daring to look her way for fear that she'd admonish him for presuming such a thing.

"Did I mention how relieved I was to find you staring down at me when I woke in Emergency?"

"Is that what they mean when they say good things come out of bad ones?" he asked, determined to keep her talking.

"It is in our case. I'm glad you and I are getting a real chance to talk. Having you back here has been unimaginably difficult for me."

His head filled with a mix of excitement and trepidation; he held his breath. "Go on."

"Even though I told myself that I was leaving for a better career and the opportunity to meet new people, your return was my biggest reason for getting out of here."

"And now?"

The only sound in the vehicle was the gentle roar of the engine as it geared down to climb the hill leading out to the bluff overlooking the water. "I called the nursing department at Portsmouth General and told them I wouldn't be taking the job."

He let the air slide from his lungs. "What's next for you?"

"Hopefully, the hospital will have a position for me. In the meantime, I'm going to continue making the adjustments I need to live with my diabetes."

"A lot of people are going to be pleased to hear you've changed your mind."

"And that includes you?" Her eyes squinted just a little.

"I'm definitely in that group. But are you sure about this? It's your future."

She sighed as she pushed her hair off her forehead. "I am. I belong here."

Here with me? Was she about to say that she wanted to be with me? It couldn't be that easy, not after all this time.

Once they reached the small community of Cranberry Point and the general store where the turnoff to the actual point was, Neill eased the SUV over the bumpy entrance to the narrow road leading down to the plateau at the water's edge. When they reached the picnic site situated above the roaring surf, he turned the vehicle around to face back up the hill before getting the things out of the back. Sherri helped him spread the blanket and placed the picnic hamper along one edge. They sat down, facing a narrow inlet of water where waves rippled and sparkled in the sun, while the gulls screamed and dived toward the water.

"All the times I've been out here, I didn't realize you could see back along the road leading in here," Sherri said, pointing to the stretch of narrow track they'd just driven over.

He followed the line of her finger. "It's a dangerous piece of road, and one that hasn't gotten any better over the years," he said.

She raised her face to the sun, exposing the open neck of her shirt and the swell of her breasts against the smooth fabric. "I can't come here with you without remembering those other trips we made here."

"Our version of a wild date," he said, feeling a rush of hot need roaring through him. She had never looked as beautiful as she did at this moment, and he couldn't seem to collect his scattered thoughts long enough to say anything intelligent.

So much for your big plan to state your case and entice her back into your life with your tender pitch.

He wanted to touch her hair, run his fingers over her neck, kiss her senseless. Instead, he said, "Sherri, I've been wanting to tell you something ever since I got back. It has to do with why I made the decision to return to Eden Harbor."

She turned to him, her eyes looking directly into his, driving him to find the words to explain his life and what it had been like these past few years. "I don't have to tell you that everyone, including me, assumed that I would continue to live and practice in a big center like

Boston. In fact, when Uncle Nicolas first suggested that I come back here, I refused. I couldn't imagine being here practicing medicine." His glance took in the sweep of green washing over the sloping ground toward the distant beach, making him wonder how it was that he hadn't missed this place all those years. And now he couldn't imagine leaving it.

"Then one night about a year ago I was working in Emergency when a young single mother came in with her daughter, who was only ten years old, a year older than Morgan is now. Despite our best efforts and all the technology available to us, the daughter died of an aneurysm before we could save her. It wasn't until I went to talk to the mother that I realized she had no family members she could call on for support, as all of her family lived out in California. There wasn't an aunt, uncle, grandparent or any family member this woman could call on to help her face the death of her daughter. I will never forget watching her walk out of the emergency department alone that night."

"Did she not have friends?"

He shrugged. "I don't know. The nurses offered to call someone for her, but she seemed too distraught to give them a name."

"What a terrible way to lose your child."

"It was awful, but it had a profound influence on me. The next time my uncle phoned and brought up the subject of me coming home again, I finally understood what he meant. Living near family is what I want for Morgan…and for me."

"Go on."

"When Lilly decided to move to Houston, I realized that moving farther away from my home was out of the question."

"I understand what you mean." She touched his hand where it rested on his thigh, sending heat flashing through him.

He leaned toward her. The floral scent of her hair, the heat of the sun on her skin urged him to kiss her. She tilted her chin up, her eyes on his, her lips parted. Giving in to the moment, he kissed her gently, drawing her lips to his, savoring her smell, the touch of her fingers on his cheek as she sighed and focused all her attention on him.

He gathered her in his arms, pulling her body against him, his hands eagerly stroking the soft skin of her throat. She pulled back a little and gazed up into his eyes, and in her expression he read her uncertainty.

Don't blow this!

He eased away from her, his eyes searching hers. "We'll take it slow. I promise."

They sat together, their arms around each other, listening to the pounding of the ocean on the rocks, the keening cry of the gulls as they swooped above the rock face. High above, an American bald eagle glided into view, its wings horizontal to the earth as it soared above the headland.

"It is so beautiful," she exclaimed, shielding her eyes from the light as she watched the huge bird float gracefully across the sky.

Neill followed the bird's easy glide over the point, his gaze drifting to the road directly below the bird's flight path. He could sit there next to Sherri for the entire day, he mused as he spotted a half-ton truck making a rapid turn onto the track from the highway, its wheels spitting gravel, the rear tires fishtailing as the truck headed down over the edge of the road. Instead of slowing down, the vehicle picked up speed, coming dangerously close to the precipice and the sheer drop to the rocks protruding below.

"What the hell?"

Sherri followed his gaze. "Oh, Neill! What's the driver doing? That truck is out of control!"

Neill jumped to his feet as the truck swerved back on the track and slammed against a boulder on the opposite side before careening farther down the narrow road. "That fool is going to get himself killed."

Sherri rose and stood next to Neill as they both watched the truck charging over the rough ground. They stared in horror as the vehicle swerved sideways, its rear end leaping into the air before the truck rolled end over end, coming to rest against a large boulder, the only thing holding it from crashing into the water.

"Sherri! Get in!" Neill ordered, pulling his keys from his pocket and running to the driver's side of his SUV. They drove as fast as the terrain would allow, the vehicle bucking and swaying beneath them. Neill passed his cell phone to Sherri. "Call 911," he yelled over the roar of the engine as they skidded back up the track to where the truck rested precariously on its side.

Sherri clicked the numbers into the phone, all the while bracing her hands against the door frame as the vehicle swerved dangerously over a knoll. The call could be heard on the speakerphone inside the vehicle. "911. What's your emergency?"

Neill identified himself and responded with the information as he reached the crash site and shut off the engine. "We're going to make our way down to the truck."

"If at all possible, stay on the line until you reach the vehicle."

He pulled his medical bag from the backseat as

Sherri jumped out of the passenger side, the cell phone clutched in her hand. They could see the occupant's arm dangling from the driver's side of the truck, and there was a patch of level ground just in front of where the truck had come to rest. Without a word, they started toward the edge, their feet slipping on the damp grass as they moved quickly over the bumpy ground, intent on reaching the vehicle. The ground dipped beneath their feet as they edged nearer. Sherri stopped suddenly, and Neill had to scramble sideways not to bump into her. "What is it?"

"I recognize the truck. It's Charlie Crawford's."

"Sam's brother? Why would he drive like that, do something so stupid?" Neill asked, going ahead of Sherri, anxious to reach the vehicle.

"Charlie's a bad alcoholic."

Sherri's words reached him just as his hands gripped the driver's door. Seeing the man slumped against the inside of the vehicle, blood streaming from his head, his eyes closed, he focused his attention on what needed to be done. "Tell the 911 operator we've reached the site."

SHERRI SPOKE TO the operator as she moved carefully toward the overturned truck, the wind suddenly yanking her hair into a frenzied mass around her eyes, blocking her view. Her feet searched for an even spot on the rough ground as she forced her mind to remain focused on the situation.

Sam's brother was behind the wheel. How could he? She'd warned him every chance she got not to drive when he was drinking. In the past few months his wife, Freda, had threatened to leave him if he didn't stop drinking, but obviously that hadn't changed much in Charlie's life. Charlie had come back from Iraq a broken man, a highly decorated member of the marine corps, and he hadn't been willing or able to accept help for his alcoholism. It was clear from what they were seeing that Charlie had followed the destructive path of his older brother.

Sherri reached Neill, her apprehension peaking as she stared into the cab of the truck. Charlie's eyes were closed and his breathing shallow. Blood oozed from an open wound on his forehead. The arm hanging out of the window leaned at an odd angle, probably broken. The cab reeked of alcohol, and a traveler—slang for an alcoholic drink—rested in the cup holder on the console between the bucket seats, its sides gripped by the rubber tabs holding it in place. The other smells were sweat and dirt from the hundreds of trips made in a truck that the owner had never bothered to clean.

Neill eased Charlie's arm back into the truck, causing him to cry out as he opened the door.

"How far away is the ambulance?" Sherri asked the operator, the cell phone braced against her ear as she watched Neill examine Charlie as much as he could without moving him.

"ETA is about five minutes," the operator responded.

"I can't move him without help in case he's sustained a back injury," Neill said, opening the door wider to gain better access. Sherri retrieved the stethoscope, blood pressure cuff and light for checking pupils from Neill's medical bag. They moved as one, assessing Charlie's condition, taking his vital signs, relaying them to the 911 operator to be passed on to the EMTs on board the ambulance.

"Tell them we'll need a neck brace and backboard," Neill said, following this request with another for IV solution. He mentioned the possibility that they might have to insert a chest tube on route.

"You're going on the ambulance with him," Sherri said.

"Yes," he answered, his voice distracted, his eyes on Charlie, whose color was ashen. His respirations were faster and shallower than a few minutes ago.

"Where's that ambulance?" Sherri muttered just as the wail of a siren could be heard coming along the highway above them. "Thank heaven." The trembling in her legs eased. Charlie couldn't die like this, not after everything he'd lived through. He was a good man. He had a wife and two children. He'd been so kind to her when Sam had died.

Neill steadied Charlie while he checked his head wound, his fingers moving confidently. Charlie groaned at his touch. "Charlie, it's Neill Brandon. How are you feeling?"

Charlie groaned once again and tried to turn away.

The ambulance stopped. The EMTs scrambled out of the vehicle and made their way toward the crash site with a stretcher, backboard, neck brace and the IV ordered by Neill ready for the patient. With professionalism and ease, they slid Charlie out of the truck and onto the stretcher, strapped him into place and did all the myriad duties required to stabilize him before starting back up the slope toward the waiting ambulance—all under Neill's watchful eye.

He was so sure, so calm, so deliberate in every move he made, every word he uttered. Sherri watched in complete fascination as he transformed from the man she knew to the doctor whose expertise had been honed in one of the best medical centers in the country.

As the EMTs made their way up the slope, he came

toward her, a look of relief on his face. "Guess we'll have to finish our picnic another time."

"I'll follow you in," she said, feeling the rush of adrenaline like a narcotic, her awareness of Neill heightened to the point where all she wanted was for him to take her in his arms and kiss her senseless.

He glanced down at her, his powerful hands clasping her arms. "Sherri…" His eyes told her he wanted to say more, but the words would be inappropriate under the circumstances.

"You'd better go."

He grabbed his medical bag and started toward the back of the ambulance, then turned back and pulled his keys from his pocket. "You'll need these."

She climbed up the hill behind him and held out her hand. "I will."

She watched the ambulance pull away. When it reached the highway, it quickly picked up speed and was gone from sight.

She put the key in the SUV's ignition; the sudden shaking of her hands on the wheel reminded her of how stressful the past few moments had been.

But it would all be worth it if Charlie was okay. And all worth it because a barrier between Neill and her had magically disappeared. In those moments of working together, of feeling the urgency of the situation, they'd become a team again.

The shock of what had occurred still fresh in her mind, she drove slowly along the curving highway, the panorama of ocean and bright blue sky, separated by green cliffs edged with rock outcroppings, soothing her in a way nothing else could.

It was hard for her to believe she'd considered leaving this place.

When she reached the hospital, she parked Neill's vehicle in the staff parking lot near the emergency entrance and went in. The space was silent, the sun streaming through the windows into the waiting area. Over in the corner near the entrance leading to the rest of the hospital, Charlie's parents were huddled together, deep in conversation.

Elsa and Greg Crawford had been part of her life for as long as she could remember. They'd run the local hardware store together, offering summer jobs to as many of the high school students as they could, including Neill. When she was married to Sam, they'd been kind and caring and ecstatic to learn that she was expecting their grandson.

Keeping the truth from them had made her feel guilty and sad, but Sam had been determined to maintain their story that he was the father of her child. Now they were faced with their remaining son's alcoholism. Charlie clearly needed professional help to get his life under control. Her heart breaking for them, she went to them, prepared to do what she could. At the sound of her feet on the hard surface, they glanced up, their faces immediately transforming from worry to relief.

"Sherri!" Elsa jumped up and came toward her, her arms extended, fresh tears tracing down her cheeks.

Sherri wrapped her arms around the woman who had for a few years been her mother-in-law, while her gaze reached toward Greg Crawford, a man Sam had both admired and feared. "How's Charlie doing?" she asked, feeling Elsa's arms tighten around her at the question.

Greg cleared his throat and smoothed his thinning gray hair. "He's in surgery. They took him up just after we got here. Freda had to go to Bangor this morning, but she's on her way back now."

"Is Neill with him?"

Elsa leaned away from Sherri, pulled a tissue from the pocket of her navy blue jacket and began to dab her eyes. "Yes, he went up to surgery with him. He said he'd come back here as soon as he could to tell us how Charlie made out."

"You were with him, I understand. With Charlie... you and Neill." Greg put his arm around his wife's shoulders, and the two of them stared at her, their eyes pleading for information on how their son ended up needing surgery.

"Yes. We'd gone to Cranberry Point for a picnic," she said, following the elderly couple back to where they'd been sitting. "We saw Charlie's accident happen and went to help."

Her words produced a fresh gush of tears from Elsa. "We're both so glad you were there for Charlie. What if you hadn't been?" She gazed up into Sherri's face, her reddened cheeks and teary eyes expressing her fear for her son.

"We were there, and that's all that matters. And Neill Brandon is the best doctor Charlie could have had at the scene," she said, searching for the words that would soothe them.

Elsa pushed her unkempt hair from her forehead and lifted her chin. "To think we gave that young Neill a job in our hardware store all those years ago, and now he's saved our Charlie's life." She glanced at her husband, a faint smile on her lips. "Life has a way of working out, don't you think?" she asked Greg.

He patted his wife's shoulder, his eyes downcast.

Sherri watched the two of them, remembering Sam's description of how life was in the Crawford household, how adamantly his parents spoke against the use of alcohol, how strict Greg had been with the two boys growing up, how much Sam and Charlie wanted to please their parents, especially their father, who was very controlling. A man who saw his sons as an extension of himself, rather than as unique individuals.

Greg's direct gaze met Sherri's. "The police were here looking for you a little while ago. They wanted you to give them a statement about what happened. What did happen? Neill was too busy to talk with us."

"We saw Charlie's half ton coming down the dirt road leading toward the point, and suddenly it swerved and went over the bank near the…cliff."

A fresh sob erupted from Elsa. "He could have gone over the cliff!" She clutched her husband's shirtfront, her eyes on Sherri.

"A boulder stopped the truck from rolling farther. We got to him as quickly as we could."

The room stilled. Greg started to say something and then stopped.

To fill the silence, Sherri asked, "Would either of you like a cup of coffee?"

"No, dear. We're fine. We're going to wait right here until Neill comes back to talk to us. Why don't you wait with us?"

"I will, but first I need to get something to drink," Sherri said, feeling suddenly faint at the realization that she hadn't eaten anything since breakfast. She needed to put something in her stomach. "I'll be right back."

She went out into the corridor to the alcove where the pop, juice and coffee machines were and got a bottle of orange juice. The cool sweet liquid slid down her throat into her stomach, soothing the jitters sweeping through her. She leaned against the wall as she began to feel less light-headed and calmer. She was still leaning there when Greg Crawford came toward her.

She glanced at him and saw the naked worry in his eyes. "Is Elsa okay?"

"She's still very upset, and that's only natural. Charlie is all she has left, and she's terrified of losing him like she did Sam."

"Is there anything I can do other than wait with you and Elsa?"

He searched the pop machine as if looking for something and then turned to her. "There is."

"Name it."

"I know that Sam was an alcoholic, and your life with him couldn't have been easy. You could have left him, and you didn't. We're both thankful for that."

"Sam was a good man and very kind to me. I loved him and wouldn't have left him," she said, hearing the words that would have been a lie if Sam had lived. There were many nights after his death when she'd wondered if the argument they'd had before he'd left the house that day had played a role in how his life had ended. Had she said something that made him careless, or had he simply decided that he couldn't go on? She swallowed hard and stared at the floor.

"And he loved you. He wasn't much for talking, but he did tell me one day that he loved you and didn't know what he'd do if you ever left him."

She couldn't tell him that she'd come very close to leaving a couple of times but had stayed more out of a sense of duty than any real love. Sam's drinking had slowly eroded their life together and had all but destroyed her love for a man who had been so kind, so charming and such a steadying influence in the chaos of her life after Neill. "Sam and I were happy together," she said, knowing Greg Crawford needed to hear those words.

"Sherri, was Charlie drinking? I realize that I'm putting you on the spot here. Charlie's wife is filing for divorce, he lost his job at the port and he's refused to move home to get his life back together. I've made some pretty bad mistakes in my life where my boys were concerned. I had problems of my own, and I took it out on them. I was too hard on them when all they wanted to do was please me." He swiped at his eyes. "I can't lose Charlie. Somehow we have to help him, get him to see that he can't keep drinking."

She saw the desperation in his eyes and felt she had only one choice. Greg Crawford might be the only hope Charlie had if he was ever going to find help with his alcoholism. "I could smell alcohol in the cab of the truck when we reached him," she said slowly, hating the anguish her words were causing this man who had once been a big part of her life.

His sigh of resignation filled the alcove where they stood. "What am I going to do?"

"Maybe this accident will be a wake-up call for Charlie. Alcohol made Sam's life difficult, and if there's one thing I'm sure of, Charlie loved Sam."

"But will this accident be enough? Will he stop, or at least try to get help?"

"I can't say. No one can." She touched his arm in sympathy. "But if there's anything I can do, you just ask."

"I may take you up on that offer. His wife has virtually given up, but she still cares and they have their children to consider. She's been seeing a counselor who has suggested an intervention to see if we can get through to Charlie about his drinking. Would you be part of that?"

"If the counselor believes it could help."

He drew her into a hug and kissed the top of her head. "You're the daughter we never had."

Feeling his arms around her took her back to the night Sam had died. She'd gone home to visit her mother, mostly to get away from another argument over the amount Sam had drunk the night before. He'd promised he wouldn't drink anymore. He'd needed to go up to his camp on the lake to get ready for a fishing trip with his friends. She'd been almost to her mother's house when she'd gotten the call from the hospital in Bangor.

"We'd better get back to the waiting room," Sherri said to keep from crying.

The three of them were waiting together, talking about anything other than what was going on in the operating room, when Neill came striding down the corridor toward them. Relief at seeing him, joy in the idea that this man had returned to her life, made her knees tremble.

They rose in unison. "Is he all right?" Greg asked, his arm automatically going around his wife's shoulders.

"Charlie came through the surgery just fine. His broken arm is fixed, the injury to his face stitched up. He has several fractured ribs and heavy bruising on his chest, but no concussion or neck injury. He's a very lucky man. He'll be sore for a few weeks, but I believe he'll come through it okay. He's in recovery, and you can see him when he gets back to his room," Neill said, his voice calm and reassuring.

As he glanced at her, the vulnerability in his eyes wiped out all other thoughts. It was as if time were suspended as she listened to him speak with such kindness to Elsa and Greg.

She waited while they finished talking, while he

calmed their fears, and realized that despite everything
that had happened between them—the emotional pain,
the feelings of loss and betrayal she'd harbored all these
years—her life had changed. She wanted Neill—not in
the adolescent, hopeful way it had once been, but in a
life-hardened realization that the two of them belonged
together. That regardless of what the past had done to
both of them, how it had changed them, the future was
all that really mattered.

EXHAUSTION TUGGED AT Neill's shoulders as he listened to
Mr. and Mrs. Crawford expressing their concerns about
Charlie. As he responded to their questions, he was
acutely aware of Sherri standing close to him, her attention focused on the relieved couple. Intermittently, he'd
feel her glance his way, and he'd feel ridiculously happy
and upbeat despite the intensity of the past few hours.

"We're so thankful you were there, Neill," Greg said,
extending his hand. "We've taken up enough of your
time. I think we'll have a bite to eat in the cafeteria
while we wait for Charlie to be taken to his room."
Elsa nodded vigorously in agreement, a smile etched
on her face.

Neill shook Greg's hand. "I'll check on him later, and
we'll be in touch. Charlie will make a full recovery,"
he said, aware that unless their son stopped drinking,
something like this could happen again. "If you need
anything or would like to talk, I'd be more than happy
to meet with you."

"Thanks so much for everything," Greg said, his
gaze flitting from Neill to his wife. "But we'll be fine,
I'm sure."

So they weren't ready to talk about their son's problem, and in a way Neill couldn't blame them. After all,

Charlie was a grown man, and he had to want to overcome his addiction. No one could do it for him.

"You take care, and don't hesitate to call if you need me. In the meantime, Sherri and I have to get to the police station and give our statements."

He turned to Sherri. "Are you ready?"

"Your SUV is outside."

They'd always been a great team, and never more so than in the past hours. He wanted to reach for her hand, to hold her close, feel her warmth.

He wanted to, yet he didn't. A sudden feeling of awkwardness crept over him.

Having said their goodbyes to the Crawfords they walked out into the brilliant afternoon sun. In ten minutes, they were sitting in the police station being interviewed by Paul Attlee, the police officer who had been called to the scene of the accident. Officer Attlee's questions were straightforward, and he, like Neill and Sherri, was sorry to learn that alcohol was involved. Paul's older sister had gone to school with Charlie and liked him, as did so many people in Eden Harbor.

Once they were finished and standing outside on the front steps of the police station, Neill gave in to his urge, put his arm around Sherri's shoulders and hugged her close in one long, delicious squeeze that felt so good, so right.

"I'm starving. You must be, too. Did you have something to eat while you were waiting?" he asked, keeping his hand on the small of her back as he led her to his vehicle parked at the curb.

"I had orange juice, but I need something else," she said as he opened the passenger door for her.

"Let's go to the bistro a few blocks from here. I've ordered takeout from them before, and they're pretty good." He started the car and headed out of the parking lot toward downtown.

"Great," she said, holding her hand over her rumbling stomach. When they reached the restaurant, he parked and they walked in together—and were greeted by the smiles and curious glances of a few patrons Neill and Sherri had known all their lives.

"Will we be the talk of the town before nightfall?" Neill asked.

"I think so, if not before," Sherri said, sliding into a booth near the back of the restaurant.

They ordered and settled in to talk. Neill had waited a long time for this—this feeling that he and Sherri were a couple again, enjoying a meal at a restaurant like other normal couples did.

"Greg asked me about Charlie and whether he'd been drinking," Sherri said, her expression solemn.

"What did you say?"

"I told him the truth." She wove her paper napkin through her fingers.

"What did he say?"

"What could he say? He knew Sam was an alcoholic. Greg knows the risks involved."

He saw the pain in her eyes and wanted to ease it, to protect her from whatever memories today had forced on her. "Want to talk about it?"

"Sometimes I feel that if I'd been more forceful with Sam about his drinking, if I'd taken a stand and left, that maybe he would have had no choice but to seek help. As it was, I just sort of went along, hoping each day that a miracle would happen, that Sam would wake up one morning and not want to drink anymore."

"No one can force an addict to change their behavior."

"As a professional I know that, but as Sam's wife, I still believed that there had to have been something I could do to help him. Sam never hurt anyone. He loved me, he loved his family and he deserved so much better."

"Sherri, you've never talked to anyone about your life with Sam, have you?"

She shook her head. "Sam rescued me, and I owed him. I was living in Bangor, a pregnant university freshman, and I was trying to figure out what to do. Then one night I ran into Sam at the grocery store down the street from my apartment. When Crawford's Hardware store was bought out by one of the big chains, Sam was offered a job in Bangor. He and I started talking and then dating and finally one night I told him what had happened. He didn't rail on about you, or about how this wasn't fair to the baby. He simply told me that he'd loved me all through high school."

"And he offered to marry you."

She finger-combed her hair in what had become a nervous habit. "Yes. And I accepted. Our son needed a father, and I needed someone to care for me. I didn't love him when I married him, but I liked him *so* much. He was aware of how I felt, but he told me he'd make it his mission to change my heart. We had a quiet wedding in Bangor with his family and mine as the only guests, and we agreed that he would be the baby's father, that no one would ever know the truth."

Remorse rose through Neill, followed by anger he knew he had no right to feel. "Why?"

"Because you were out of my life. Because Sam wanted to be the father of my child. Because I wanted him to be. My child deserved two parents who loved him and who would do anything for him. After we were married, I began to see how devoted Sam was to me and to our baby. When Patrick died, Sam was so supportive even though his heart was as crushed as mine was by the loss. It was during the weeks after Patrick's death— weeks when I learned what it meant to have someone care as much as I did—that I came to love Sam, not in the way I'd always imagined love to be, but in a way that offered happiness and security."

Neill reached for her hand.

Hesitantly, she twined her fingers with his. "What I didn't realize was that Sam started drinking heavily the night after I lost Patrick, and he never stopped. Before that, he just used to drink socially, or when he went out with the guys. Or maybe it was more often." She squeezed his fingers. "I don't know. As far as I knew, he didn't have a problem with alcohol when I married him."

"Alcoholics often hide their addiction."

"It got bad enough that we both had to face reality. And I changed, as well. Without Patrick, I went back to finish my nursing degree and then found myself becoming even more restless, more dissatisfied with my life. It was one of the saddest times for both of us. To think that a man as caring and kind as Sam could also be an alcoholic was devastating. Sam's drinking became the one conversation we couldn't have with each other. I wanted to leave, but I felt I owed it to him to stay. He helped me out and I had to do the same for him. As much as I tried to get him help, he kept resisting until the day he lost his job and came home to me completely despondent. I should have taken him straight to the doctor, but I didn't."

"And he had a fatal accident on one of the lakes north of Bangor." Neill searched his memory for his mother's description of what had happened.

"And I'll never know if it was intentional or truly an accident."

Neill was speechless with remorse. What Sherri had lived with, how she'd tortured herself over what alcohol had done to her husband, would never have happened if he'd manned up and married her. He'd let his drive to succeed, his plans for his life, determine the fate of so many people. But he could at least attempt to ease her fears that somehow she'd failed Sam.

"Sherri, you had nothing to do with Sam's behavior. We all make choices, and he made his when he took that first drink. He could have sought help. He had you to support him through any treatment or therapy needed to put an end to his addiction. He, not you, chose to ignore the warning signs that his drinking was out of control. You couldn't have changed him. He had to make the changes himself."

"But I feel guilty. He'd done so much for me, and I failed him."

"You didn't." He grasped both her hands in his. "You didn't fail him or anybody else. What Sam did was his responsibility."

"It's so easy for you to say when you weren't involved."

"And I will have to live with that."

She closed her eyes, tears sliding between her lids and resting on her cheeks. She wiped the tears from her face. "I want all these feelings of loss, of lost opportunities, to be over. Sam wasn't the only one who didn't take responsibility. You and I didn't, either. We had all these plans for the future, and yet neither one of us took precautions that night on the beach."

"You're right. But in our defense, we were teenagers in love."

"Who didn't consider the possibility that I might get pregnant."

"There's no going back in life, only forward," Neill said, wishing with all his heart that from here on in, they would be together as they were now.

CHAPTER TWELVE

SHERRI WAS STARTLED out of her worried thoughts when the server arrived at her elbow with a plate of food she couldn't remember ordering. But the sight of the soup and toasted Western sandwich made her stomach growl in appreciation. She picked up her spoon and ate hungrily.

Neill waited for his plate to be put in front of him and for the server to leave before he spoke. "You're right about the birth control and our lack of responsibility, but there's something else here that needs to be acknowledged."

She glanced at him over her soupspoon. "What's that?"

"After you called my dorm room in Boston, I tried to call you back, but you wouldn't take my call."

"Because I was in Bangor, trying to pull my life together while waiting for my baby to be born."

"And I was alone in Boston, trying to figure out what I could do to make up for my mistake."

"We've been over this," she said, lowering her voice as she glanced around. The loss of her baby might be old news, but it would be news again if people overheard them.

"But not like this. Not with both of us willing to take responsibility. If we're ever going to have a chance at a future together, we need to have this conversation."

She didn't agree, but then again, she'd been the one who'd taken refuge in another relationship in another town. Hardly the history of someone wanting to confront a problem, she reminded herself.

"Sherri, I couldn't make my life right, no matter how hard I tried. Being a doctor without you wasn't how I imagined my life would be when I left high school."

"You married Lilly."

"Lilly and I started dating a year after you refused to have anything to do with me."

"During the same time I was trying to get Sam to stop drinking. When Sam died, my first thought was to find you, to confide my sorrow in the one person I could trust to understand—" The threat of tears blocked her throat.

"But I was already—"

"Married."

They sat silently staring at each other, their food cooling on their plates. "Timing is not one of our strengths," Neill said at last.

"That's the understatement of the century." She smiled ruefully, catching the light in his eyes as they stopped eating, aware of how easy it was to talk to him still, all these years later.

"Somehow, I'm going to make this up to you…to us," he murmured, his eyes dark with determination. "We deserve another chance at making each other happy. We didn't succeed last time, but this time it will be different, I swear."

She saw the sincerity in the depth of his gaze and was overwhelmed by the thought that if she'd been able to get past her hurt, if he'd been willing to come home to her, to take responsibility for what they'd done together, they would have been happily married for all these years. "We've come full circle, haven't we?"

"How so?"

"Well, it was Sam who rescued me when I needed rescuing, and it was you who rescued Charlie. If you hadn't become disillusioned with your life in Boston, you might not have been here when Charlie had his accident."

"And if Charlie can see how lucky he is, how much he needs to believe in his good fortune and turn his life around…"

"Do you think this means we're meant to start over, as well? To rescue each other?" she asked, the hope in his eyes easing the air from her lungs.

"Sherri, there is one event I wouldn't change, and that's the arrival of Morgan in my life."

Envy made her heart beat against her ribs. What if their son had survived? Grief slammed into her with the force of a hurricane. It had been twelve long years since she'd lost Patrick, and still the memory of him could shatter her in a matter of seconds. "You're so fortunate to have Morgan."

"In so many ways. Morgan has shown me that there is so much more to life than making money and hoarding power. Lilly found parenting difficult, but for me it was rewarding, a natural extension of who I was. When Morgan was diagnosed with epilepsy, I wanted to put my career on hold, at least for a few years until Morgan's health issues were stabilized and she'd become accustomed to her new life."

"And Lilly?"

"Lilly was already making plans for moving her company to Houston. It was assumed that any change of plans would be mine, not hers."

"Why would you let Lilly make decisions for the two of you? You had as much right as she did to your career and your happiness."

"That's the whole point. I saw in Lilly what I wanted to see."

"Meaning?"

"Lilly liked to live life on her terms." He went on to explain the call he'd received from Dr. Reynolds and Lilly's attitude toward Morgan's care. She could understand Neill's anger at his ex-wife.

"Morgan's been through a lot," she offered.

"Yes, but she's still trying to get her parents back together, to be a family again. She is still convinced that her mother and I will be living under the same roof again someday. When Lilly was here, all she talked about was getting her mother to move here with us. Sometimes I wish that Lilly and I had fought more during our marriage."

"Why?" Sherri asked, surprised.

"Morgan has never understood why we couldn't go on living together. It might have been easier for her to accept if we'd been fighting a lot."

"Do you really believe that?"

He ran his hands through his hair. Her eyes followed the movement of his fingers. "Not really, I suppose. No, I wouldn't want Morgan to go through what a lot of kids go through when their parents fight."

"And do you think she'll start to feel any differently now that Lilly lives so far away?"

"Time will tell, I guess. Meanwhile, I'm a little anxious about the preteen dating scene."

"Dating? She's only nine—she's not old enough to date."

"I know, but she wants to be popular, like any kid,

and the kids in her class are already talking about boys, or so Mom says."

"Apparently I need to brush up on my knowledge of the lives of nine-year-olds," Sherri said.

"Me, too. That's my point. Morgan and her mother love to talk about clothes and school, which has always left me sitting on the sidelines if not outside the dressing room door." He shrugged and smiled, a mannerism Sherri remembered from years ago. Whenever Neill was worried, he'd try to shrug it off or smile it away.

"Does Lilly plan to spend much time in Eden Harbor?"

"Small towns are not Lilly's cup of tea, so I suspect that she'll want Morgan in Houston more often so they can go shopping together."

"How will we manage all this?"

"We?" A grin suffused his handsome features. "I like that particular pronoun where you and I are concerned."

She could feel her cheeks beginning to glow. "And you didn't answer the question."

"I had an interesting conversation with Morgan a couple of days ago. Someone in her class told her about you."

"They did? How did you handle it?"

"She wants to meet you, and I told her she'd already met you in the hospital."

"But if we're getting back together, she'll need to be told what's going on between us."

"She will, but maybe we can let it wait for a while. Maybe we should meet somewhere outside of town for dates."

"I'm not sneaking around! If you and I are going to be together, we're going to be honest about it. Besides, if Morgan finds out that we're dating from someone else at school, she'll be hurt. And I can't blame her. You said she's already missing her mother not being a part of her daily life, and if she finds out you've been sneaking around with me, she might act out."

"Act out how? Run away?"

"It's a possibility. Morgan deserves to be treated like the smart young woman she is." She saw the look of surprise on Neill's face and softened her tone. "I want my relationship with Morgan to start off well. And she's right. Do you realize that someday we may find ourselves wanting to tell her about Patrick?"

"Can I ask you something? Did you name him Patrick after my cousin?"

Patrick Brandon had died of AIDS back when there were very few drugs available to control the disease. "I remember him as a funny, older teenager who we all looked up to when we were in grade school."

Neill reached across the table and cupped Sherri's chin in his hand, brushing her skin with his gentle fingers and driving her desire for him. As he leaned across the table and kissed her on the lips, his mixture of sweat, need and exhaustion fueled the heat rising through her.

He smiled as he kissed her again. "As your doctor, I'm prescribing bed rest for you, with a little extracurricular activity on the side during which you don't have to leave the bed."

"That sounds perfect. There's only one tiny little problem."

"What's that?"

How much she wanted this man, how easily his touch could leave her wanting more. "With the news of Charlie's accident making its way around town, my mom's probably got one of her pals posted on my street watching for me so she can pry information out of me."

"Your mother would have made a great detective."

"I couldn't agree more. Remember how she always seemed to know the exact second we reached the veranda at my house?"

"I do." He kissed her again quickly. "It's time for us to make tracks to my house. There's no one there, only unpacked boxes."

Her control was slipping with each inviting touch of his hands. "Where's Morgan?"

"She's going to her grandmother's house after school. Mom's going to bring her back later. Those two are thick as thieves, and Mom is so happy to have her granddaughter in the same city."

Her heart pounding in delight, Sherri checked her watch. "We'd better get a move on, then."

THE DRIVE TO Neill's house on the edge of town passed in a blur. He drove with one hand on the wheel and the other in hers, his fingers tracing circles on her palm while his gaze flicked from the road ahead to her face, an eager smile on his lips.

Once in his house, he gathered her in his arms and started for the stairs. "I've wanted this ever since I signed the purchase agreement for this house."

"Only that long?" she teased.

He hugged her close to his chest, his eyes locked on hers. "A man spends most of his natural life wanting a woman, and she makes light of his ardor?"

She nuzzled his neck, pressing her mouth into the soft skin in front of his ear. "I'd be more than happy to show you *my* ardor," she whispered and was rewarded with his arms forcing her body closer to his.

He nearly dropped her on the bottom step in his eagerness to get up to his room. "Got to pay more attention," he said, a smile tugging at the corners of his mouth. How long had she waited for this feeling of connection? A feeling she'd only ever had with Neill.

At the landing, he turned and strode down the hall toward the bedroom at the back of the house. He nudged the door open with his shoulder and let her slide down the length of him. Her feet touched the floor just as he kissed her lips, his tongue pushing into her mouth. Her fingers slid over his muscled chest as she reached up and pulled him down to her, kissing the soft skin of his throat as her lips moved up his heated skin.

A lifetime had passed since she'd held him, touched him and reveled in the thought that he was hers.

"Kiss me," he ordered, his voice a soft rasp.

Leaning her body into his, she kissed him, arching toward him as she undid the zipper of his jeans to his thunderous groan of pleasure. Without a word, he lifted her up and placed her on the bed, his hands palming her breasts as he eased down beside her. Making love to him again would be different from any other experience she'd ever had. She gave a catlike stretch, pulling her T-shirt over her head and tossing it to the floor. His fingers working quickly, he undid the front fastening of her lace bra. He looked at her through eyes darkened with lust and need, the moment stilling between them.

The air was quiet, the room warmed by the afternoon sun streaming through the windows. Neill lowered his head to hers, kissing her neck, the bare skin of her shoulders, freeing her mind of all concerns except for the man who was driving her crazy with his touch. All the while he whispered his need for her, his longing. She drew his words into her heart, into the secret place that had held all her pain for so long.

His hands moved down her body, undoing her jeans,

working his fingers beneath her panties. His fingers traced their heated advance over the narrow width of her pelvis while his mouth teased her lips. Her body writhed beneath his as he pulled her closer, his jeans barely containing his erection.

Eagerly, Sherri returned his kiss while she frantically raised her hips and pushed her jeans down her legs, then kicked them off. She breathed a moan swallowed by his kiss—a burst of need, raw and urgent, rushed past her lips as his fingers found their mark. "Don't stop!" she whispered, pulling him on top of her.

He raised his head up, his breath coming in short gasps. "Damn!"

"What?" Sherri asked, her words scraping past her throat.

"We need protection," he said, his voice barely above a whisper. "In the bathroom," he said, climbing out of the bed.

She watched his lithe body with all its angles, the length of his powerful legs as he moved toward the bathroom door, her mind going back to another time, to the night they'd first made love, the night Patrick had been conceived.

As she waited for Neill, memories of that night flooded her. The prickling sand beneath her hips, the unbridled lust, the awkward joining of two bodies in the night. And, afterward, the sweet entwining of their limbs as they lay together beneath the night sky.

She watched in wonder as Neill came out of the bathroom, his eyes searching for hers as he moved to lie down beside her once again. "Sherri—"

"Dad?" Morgan's excited voice rang out from somewhere below. "Dad, I'm home. Gram's with me, and I've got great news!"

They gasped in surprise. "Oh, no!" Neill grabbed his jeans. "What's she doing here?" He glanced at his watch. "Damn!"

Sherri scrambled off the bed and found her T-shirt, pulling it over her head. "Where are my jeans?" she asked, her voice a muted wail.

He pointed to the floor on the other side of the bed. "There!"

Forgetting her panties, she yanked the jeans up her legs and over her hips, wrenching the zipper closed. Her heart pounding, she finger-combed her hair. "What do we do now?"

"We go downstairs," he said, smoothing his hair after pulling his shirt back over his head. "Like you said, we're not hiding our relationship."

"How do we explain that we were in your bedroom?"

"We don't have to," he said, just as they heard Morgan call out again from the hall below.

"Dad! Where are you?"

"Maybe your father's in the kitchen," Donna Brandon could be heard saying, her voice echoing along the stairwell.

Neill held out his hand to her, his gaze steady. "This wasn't how I planned to announce our relationship to my mother and my daughter, but it will have to do." Twining his fingers with hers, he opened the door and started down the stairs.

His mother glanced up, and her face blanched. "Neill. Sherri," she said, clutching her purse and placing her arm protectively around Morgan's shoulders.

CHAPTER THIRTEEN

SHERRI WALKED BESIDE Neill down the long stretch of stairs that brought them face-to-face with Donna Brandon. With each step, she made herself believe that this would go well, that they would find the words to explain, words that would somehow ease the humiliation encompassing her every step toward the bottom, where Neill's mother and daughter waited.

Sherri's courage deserted her when she saw the look of displeasure in the woman's eyes. She turned to Neill. "I'd better go."

He squeezed her hand. "No, I want you here with me."

Sherri waited, hoping Neill could distract Morgan with the opportunity to watch TV or play a video game, or anything that would allow the conversation between his mother and them to take place. She calmed her discomfiture with thoughts of her condo, her ever-patient cat and the quiet solitude of her own private space.

"Dad! What's going on?"

His mother squeezed her granddaughter's shoulders. "Morgan, honey, why don't you get a snack from the refrigerator?"

"No!" A pout formed on her lips. "I want to see Dad." She went to her father, ignoring Sherri as she wrapped her arms around his waist. "Who is she?" Morgan squinted at her father. "Is she the nurse from when

I was in Emergency? What's she doing in our house?" she demanded accusingly.

"Morgan, this is Sherri Lawson. She and I had lunch together, and—"

"You said you were going on a picnic. You never said she was coming to our house. Why is she here?" Morgan scowled at Sherri.

Sherri looked to Neill for support. "I came to see your father."

"In his bedroom?" She turned on her father, tears spilling down her cheeks. "You were having sex with her, weren't you?"

"Morgan, that's none of your business," he said.

Her cheeks hot with embarrassment, Sherri started to move away from Neill. "I shouldn't be here. You need to be with your family."

"Neill, I agree with Sherri. Can we discuss this in private?" his mother asked.

"Dad, I want her out of here now," Morgan said, sobbing.

"I'm leaving," Sherri said.

Neill's eyes implored her. "I don't want you to. You came in my car, remember?"

"I can walk back to town. It's not far." Sherri let go of his hand.

"No," he said, reaching for her.

Morgan edged closer to her father. Wrapping her arms tighter around him, she hugged him. He hugged her back, and then held her at arm's length, his voice gentle as he said, "Morgan, go to the kitchen like your grandmother asked you to do."

Morgan started to object, but the look of determination in her father's eyes must have stopped her. "I don't want her here," she said as a parting shot, her heels hitting the floor hard as she stomped down the hall toward the kitchen.

"Neill, what you and Sherri do together is your business, but why would you be having sex in the middle of the afternoon when you knew your daughter was due home?"

"We didn't know you were coming over. Morgan was supposed to be at your house. I wish you'd called first."

"Morgan wanted to come home. If I'd known about this…" Her voice was stiff, her eyes on Sherri. "My son denied being involved with you when I asked him. I—"

"Mom, Sherri and I love each other." Neill's jaw worked. "We've had a hell of a hard day and we needed a little downtime."

Donna turned to him, her hand strangling the strap of her purse. "And your daughter has had a rude shock."

"I didn't want her to learn about Sherri this way, but now that she has, I'll explain everything to her."

His mother waved her free hand in disgust. "You've barely gotten settled here. Your daughter's only begun to adjust to all the changes in her life, and yet you two can't keep your hands off each other. Do you not see how upsetting this is for Morgan? Surely you could have waited."

Neill rubbed his face. "Mom, please try to understand. We all need a little time to work this out, and Morgan will be better once I've been able to explain it to her. You know I'd never intentionally hurt my daughter," he said, his weariness showing in his voice.

His mother seemed to shrink into the hardwood floor, her expression one of sadness. "Neill, all I've ever wanted was for you to be happy, and I've no right to interfere in your life. All I can say is be kind to Morgan and realize that she's still not truly settled and she misses her mother. She wants her mother to visit her."

"Lilly is welcome to see Morgan anytime she wants. I want Morgan to spend time with her mother. I want my daughter to be happy."

"Happy? The child needs a normal life with two parents." His mother shifted her weight from one foot to the other, her grip on the strap of her purse easing. "What I don't understand is why Lilly would give up custody. What mother does that?"

"Mom, the only one who can answer that is Lilly. As for Morgan, I'm trying."

"I know, Neill." She sighed, a look of contrition in her eyes.

"Thanks for looking after her this afternoon."

"I love Morgan, and having her with me is a joy." His mother's expression softened as her eyes searched Neill's face. "I only want what's best for you and Morgan. I just wish you'd taken a little more time to settle in here before…before this." Her eyes swept the foyer before coming to rest on Sherri. "I may have spoken out of turn, but I'm worried about my granddaughter. She needs her father, now more than ever."

"We didn't mean for this to happen the way it did. We've both had a long day," Sherri said, feeling chastised by this woman's attitude. At the same time, she understood her concern. She'd feel the same way if it were her granddaughter.

"Well, I've said enough. Do you want me to stay for a little while?"

"I do, if you don't mind. I have to drive Sherri home."

"Then I'll go to the kitchen and make Morgan a snack if she wants one." She walked down the hall, her head held high.

After watching her go, Sherri turned to Neill. "I feel so guilty."

Neill hugged her close and kissed her upturned face, his lips lingering on her mouth. "Don't feel guilty. We're entitled to our happiness."

"Hmm. You're right," she murmured, soaking in his closeness, his lips hovering over hers. "It might be better if I went back to my place, though, until you and Morgan talk this out."

He sighed, pressing his forehead against hers. "I guess so. I'll call you later."

"Dad, when's dinner?" Morgan demanded.

They jumped apart, but Neill kept his arm around Sherri's shoulders. "Just as soon as I take Sherri back to her house."

"Dad!" His daughter's tone held resentment.

"Morgan, were you listening in on our conversation?"

"How could I help it?"

His lips formed a tight line. "Morgan, I'm going to drive Sherri home, and then I'll be back."

Morgan's face was distorted by an exaggerated pout. "I got Grandma to drive me home early so I could talk to you. It's important."

"I'll be right back, Morgan."

"You promise?" she asked, and the vulnerability in her eyes made Sherri wince.

"Promise. You wait here and we'll talk. Gram is going to stay until I get back. Or do you want to come with us?"

"No." She shifted her gaze to Sherri. "I want to talk to you in private."

"See you in a few minutes," he said, leading Sherri toward the door. "I'm sorry about all this. We started out with such a great plan for today, and then the accident happened, and I had to be in surgery with Charlie. And now…" He left the thought unfinished.

"Like you said, we're in this together," Sherri said, but it wasn't really the truth.

She wanted Neill to explain to Morgan, in front of her, what she was doing in his house, what she meant to him and how they were going to be part of each other's lives from now on. She could understand how a child's health issues might make a parent feel very protective, but to Sherri, Morgan's impertinent attitude was unnecessary. If Morgan were her daughter… But she wasn't. Nor did Sherri have any role in the girl's life.

Was she just being overly sensitive? Or was this the fear she'd lived with all this time? That Neill would put his interests ahead of hers yet again.

AFTER OPENING THE car door for Sherri, Neill climbed in behind the wheel, his thoughts jostled about what had happened with Morgan and what would have happened had Morgan not shown up. They'd nearly made love, and he still wanted Sherri, badly. But his daughter had come home, had found them together and had been hurt by what she'd witnessed. It was hardly surprising. Children didn't expect to find a strange woman in their house, and it was made worse by the fact that Morgan still held on to the hope that he and Lilly would reconcile.

"Sherri?" He offered her an encouraging half smile and was relieved to see her return it.

He started the engine and pulled out of the driveway. "I didn't do a very good job back there. Of all the times for Mom to bring Morgan home without calling me first."

"It wasn't fun for either of us," she said quietly. "But it's not often that a daughter walks in on her father when he's about to have sex with an old girlfriend." Her attempt at a lighthearted tone failed miserably.

"I wasn't going to have sex with you. I was going to make love to you. I love you, Sherri."

He glanced over to see a startled look on her face. "You believe me, don't you?"

"Yes, I do. It's just that I wasn't expecting you to say that. After the way your mother behaved back there, I had the feeling I was in the way."

"Never again will you ever feel that you're in the way if I have anything to say about it. When Lilly left for Houston, Morgan needed me, and I needed her. We've been a team for a while now. I didn't realize that she felt so possessive, and I definitely didn't realize she'd react this way."

"Why not? She's become accustomed to being the one person in your life. I can see how she'd see me as an interloper. Did she not know you had a date with me?"

"I told her about the picnic with an old friend, but she didn't seem very interested."

"Did you say who you were going on the picnic with?"

"Yes. Maybe seeing us together made it more real. I don't know. With her busy school schedule, she probably hadn't thought about it until she saw us together," he said defensively.

"And when you get home, are you going to talk to her about me?"

"Absolutely." Out of the corner of his eye, he saw Sherri relax back into the seat.

"Today was a shock for her, and it would be for any child who still thought of her parents as a couple," Sherri said. "Did you not date anyone after you divorced Lilly?"

"No. I was too busy." He turned up Sherri's street. "And quite frankly most of the women I worked with were married, and my after-work hours were taken up with looking after Morgan," he said as they pulled up in front of her condo. He turned off the engine, feeling let down and a little dejected. He'd had such plans for today. Everything seemed so chaotic, and he was tired of it. "This is not how I wanted our day to end."

"Me, either."

He touched her cheek, feeling the warmth of her skin, the sense of security her presence gave him. He leaned toward her. "I'm putting you on notice. We are going to start dating, and we are going to have a life together. I've made some major blunders, but from now on, it's you and me."

She unfastened her seat belt and slid her arms around his neck, her breath warm on his cheek, her hands caressing the back of his head in a long-remembered movement that filled him with longing for the love that had once flowed so easily between them.

"Neill Brandon, I'm going to hold you to that." She kissed his mouth, an open kiss filled with promise as her fingers worked into the collar of his shirt, moving down his chest, making his blood hot. After all these years and everything they'd missed out on in each other's lives, all he wanted was to take her home with him and make love to her. He wanted to reclaim her, body and soul.

But he had a daughter at home who needed him, who had always needed him.

As much as he wanted to go with his heart, his instinct to care for his daughter won out. "I'll call you as soon as I get home and see what's going on with Morgan. Will you be all right?"

She touched his cheek and tapped the end of his nose as a smile warmed every part of her face. "Yeah, but you'd better call. You now have two women to keep happy in your life, and neither of us is good at being ignored."

In that moment, suspended between his love for his daughter and for the woman who had been part of his dreams, if not his life, for as long as he could remember, Neill succumbed to the force of his feelings. "I could never ignore you. That would be totally impossible for me. What I wouldn't give to run away with you right this minute and start making up for lost time."

She took his face in her hands and kissed him, a slow kiss filled with a simmering demand for so much more. "No running away for either of us ever again."

"Got it," Neill said, remembering other days when he'd dropped her off at her house, reluctant to let her go. He returned her kiss, pulling her against him across the console, his hands sliding down her back.

"I've got to go," she said, easing away from him. "For both our sakes."

He came around to her door and opened it, once again pulling her close and kissing her. "I'll call you after I talk to Morgan."

She clung to him, her heart pounding with anxiety. Despite her brave words about not running away, she knew the power Neill's mother had exerted over him when they were teenagers. Donna Brandon's love for her son had been evident since the first time Sherri had gone over to Neill's house with him after school. Sherri could still remember the look in her eyes when she gazed at her son, the solid devotion she demonstrated. Neill had often seemed embarrassed by it, but whatever his feelings were toward Donna, his mother's love was unconditional.

CHAPTER FOURTEEN

SHERRI UNLOCKED THE door to her condo and heard the phone ringing. She hesitated before answering and was relieved to hear Gayle's voice.

"I've been calling, trying to reach you. Everyone is talking about what you and Neill did today. Where have you been?"

Sherri had all but forgotten the incident on Cranberry Point in the aftermath of what had happened at Neill's house. "I was over at Neill's."

"Seriously? I knew you two would get together."

"Not that way." She explained what had gone on at Neill's house, her anxiety rising with each exclamation Gayle uttered.

"I'm so sorry. To wait all this time, and then to have his mother and daughter show up under such embarrassing circumstances. Life sucks sometimes, doesn't it? Where's Neill now?"

"He drove me home and went back to talk to Morgan."

"That can't be fun."

"And if he feels as guilty as I do..."

"You're afraid he'll decide not to date you."

The thought had been circling around in her mind. "Neill's life is complicated."

"And what about you? What do you want?"

"I was so embarrassed, Gayle. And the look in his mother's eyes…"

"Sherri, don't get down on yourself. I saw the look in Neill's eyes the day he got the call from your mother that you were headed into Emergency. I saw the love he has for you. It was so obvious. I never felt as sorry for anyone as I did for him that day."

"Gayle, I love him, but love isn't always enough. Neill's back, and maybe we have another chance, but if anything should happen to Morgan over this… If she has another seizure, Neill will take her back to Boston. He'll have no choice. He has to look after his daughter, and I have no role in any of that."

"And you'll be left behind again. Is that what you're worried about?"

Her friend knew her so well. "Yeah."

"Have a little faith in your love for each other. I recognize how difficult that might seem at the moment. But for what it's worth, I truly believe you'll be together."

"You're such a romantic," Sherri said affectionately. "You're also my best friend."

"That I am. And as your best friend, I want you to look after your health. How's your blood sugar doing?"

"I haven't checked for a while."

"Then I'll let you go so you can do your blood check. Talk to you tomorrow."

"For sure."

As much as she worried about Neill's talk with his daughter, she had her own issues to deal with, the major one being her diabetes. After she filled her cat's bowl and gave him some fresh water, she checked her blood sugar. The test strip showed it to be a little elevated but still in the acceptable range. Satisfied, she decided to give her mother a call before starting dinner. Her mother answered on the first ring. "I've been waiting for you to call. I heard that you and Neill saved Charlie's life. I'm so proud of you, dear," Colleen said hurriedly.

"Thanks, Mom," she said, forcing herself to sound upbeat. "I was wondering if you might like to come over and have dinner with me?"

"I've got an even better idea. Linda and I were just sitting here thinking that it's time the three of us had dinner together—an impromptu girls' night in. I've got stew simmering on the stove, and Linda's made a peach cobbler with no added sugar for dessert. What do you say?"

How long had it been since they'd had a meal together? Sherri wanted to change all that. After her trip to the hospital and her diagnosis, she'd intended to spend more time with her mother and her sister. "That sounds fantastic."

"Well then, get on over here," her mother said.

There was something so comforting about going over to her mother's. Although there had never been much money for extras, there had always been lots of good food, and her mother always met her with a smile. But most of all, there had never been any doubt in her mind that her mother loved her, a basic fact that many people couldn't claim as being true in their lives.

When she reached the door of her mother's house, she was met with a hug from her sister. "Tommy and Michael are sleeping over at friends', so we have the whole evening," Linda said, pulling Sherri toward the kitchen. "And Mom's in her glory with people to cook for and fuss over. Right, Mom?"

"You got it," Colleen said, smiling at both of them across the kitchen island as they pulled out stools and sat down to watch their mother put the finishing touches on dinner.

Linda settled in next to Sherri. Tonight, she was wearing a pair of hot pink glasses and had magenta stripes in her hair. Linda changed her hair color as often as she changed her glasses, but it was all part of her sister's drive to prove that she was more than simply a woman who was overweight.

Her smile was enthusiastic. "We've got lots to celebrate. Not only are you the heroine of the day, but I got a promotion at work. I'm now the information officer for the town."

"That's great!" Sherri hugged her sister again, so pleased to see Linda enjoy her success. Linda had always worn her emotions on her sleeve, while Sherri had been the quiet one. As a result, Sherri seldom confided in her sister, uncomfortable with Linda's over-the-top reactions. Observing her sister's enthusiasm, she wondered if their relationship might have been different if she'd shared her disappointment over Neill all those years ago. Would her sister have been supportive? She shrugged mentally. She'd never know the answer to that question, and she couldn't change what she'd done.

Colleen set the ladle down on the ceramic mat next to the stove and turned to face them. "I haven't felt this good in years. Both of my girls here with me, and both doing so well in their lives."

"Makes up for all the bad times, doesn't it?" Linda asked.

"Yep. We're the unbeatable Lawson women," her mother said, her voice brimming with pride.

In that instant, Sherri was overwhelmed with love for her mother. Colleen had always felt she had to hold up the family name, in memory of the husband who'd died of a heart attack when Sherri and her siblings were in school. Her mom had been lucky to find a job that paid her enough to keep the house on Mark Avenue. "But none of it has been easy, has it, Mom?"

She sighed. "No, but it doesn't matter. As the saying goes, 'It is what it is.'"

"So tell us about you," Linda said, turning to Sherri. "Tell us about what happened today."

Sherri related her morning: the trip to Cranberry Point, the frightening sight of Charlie's truck coming down the hill and flipping on its side, Neill's quick action and the surgery that followed. "I stayed with Charlie's parents in the waiting room. They're really worried about Charlie's drinking, or at least his dad is. I'm not sure how much his mother knows."

Linda turned in surprise. "How could she miss it? His truck's always parked at one of the bars downtown once the fishing trawler has docked. No one thinks he goes in there for the food, for heaven's sake!"

In all the times Sherri had been around Charlie's parents, she'd never heard his mother mention anything about Charlie's drinking. "Greg is worried, and after what happened with Sam, I can understand. I'm worried, too."

"Do you miss Sam?" Linda asked.

She'd never talked much about her life with Sam because it all took place in Bangor, and she'd been afraid to talk about it for fear that she might accidently give away the fact that Neill was her baby's father. "Yeah, sometimes."

"I'd always hoped you and Neill would marry. Still, I was so happy when I married Sam," her mother said.

"He used to drink, didn't he?" Linda asked. "I remember being a kid and seeing him and Eldon Patterson sneaking beer out of the Patterson kitchen when Honey Patterson and I used to play together."

"Not really. Not until later."

"That's not what I heard, but I guess it doesn't really matter now. Why *did* you marry him so soon after you moved to Bangor?" Linda asked, a slow smile filling her face. "You didn't have to get married, did you?"

For a moment, Sherri considered telling her sister and her mother the whole truth about that period of her life—about her breakup with Neill, her near-disastrous breakdown after Patrick died—all of it. She wanted to get it all off her chest, to tell them why she'd had to lie about Patrick's biological father. It would feel so good to finally share the most difficult period of her life with them, but as she looked from her sister to her mother, she couldn't do it.

She couldn't betray Sam that way. Sam Crawford had been there for her during the worst time in her life. He'd promised to care for her and her child, and to be a good husband. He had loved her, and she had loved him for a brief period of time. She would protect his memory.

And wasn't her need to tell her family about Neill's behavior just a little too much like revenge? And what would it accomplish, other than to divulge to her mother and her sister a lot of potentially hurtful things about the only two men she'd ever loved. Things that could end up hurting her mother along the way, the last thing she wanted to do.

If she and Neill were going to embark on a new life together, if she genuinely wanted to put the past aside and focus on the future, she needed to do what was right for those she loved. And that included Sam, Neill, her mother and her sister.

"We were expecting Patrick before we were mar-

ried. We fudged my due date just a little. Sam wanted
it that way," she said, remembering how carefully she
and Sam had worked to get the story straight, the one
that would satisfy everyone's curious questions.

Linda gawked at her. "Sam? Sam was as straight as
an arrow. Sam Crawford was a member of the Baptist
Church."

"But it's true." Sherri glanced from her mother to
her sister.

"Oh!" Linda's mouth popped open. She and her
mother exchanged quick glances.

"It's time I told you what a really fine man Sam was."

"Then let's go and sit down where we're comfortable," her mother said, turning the burner off under the
stew. "Food can wait."

After they'd settled into the sofa in the living room,
Sherri took the chair across from them. "When I got
to Bangor to start my nursing program I started dating Sam. He was a wonderful man, and someone who
always saw the good in others. After we lost Patrick,
Sam began to drink. As you said, Linda, he would sneak
beer with a friend in high school, like so many teenagers did, but that was about it. When we began dating in
Bangor, he was strictly a social drinker. After Patrick
passed away, Sam changed."

"It must have been so difficult for you," her mother
said. "Why didn't you confide in either of us?"

"Sam didn't want people to know, and I thought I
was helping by protecting his behavior. The worst part
was watching him harm himself that way and feeling
powerless to do anything about it. That's why I want to
be there for Charlie, if I can help him."

"How?" her mother asked.

"I'm not sure at the moment. All I can think about

are Charlie's wife and family. They love him, and he's about to ruin everything with his drinking. Who knows how much worse it will get?"

"I hope you didn't keep your problems with Sam's drinking from me out of some misplaced sense that I couldn't handle it," her mother said.

Sherri nodded.

"I can understand your concern for me, and it was very thoughtful of you but unnecessary."

"Mom—"

"Yes, I worried about what people thought of me, and with reason, after the way your father's family behaved when I married him. Still, I would rather have been able to support you through all of this. I'm so sorry you felt you couldn't confide in me."

"Please don't feel that way. It's over, and I survived."

"On the subject of men, how are you and Neill getting along?" Linda asked.

"Neill and I have been working on our relationship. He says he loves me and wants us to get back together."

"And you want that, too?" Linda asked.

Did she? When he was around, she wanted to get back with him, but sitting there in her mother's kitchen, she wondered if she might be making a mistake by letting Neill into her life again. After all, he'd only been home a short time, and he had to be lonely. And like he'd said, he was feeling guilty. Was guilt his real reason for wanting back into her life? And how would he feel if Morgan continued to behave toward her the way she had that afternoon? Had she allowed herself to be swept up in the excitement, the hope that she might reclaim her dream?

How easily she'd accepted his sudden presence in her life while never really questioning any of it. Wasn't that how it had been when he hadn't come to Bangor? She hadn't questioned him then; instead, she'd let him walk away from his responsibility.

All the more reason to take it slow where Neill was concerned.

As much as she loved him, there was so much history to overcome. If they were going to succeed in getting back together, they still had lots to work out between them. "We'll see. Right now we've agreed to date."

"I'm so happy for you," her mother said. "And I don't want you to ever think that whatever happens in your life is cause for you to worry about how it affects me."

Linda squeezed Sherri's hand in a show of support as she turned to her mother. "I understand where Sherri's coming from. Don't forget how upset you were when Doug walked out on me. Sherri's right. You've had lots to deal with when it comes to your kids.

"I see why you did what you did, Sherri. If I'd had any way of keeping my life a secret and saving Mom from the gossip mill, I would have. As it is, she's been my rock, and my boys wouldn't have the life they have if it wasn't for her support."

Linda leaned over to her mother and hugged her. "I love you, Mom, and thank you so much."

"You girls have got to stop worrying about me." Colleen patted Linda's shoulders, her voice shaky. "I'm past all that. When I was younger, all I wanted was for my children to be successful and happy, but Ed taught me that's not always going to be possible."

Linda gave her mother another big hug. "You didn't have any control over what Ed did, Mom. Sure, he grew up without a dad, but so did a lot of teenagers, and they turned out okay. Ed made bad choices and he's paying the price. End of story."

"I've come to realize that over the past couple of years, but there are still times when I wish I could have done more, maybe seen just how offtrack his life was, but he was always so good at keeping secrets."

"Amen to that," Linda said ruefully.

"While we're on the subject of secrets, I have one of my own."

"You do?" Linda said.

"What is it?" Sherri urged, anxiety coiling in her belly. "You're not ill, are you?"

"No, nothing like that. I should have told you months ago. I've been seeing someone. Well, not out in public so much as at the store." She smoothed the hair from her face. "This is hard to say because I've worked with this gentleman for years."

"Are you talking about Leonard Hayworth at the supermarket?" Linda asked.

"He got me my job, and he's been there whenever anything went wrong in my life. I don't mean that we had an affair, nothing like that. But after his wife died two years ago, we started going on dates out of town. He wants to stop sneaking around, as he calls it, and he's finally convinced me that I don't have to hide from what people think about me. And I did hide for years, he made me see that."

"You've been seeing Leonard, and I didn't know about it?" Linda said, incredulous. "I live with you, and I didn't know you were in a relationship. How did you manage that?"

Colleen gave her a sheepish glance. "You were busy and didn't notice."

"Those trips to Portland to meet high school classmates from upstate." Linda chuckled. "Well, who would have thought that my mom would do something like that?"

"It doesn't matter anymore. We're going to start acting like the couple we are. We simply decided that life's too short to deny how we feel."

"Are you talking about marriage?" Sherri asked.

"Oh, no. At least not yet. Leonard wants me to move in with him, but I'm not ready to go that route just yet. Besides, living together is not my style."

"Why not, Mom?" Linda asked as she leaned closer to her mother. "After all, it is the twenty-first century, and you're not getting any younger."

"No, I'm not. But I have my plans for this house." She glanced around at the high ceilings, the elaborate crown moldings and arched windows. "I also don't want to rush into anything."

"Rush into anything? Mom, you've been a widow for over twenty years! I'd hardly call that rushing," Sherri said.

"Now, don't you two gang up on me! Besides, if you must know, I nearly invited him here tonight, but I wasn't sure how you girls would feel about it."

"Feel about it? We're happy for you, Mom," Sherri said, joining her mother and sister on the sofa and wrapping her arms around her mother. "You deserve every moment of happiness you can find. And if Leonard makes you happy, we're all for it. Aren't we, Linda?"

"Of course! But it's ticking me off that you've both found someone while I'm still single. It's not fair," Linda said.

"Honey, your day will come. In the meantime, that's enough about my private life. Let's eat. One of you set the table and the other one can make the salad. The ingredients are in the fridge."

"You take the table—I'll get the salad ready," Linda said to Sherri before heading to the kitchen, catching up with her mother and hugging her again. "It's been a long time since the three of us spent an evening together like this."

They ate, laughed and chatted all through dinner. When it came time to go home, Linda walked her sister out to her car. "Sherri, I've never seen Mom so happy. Have you?"

"When your kids were born, and when I graduated from nursing were the only two occasions that come close. But you're right, Mom's life has not been easy. I want her to have the kind of love that makes up for all of it."

"Always looking for perfection, aren't you?"

Her sister's words took her by surprise. "Do you really think that?"

"Yes, of course I do. You always had to have the best grades in school, the best summer job, the perfect dress for prom night. And now look at you. You're perfect—perfect figure, perfect hairstyle and hair color. No one will ever be able to say you didn't do everything as perfectly as you possibly could." Linda wagged her finger at her. "I'll bet there's not a cup out of place in that kitchen of yours, am I right?"

"Just because I like things neat and tidy…"

Linda laughed and kissed her cheek. "Face it. You're perfect. A pain in the butt sometimes, but still perfect."

"If you say so." Sherri fluffed her sister's hair.

"Hey, don't knock it. I wish I had your perfect genes."

Her sister seemed to take life in stride, as if whatever was thrown at her was meant to be. Sherri didn't understand that sort of thinking, but maybe her sister's approach would rub off on her. "Trade you one perfect gene for your hot pink glasses."

"Wait till you see the pair I bought in Portland. They're tiger-striped."

Sherri chuckled. "I can't imagine. I'll talk to you tomorrow."

"Want to do lunch someday soon? Now that I've been promoted, I plan to treat myself to the occasional day when I don't brown-bag it to work." She gave her magenta bangs a pat.

"You're on. Call me when you're ready to hit the lunch spots." With that, Sherri climbed into her car, started it up and eased down the driveway and onto the street.

Feeling content and relaxed, she drove home slowly, listening to a classical radio station, reliving the past few hours with Neill and his family, and then with her family. How different they were, yet how similar. Why did she worry so much about what people thought? If there was one thing she'd like to change, it was her need for acceptance, for proof that she was good enough. Was that where her need for perfection came from?

Once in her driveway, she parked the car and sat there for a few moments while the announcer finished the weather report. It was going to be another sunny day tomorrow, and it made her think of Neill and whether they'd be able to spend time together. Obviously, it would depend on how things went with Morgan. In the quiet of her car, she gave in to her apprehension. Having Neill's mother and Morgan arrive at the house had not only been embarrassing, it had brought back all her old feelings of inadequacy.

She checked her watch and realized that it was getting late. Neill had promised to call her, but she hadn't

heard a word from him. She checked her cell phone.
No missed calls and no text messages. Had something
gone wrong?

CHAPTER FIFTEEN

AFTER HE DROVE Sherri home, Neill returned to his house, his thoughts clouded with worry. How was he going to explain to Morgan why Sherri had been at the house? Sure, he had a right to a personal life, and he wanted Morgan to know about Sherri and to share in the life he wanted for the three of them, but he'd never intended that it start off like this.

Trying to avoid upsetting his daughter after her seizure, he'd kept his feelings and thoughts about Sherri to himself. He probably should have sat down and talked to Morgan about his life, about Sherri. Hadn't Morgan shown an interest in his life when she brought up the fact that Tara had mentioned Sherri?

He should have been more open. He realized that now. Morgan was a bright, intuitive child who needed the security of being part of what was going on, a child whose curiosity about life had brought her to the attention of the teachers back in Boston.

As he drove down the shore road toward his house, he decided that he would start today, right now, and talk openly to his daughter. No more hiding behind the idea that telling her the truth about what was happening in his life might be too stressful, or that she wasn't old enough to grasp the situation. She'd certainly grasped what was going on a short time ago.

He'd put the barbecue on and make his special burgers, one of Morgan's favorite meals. Then he'd answer all her questions, no matter how difficult or embarrassing.

With that thought uppermost in his mind, he pulled into his driveway, noting that his mother's car was still there as he'd expected. His mother had never really understood why Sherri and he had broken up, and he'd avoided talking about it, believing that somehow things would all work out between them.

He pressed the garage door opener and eased into his parking space, careful not to get too close to the lawn mower. He closed the garage as he opened the door leading to the breezeway at the back of the kitchen.

His mother met him at the door. "Oh, Neill. I was just about to call you. Morgan's gone off somewhere."

"What do you mean?" he asked, placing his keys on the counter.

"I sat down to read the paper, thinking she was in the family room. When I called out to her, she didn't answer."

"Did you check her room?"

"I did, but she's not there."

"I'll check. She wouldn't have left the house. Did you look in the attic playroom?" he asked as he climbed the stairs and followed the hall down to his daughter's room at the front of the house. When he opened the door, the room was empty, silent. His chest contracted in fear. "Morgan!" he yelled, striding down the hall to the stairs, ducking into the bathroom on his way past to be sure she wasn't in the shower. Not there. He climbed the narrow stairs to the attic. The air was stifling as he opened the door to the large room that ran the length of the house. The room was eerily quiet.

He raced down the two flights of stairs, going from

room to room, his heart accelerating with every room he searched. She was nowhere to be found. Had she had another seizure? "Mom, did you call Tara?"

"She couldn't have gone over there on her own," his mother replied, her voice radiating anxiety.

He scooped up the phone, clicking on Tara's number in the call list and waiting impatiently while it rang. "Mrs. Williams, I'm sorry to bother you, but is Morgan there?"

"No. Tara is at gymnastics class, and I'm picking her up in about half an hour. Is Morgan missing?"

"She was here a little while ago, and when I got back, she was gone."

"Was she there alone?"

"No." He saw the anguish in his mother's eyes.

"Can I help?" Tara's mother asked.

"No. I'm sure she's just gone—"

Through the window over the kitchen sink, he saw that the door of the barn was ajar. "I think I know where she is."

He went out the back door, across the lawn and into the garage, his mother following right behind him. "What is it, Neill?"

"Morgan, are you in here?" he called, the warm air of the barn closing around him. "Morgan!"

The door of the old tool room opened, and Morgan walked out. His heart leaped in relief. "You gave me an awful scare," he accused, going to her and folding her into his embrace, happiness washing through him.

"I'm sorry," she whispered, her tone contrite.

"I was worried sick," her grandmother said, her shoulders slumping, her expression forlorn.

Neill held out his arm, and his mother moved into his embrace. "We were both worried, but that's all over."

He held his mother and his daughter close, thankful that he had them both in his life. "I came home prepared to make my world-famous burgers. Anyone interested?"

"I'll have two," Morgan said.

"I'd love to stay, but I have to do some baking for the church bake sale tomorrow. Maybe another time," his mother said.

"I'll hold you to it." Neill walked with the two of them out of the barn and closed the latch on the door, feeling the tension ease in his shoulders.

"Call me later, will you?" his mother asked.

"I will."

He and Morgan watched his mother go to her car and drive away.

After they'd gone back in the house, Morgan turned to him. "Is *she* here?" she asked, then went straight to the fridge and took out a can of apple juice.

"No, Sherri's not here."

Morgan gripped the can of juice as the fridge door closed behind her. Snapping the tab, she took a sip. "I don't see why you brought her here."

"Let me explain, Morgan."

"This had better be good, Dad." She sat down at the table.

He sighed as he sat down across from her in the awful chairs that Lilly had insisted they buy when they moved into their first house in Boston. The tabletop was glass, revealing chrome legs that sprawled out under the top, making it virtually impossible to sit comfortably. The chairs were all chrome and white faux leather with hard edges. He'd taken all their furniture from the house in Boston, hoping that by doing so, Morgan would feel less anxious, more at home in her new surroundings. Morgan needed as much of her life as possible to remain the same. He adjusted his long legs beneath the table, searching for a comfortable position. "I didn't mean to have you meet Sherri under such awkward circumstances."

"Awkward? Dad, you and she were in bed together!"

"Not quite."

"But you planned to be."

"And I'm sorry you had to walk in on that, but what happened earlier doesn't change the fact that Sherri and I are… We care for each other."

"You just met her. We've only been here a few months. How can you have sex with a woman in our house when you don't even know her? What about me? What about how I feel?"

"Morgan, I want you and Sherri to get to know each other. You'll like her, I promise."

"I want her out of our lives. She doesn't belong here with us. I need you, Dad. When we moved here, you said that we'd have lots of time together, not like it was in Boston. You promised me that you'd be home more, not at the hospital all the time. You never told me you'd be up in your bedroom with some woman when I came home from school," she said, her voice rising, her eyes glistening.

He wanted to hug her close and tell her that everything would be all right, but Morgan was too smart to be fooled by platitudes. "You're right. I did promise that we would be able to spend more time together after we moved here. I also promised you that you'd get to know your grandmother and make new friends, and you have," he said, feeling so inadequate in the face of his daughter's angry scrutiny.

"So what's this woman hanging around you for?"

"Morgan, it's time I explained something to you."

Morgan took a long drink from her juice, her eyes angry as she placed the can near the center of the table. "This had better be the truth," she muttered.

He ignored the tone and the bravado his daughter exhibited. He understood what was going on with her. She was angry, and she had a right to be. But she also needed to hear what was going on in his life, as he had no intention of giving up Sherri. "Sherri and I knew each other in high school. We started out as best friends, and the more we got to see of each other, the more we wanted to spend time together. She was so smart and outgoing and I was shy, not athletic like you. I didn't have many friends."

"Dad, the nerd," Morgan offered, a smile twitching the corners of her mouth.

"Yeah, your dad was a nerd. Probably still is. Sherri was popular and funny, and she really liked me, much to my surprise."

"Did you date back then?"

"Yes, we dated our last year of high school. And when it came time to decide what we'd do with our lives, we decided that I would be a doctor and she would be a nurse. We'd set up practice somewhere around here, and we'd have a family and build a house together."

"Dad! That's so old-fashioned. Did you really think you'd be together forever? No one does that anymore."

"When did you get so cynical?"

"It's real life. No one expects to stay together. Mom says that people change and so do their feelings, so it's not reasonable that two people would stay married forever."

He wanted to strangle Lilly right about then. What a harsh thing to tell a daughter struggling to accept her new life without both parents. But had he done any better? "Yes, things can change, and people can grow apart. And it's also true that sometimes when you least expect it, you can rediscover someone."

"And fall in love again, you mean?"

"Sure. Why not?"

Morgan shrugged and chewed her lip. "I will never figure you adults out. You're always screwing up."

"Morgan!"

"Well, it's the truth. Every one of my friends has at least one parent that's a nutcase. No one gets to go home and just hang out because there's always someone upset or unhappy. My friend Kirsten—her mom takes tranquilizers. Did you know that?"

"No, I didn't."

"Well she does. I've seen the bottle of pills. Kirsten showed it to me." Morgan reached for the juice can and twirled it in her fingers, then took a quick sip and returned it to the center of the table. "I suppose now you're going to tell me that Sherri's life is a total mess and you want to help her, right?"

"No, that's not it at all. Don't talk like that."

"Why not? It's reality, Dad."

"Well, it probably is for some people, but not for you and me. And not for Sherri."

"If you say so." Morgan looked at him doubtfully.

"I'd like you to meet her under different circumstances than today."

"Well, don't expect me to like her."

"I like her."

"How much?" she asked, defiance shining in her eyes.

Did he dare tell his daughter the rest of the story? And if he did, how would she take it? But hadn't he decided that he'd tell her the whole truth? "When I moved from here to Boston, I was in love with her."

"And what about now?"

"We're getting to know each other again." Why had he said that? He wanted his daughter to share in his happiness. "No, that's not the complete truth. We still love each other. We probably always have."

"You married Mom and had me while you loved someone else?"

"No, that's not true. I loved your mother very much in the beginning."

"But you don't love Mom now, right?"

How could a nine-year-old be this mature? Was that what happened to children of divorced parents? "No, I don't love your mom anymore. I care about her, and I'm glad she's your mother, but sometimes love doesn't last."

"Why?"

"I wish I knew, sweetie."

Her intense gaze remained focused on him. "Then I don't get it. How could you still love this woman?"

Not knowing what to say and seeing the anxiety in her eyes, he came around the table and knelt down next to Morgan. "I know it's complicated, but sometimes life is just that. Complicated." He put his hand over hers where it rested on the table. "I want you to understand that regardless of my feelings for Sherri, I love you, and I will always love you."

"How do you know? Lots of people fall out of love, and into love for that matter," she said, her eyes searching his while she sat perfectly still.

"Because my love for you is completely different from any love I feel for Sherri, or the love I once felt for your mom. You're my daughter, and that will never change. We will never stop being a part of each other's life. Just like it is between your grandmother and me. Although I went away to college, became a doctor and then moved back here, Mom never stopped loving me, and I never stopped loving her. That kind of love goes on forever."

"But I know kids who say they don't love their parents. Does that mean their parents don't love them?"

He stared at his daughter. "Have you been thinking about this a lot lately?"

"Yes, Dad. All kids think about this."

He sighed, his hand still on hers. "Sometimes our love for one another gets messed up with other painful things going on in our lives. When that happens, love can get buried in the troubles a parent or a child might be going through."

Relieved to see the look of understanding in Morgan's eyes, he pulled her into his arms and held her close. "Face it, kid," he growled as he hugged her. "We'll always be together."

She laughed, a deep belly laugh, and hugged him back. "Dad, I'm hungry."

"I am, too," he said, relieved that Morgan seemed to be okay, that he'd handled the situation the best he could. Still, it had been a close call—the look in his daughter's eyes had told him that.

"And by the way, what were you doing in the barn?" he said, happy to have made it through the conversation without a major upset.

"Did you know that the place is filled with stuff for building things? There are saws and hammers and a table with a saw in it."

"Morgan, you didn't touch any of it, did you? You could hurt yourself."

She gave him an exaggerated frown. "Of course not. Are you going to take up woodworking?"

He'd been so excited to find the property for sale that he'd only given the barn a cursory glance. "I hadn't planned to."

"I've got an idea. Let's have a yard sale and clean out the barn. It would make a great place for me and my friends to hang out. What do you think, Dad?"

"You're brilliant. We'll start on it next weekend. Get it cleaned out and go from there."

Morgan gave him a high five. "Cool."

"Now it's time to fire up the barbecue."

"I'll help you make the patties."

He'd assembled all the ingredients for his burger recipe when he remembered he hadn't called Sherri. *Damn!* He scooped up the phone and dialed her number. She answered on the first ring. "Sorry for not calling you sooner," he said.

"How did it go?"

He glanced around, relieved to see that Morgan was not in the kitchen. "We talked, and she seems okay," he said tentatively, still not 100 percent sure that Morgan understood how serious he was about Sherri.

"Well, I'm relieved Morgan knows about us and how we feel about each other."

"She does."

He could hear her sigh and wished he were there with her. "While you were talking with Morgan, I had dinner with my mom and Linda. We had a great time, and I feel so much better about everything. Do you really think it's our turn for happiness?"

"I definitely do."

"Will I see you after my shift tomorrow?"

"We can have dinner over here," he affirmed as Morgan came through the back door. "The other woman in my life just appeared. Talk to you tomorrow."

"Love you."

"Love you, too," he said.

"Was that Sherri?" Morgan asked as he hung up the phone.

"Yes."

"You said you loved her," Morgan said, her voice low as she came toward him.

"I do love her."

Morgan swerved away from him. "Love is so dumb."

"Wait until you fall in love and we'll see if you still feel the same way."

She gave him a sideways glance. "I'll never understand old people."

"I'm not old," he protested, and then he saw the silly smile on her face.

"Let's get the barbecue going. I'm famished."

"Me, too." Morgan followed him out to the back patio, and the familiar act of barbecuing calmed Neill down. It had been such a stressful day—yet a good day in so many ways.

THREE DAYS LATER, Neill and Sherri were finishing up a surgical clinic where people came to have dressings or incisions checked by the surgeon. Their last patient of the day was Charlie Crawford. His bruises had begun to fade. His ribs were still sore, and his arm would need physiotherapy and possibly occupational therapy, both of which Neill had ordered.

"Well, that's about it for today. I think you're making great progress," he said in an attempt to lighten the sorrowful look on Charlie's face. He liked the man. Charlie's wry sense of humor had provided some funny moments during those summer months when they'd both worked in Crawford's Hardware store.

"That's good to hear. I want to thank you and Sherri again for being there. I could have died."

"We're glad we were there for you, too, Charlie. It looks like you'll make a full recovery, and that's all that matters. Is there anything else I can do for you?"

Charlie didn't answer.

He noted that Charlie's hands shook a little and he seemed somewhat agitated. Was he beginning to suffer from withdrawal? "Charlie, are you feeling okay?"

"Sure, Neill, I'm fine." Charlie sat up straight and drew air deep into his lungs.

"You're sure?" Neill pressed.

Charlie looked down at his work boots and then stared at his hand where it rested on his jean-clad thigh. "Is Sherri here today?"

"Yes, she is. Did you want to see her?"

"I would, if you don't mind."

"I'll get her."

Neill went out to the desk, placing Charlie's chart on the raised counter in front of Gayle as he waited for Sherri and Gayle to finish their conversation.

Sherri's eyes met his and the old warmth generated by seeing her washed through him. "Charlie wants to see you," he said. "He's in Exam Six."

Sherri put the chart she'd been holding down on the counter. "Thanks."

She walked past him down the hall, and he couldn't help watching her—the way her body moved, the sway of her hips. Heat rose through him. He'd been busy the past two days, and the dinner they'd had seemed like such a long time ago. He intended to invite her to his house tonight. He'd already talked to her about getting together that evening for dinner. He'd initially wanted to invite Morgan along, but she and Tara had a test for the next day, and they were going over to their friend Kirsten's house to study together. Morgan was going to go to his mom's place for dinner, and he'd agreed to pick her up there after he took Sherri home.

He needed to tell Sherri about his conversation with Morgan, but he hadn't found the right time, and she seemed to be avoiding the subject. But he'd see what she had to say tonight when they had an evening alone together.

He was looking forward to being with her, to having her focus solely on him. It was selfish, perhaps, but he'd missed her over the years and he was desperate to rekindle what they'd once had. He was convinced that they had so much to look forward to, once they sorted through their problems. And they still had a major one—she had to trust that he would put her first—that he would never walk away from her again.

Proving that he had changed would take time, but he would manage it because seeing her again, being around her, had driven home the fact that there was no one else in the world who could make him happy the way Sherri could. It was a realization that was both exhilarating and frightening at the same time.

His life held such hope now, such opportunity, which was strange because when he'd first come home, he'd wondered if he would feel stymied being in a small town. But he didn't, because he had realized how appreciated he was by the people he looked after, many of whom he had a personal connection with.

He was finally beginning to understand why his uncle Nicolas, a brilliant surgeon, had become a family practitioner in a place where no one would ever realize just how great an impact he might have had on the field of surgery had he opted to remain in a large medical center affiliated with a great medical school.

In Exam Room Six, Charlie's sobs filled the room. "I'm sorry. I didn't mean to cry. It's just that it's been *so* hard these past few days. I want a drink so bad, but if I have one I'll break my promise to my wife. I promised not to drink, and I meant it, really."

He scrubbed his face with his hands, and Sherri noted the lines on his forehead, the sallowness of his skin, the way his fingers trembled. "Charlie, you have to get professional help. You can't go on like this any longer."

His head down, his dark hair curling around his face the way Sam's had, reminded her of the nights Sam had come home vowing never to have another drink. He'd never been able to keep the promise. "Sam didn't get help. But if he was here now, he'd want you to listen to me. To get the professional help you need."

Charlie's dark eyes met hers. "You think I'll end up like Sam?"

"You won't. Not if you decide to get help."

"But I don't want to go to the local AA group. I've tried to keep my drinking a secret. After the accident, Dad came to see me and wanted to know what he could do to help. He's trying to keep it from Mom since her heart isn't good. Dad told me she doesn't know how bad my drinking is, and I'm afraid Mom will find out." He stared at Sherri, his eyes watery. "I'm afraid of everything these days, and I hate the feeling."

"Would you go to Bangor or Portland to the AA meetings there?"

"I could try." He resumed looking at his feet, his

hand resting tentatively on the exam table. "My whole life changed when Sam died. He was there for me, no matter what. I miss him."

"I do, too. He was a good person, and he loved you."

Charlie's shoulders shook. He gripped the table. "My wife wants a divorce, and I don't want that. I love her. We went to school together, and having Cassie and Cindy made me the happiest I can ever remember being. If Freda divorces me, I—"

He got up, went to the window and stared out. "I'm a mess, and I don't... I can't seem to fix it."

Sherri wished there was something she could say, some magic solution she could offer. Watching Charlie brought back all the memories of listening to Sam, to his pleas for understanding and support. All of which she'd offered, only to come home from a shift at the hospital to find him in the family room too drunk to make it upstairs to their bed.

"Charlie, I don't know what else to say to you other than please get help before it's too late. I don't want to lose you like I did Sam."

He looked at her with the same pleading glance Sam had offered so many times during the last year of their marriage. "I'll sign up for AA outside of town, but I may need more than that to get better." He glanced at his trembling hands.

"I'll look around and see what I can find. Would you go to see a psychologist?"

"Anything to save my marriage," he said, and Sherri knew he meant it.

NEILL COULDN'T STOP his gaze from searching the corridor, waiting for Sherri to return.

"Sherri's a beautiful person, isn't she?" Gayle said, looking up from her computer.

"What?" Neill glanced down at her.

"I saw you watching her. It's clear to everyone how much you care about each other."

"I do care," he said, forcing his attention back to the chart he was holding.

"Sherri told me about your relationship in high school. I'm so happy that you've decided to try again. What you have is special." She peeked up at him from under her voluminous hair. "You really love each other."

He couldn't stop the smile forming on his lips. He liked this woman. "We'll get it right this time around."

"She really wants it to work out," Gayle said.

The phone rang and Gayle answered it. Neill wished he could go down to the exam room to see what Charlie and Sherri were talking about. He had no right to know, but he wanted to all the same. He tucked the chart under his arm and started for the doctor's dictation space along the corridor leading to Exam Six. He could always dictate while he waited for Sherri; better that than standing at the desk like a lovesick teenager. He was nearly at the dictation room when Sherri appeared. "How did it go?" he asked her.

Neill knew by the look she gave him that she was upset, and he opened his arms to her. She walked into them, her head coming to rest on his shoulder, his heart swelling in his chest as he gently put his arms around her.

"Neill, Charlie wants to stop drinking, but he's afraid he can't do it."

"But there are organizations out there whose sole purpose is to help. All he has to do is take the first step."

She pulled away from him, her fingers reaching for

the tiny heart necklace at her throat. "It's not that simple, Neill. Charlie and Sam grew up in the same house and faced the same issues."

He didn't want to argue with her because he wanted to talk to her about tonight and his plans for their dinner. But her expression made it clear that she was too worked up about Charlie to focus on anything else. "Sherri, you can't get involved in this. Charlie is a grown man with a wife and family. He has to work out his own issues."

"Well, he's doing a lousy job so far."

"And you think you can change that?"

"I don't know. He's Sam's brother, and I feel responsible in a way."

Neill believed that addiction could only be treated if and when the afflicted person wanted to change, but he loved Sherri, and he intended to see that she was happy. "Okay, why don't we sit down in the dictation room and see what we can do."

They went in, and he closed the door. The scent of her skin, the anxiety evident on her face, made him want to hold her close. He settled for taking her hand. "Tell me why you feel Charlie's case is different, why he needs more support."

Sherri sighed. "Because Sam and Charlie grew up in a very strict household where the boys were always expected to work harder than anyone else, to obey their parents no matter what. They were never allowed to have friends over or to go out, except on Saturday night, and then only until midnight. They endured a lot of teasing and felt singled out by their peers as being weird, and as a result neither boy was popular growing up."

"But they had everything—cars, snowmobiles, fancy clothes. I remember they went on a lot of trips."

"Sure they did, but only after they did as they were

told. Alcohol was completely prohibited. Sam told me about the one time he'd come home drunk and what a horrible scene it was. He never did it again. He made up for it by drinking like a fish once he got to Bangor."

"But that's in the past, and there are people who can help Charlie, professionals with experience. Why do you feel so responsible?"

Sherri didn't answer for a moment. "I owe Sam's brother. I told you if Sam hadn't been there for me, I don't know what I would have done. And Sam loved Charlie very much. When Sam started to drink, his big concern was that Charlie not find out. Most of all, I feel guilty that I didn't do enough for Sam when I realized that he was drinking more than just socially. At first, I pretended that he was only doing it because he was worried about me, or about his job, or about the baby. After Patrick died, I knew that his drinking was getting out of control, and still I did nothing."

"What could you have done?"

"I could have talked it out with him, made him see what he was doing to himself and to us. But a part of me didn't want to talk about our relationship because I had come to realize that with the baby gone, I didn't have any real feelings for Sam beyond friendship. I had thought that I loved him but I couldn't have or my feelings wouldn't have changed so easily. And worst of all, Sam became even more loving after the baby died, and I started to feel smothered by his affection. I was afraid he wanted to have a child with me, and I couldn't face the idea. And I couldn't ask for a divorce, because I couldn't hurt him. I was sure Sam knew how I felt, which made me feel even worse." She stared down at her hands. "To this day, I believe that had I been more caring, or had I seen the signs earlier, Sam would still be alive. When they found his body, I couldn't help but wonder if I'd been more responsive, or if he'd married someone who truly loved him, then he wouldn't have died."

Neill gave in to his need to take her in his arms. "Sherri, you did what you could for Sam, and there's no point in dwelling on the past. It won't help Sam or you."

She shoved him away, her eyes shimmering with unshed tears. "No, you don't understand and you never will. I wanted to love Sam. Forever. I wanted to be his wife, and to make him happy. But because of you, I never really committed myself to the marriage. I was always holding out, waiting for you. And I hate myself for that!"

He reached for her. "Sherri—"

"Please don't."

"Okay. How about this? I'll take you home and make dinner. You need to eat."

"What about Charlie?"

"We can't do anything for him today. I'll set up a follow-up appointment for him, and I'll talk to him about his issues around alcohol. If he's receptive, I promise you I'll get him in with the best psychologist in Boston, where he'll get the help and support he needs to deal with his problem away from here. The psychologist I have in mind has treated substance abusers for most of the years she's been practicing, and if anyone can help Charlie and his wife, Dr. Sharp can. How does that sound?"

"Thank you," Sherri murmured, wiping the tears off her cheeks.

"You're welcome." He wanted to take her home with him, feed her and tuck her into their bed, the way he would if they were married. But they weren't, and he had to live with that for the moment. "It's time for us to finish up here. I have big plans for you this evening."

She stood up, smoothing her hair from her face. "I'm so hungry."

The need to make love to her made his arms shake. He craved her touch, the feel of her hands on him, the urgency of her smile. Instead, he put his hand on the curve of her back and led her out of the room. "I'm going to set a record here on how fast I can complete this dictation. Then I'll pick up all the ingredients to make you a dinner you'll never forget."

"Thank you for everything, and especially for helping Charlie. With your help, he'll recover. I know he will."

CHAPTER SIXTEEN

ONCE HE FINISHED his dictation, Neill made a quick stop at the grocery store and picked up fresh pasta, salad makings and frozen low-fat yogurt for dessert. He intended to be there for Sherri that evening by simply offering his love and support.

He'd done so much damage to so many people by his careless, thoughtless behavior all those years ago. If only he'd acted differently, been there for Sherri back then. They would've gotten married, moved back to Eden Harbor, set up a family practice together as they'd planned and maybe even been friends with Sam and whoever he'd married.

Instead, Sherri and Sam had had their lives changed forever because of his behavior. It was frightening to think how easily a person's life could be altered by the simplest and sometimes most careless decision, the kind of decision that ended up having huge repercussions.

When he arrived at her condo, her car was already there. Carrying his two paper bags of groceries, he went up the steps to her front door. "That was fast," she said, taking one of the bags from him and setting it on the counter in the kitchen.

He followed her, placing his bag on the counter before pulling her into his arms and kissing her.

She responded instantly to his touch, her arms going

around his neck. "You have no idea how long I've waited for this," she whispered against his lips.

"Me, too." He kissed the corners of her mouth, trailing his lips along her chin, molding her body against his. "I have a confession to make."

"And that would be?"

"I wanted to make love to you in the dictation room so bad."

"You did?" She leaned back in his arms and gazed up into his face.

"Yes. Actually, it was the second time I wanted to make love in the dictation room."

"Really?"

He nodded, tucking a stray strand of her hair behind her ear. "The other time was the day we had our first clinic together, the day after Morgan was brought in to Emergency."

She touched his face, her fingers stroking his neck down into the V of his sports shirt. "That day is forever burned into my mind." She kissed his throat. "Making love in the dictation room. Isn't that just a little perverse?"

He moved his body against hers. "You do strange things to me."

She groaned in pleasure. "If only I didn't need to eat."

"You're talking about food? Now?"

She sighed and looked up into his eyes. "I'm afraid I am."

"I did promise dinner, didn't I?" he said, harboring an irrational hope that somehow she was kidding about needing food. He knew better, and he wanted her to be healthy and happy and everything else good in life.

"You did, but if it will make you feel any better, I'll

get showered and changed and help you. I'm really good at setting the table."

He put an arm around her shoulder and walked her down the hall to her room. Kissing her, he whispered, "I'll be waiting."

He busied himself with finding where she kept her pots and pans, filling a pot with water for cooking the pasta and assembling a salad. All the while, he listened for the sound of her coming down the hall, his body heating as he imagined the water sluicing over her wet skin, the sweet scent of her shampoo as she lathered her hair, her neck stretched back as the water cascaded over her body. He considered joining her, but he remembered his promise to himself that he would go slow and make what she needed his top priority.

He was grating Parmesan cheese when he felt her arms wrap around him. She pressed her body into his. "You smell delicious," he said, turning in her embrace and kissing her, feeling a wonderful sense of connection when she smiled and touched the hair on his forehead.

"Thank you, and it's so nice to have someone make dinner for me." She gathered the plates, knives and forks and took them to the table near the window that looked out onto a small flower garden. "I'm thinking about converting my flower garden into a vegetable garden so that I can have fresh salad greens during the summer. I'm going to concentrate on eating healthy to stabilize my blood sugar."

"Always working on self-improvement. I remember that about you," he said, realizing that his property had huge overgrown herb and vegetable gardens that he could picture the two of them working in on long summer days. "I've never successfully grown anything. Houseplants wilt at the sight of me."

Sherri laughed. "I could show you how it's done, city slicker," she teased.

This was the woman he'd fallen in love with. "You're on," he said, feeling the tension ease from his shoulders at the prospect of what the evening might lead to.

Once dinner was ready and they were seated, they ate in companionable silence. "I have another confession to make," Neill said finally.

"What's that?"

"I had this really special date planned. I was going to take you out to an expensive restaurant this evening, and then we were going to go dancing somewhere."

"In Eden Harbor?"

"No, we were going to go to Portland. Really live it up."

Sherri placed her fork and knife beside her plate. "That was delicious. We can do your fancy date another time, right?"

"Whenever you're ready."

"I've started using the insulin pump you recommended, and it's so much easier than before."

"Oh, that's great," he said, almost having forgotten about Sherri's diabetes.

"And you know, it's not so bad. When I first started on insulin, I was worried that I wouldn't be able to give myself the injections, despite my years of instructing others how to do it. I know how silly that sounds. So I had a little talk with myself. How could I expect my patients to adapt to testing their blood if I couldn't do it myself? It's going quite well now, so you can drop that concerned look of yours," she said, her eyes reading him like a book, something he'd never really gotten used to when they were together.

"Sherri, I want to apologize for implying that you

shouldn't help Charlie. I didn't realize how much you had to deal with during your marriage to Sam."

"There was no way you could have known. No one did. Not even my in-laws. They were just happy to have Sam married to someone they liked, and Sam never wanted them to find out about how bad his drinking had become. I'm sure they were aware that he drank socially, but that was the extent of it."

"It must have been really hard to come to the realization that you didn't love Sam."

She sighed. "What's so disheartening is that Sam never really had a chance at life. Sure, he had money and he had a good job, but he didn't have many friends except Charlie. His parents were so determined to see both their sons be successful that they lost track of the fact that they both had their own dreams of what they wanted from life."

"You weren't responsible for his unhappiness."

"No, but in a way I did the same thing to Sam. I was willing to accept his offer of marriage for the wrong reason, and he ended up paying the price."

"But you were willing to stay in the marriage out of loyalty to him." Neill couldn't stop himself from saying it.

"My penance, you mean?"

"No...well, maybe." He pushed back from the table in an attempt to hide his remorse at his role in all of this. "Let's talk about something else. I'll get the dessert and make coffee."

She cleared off the table and loaded the dishwasher while he got the frozen yogurt out of the freezer. He was about to load a tray to take to the living room when his cell phone rang. "It's Mom," he said, hitting the button.

"Neill, where is Morgan?" his mother asked without preamble.

"Isn't she at Kirsten's?" he asked. "I thought she was going over there to study."

"She did, but once I got dinner ready and she hadn't shown up, I called Kirsten's house and neither of the girls is there. Kirsten's mother didn't seem particularly concerned and thought they'd said something about going to Tara's. But they're not there, either."

"She has her cell phone. Did you trying calling her?" he asked.

"I did, but there's no answer. Are you home?"

Where could Morgan have gone this time, and why wasn't she answering her phone? "I'm at Sherri's condo. We're having dinner."

"Sherri? You talked to Morgan about her, didn't you?"

"I talked to her about Sherri, and she was fine with it." That wasn't the complete truth, but something in his mother's tone put him off. He felt as if he were sneaking around, and he wasn't. Sherri's arm snaked around his waist. He smiled down at her, glad she was there with him.

"She didn't give me the impression that she was at all happy about you dating someone."

What had gotten into his mother? She'd always been so supportive, but she was making it very clear that she wasn't happy about Sherri being back in his life. "I'll head over to the house and see if she's there. I'm sure she just stopped off at another friend's house and forgot to call," he said as much for his own peace of mind as for his mother's.

"Neill, please understand I'm not trying to interfere, but at the risk of repeating myself, I think you need to give Morgan a chance to get used to the changes in her life. Your daughter misses her mother, and now she's mixed up about where she stands with you."

"Did she tell you that?" Neill asked. It hurt him to think that Morgan had shared those feelings with his mother and not with him.

He started getting worried. What if Morgan had had a seizure? What if that was the reason she hadn't shown up at his mother's? "Mom, I'm going to my house to see if Morgan is there. Will you call her other friends and see if anyone has seen her?"

"Of course. Are you taking Sherri with you?"

"Yes, Mom. If anything has happened to Morgan—"

"You don't think she's had a seizure, do you?"

Suddenly that was all he could think about.

"Mom, I'll call you when I get to the house."

His mother sighed before hanging up.

"Where's Morgan?" Sherri asked.

"I don't know." He took a deep breath to ease the worry lodged in his chest. Nothing could happen to his daughter. Despite his feelings around his mother's quiet condemnation of his involvement with Sherri, he certainly didn't want his daughter to be harmed by his choices in life.

"You'd better get over to the house to see if she's there."

He ran his hand through his hair, his mind wrestling with his thoughts. "I can't believe that she's done anything more than taken off for home without telling anyone. She's been so happy being able to visit friends and stay at her grandmother's without having to be driven around like she did in Boston."

"You go, and call me when you get there."

His heart filled with worry, he said, "I need you with

me. I've been alone these past two years trying to deal with my daughter on my own, and I'm so tired." He rubbed his face, guilt and worry wiping out the evening of relaxation he'd needed so badly.

She reached for him. "I'll go with you." As he held her, soaking in the scent of her, the warmth of her body pressed to his, he wished... He wished for a lot of things lately. Most of them revolving around the woman in his arms.

He looked down into her eyes. "I'm so glad you're back in my life," he said.

"Me, too." Sherri whispered.

He reached behind him to where his keys rested on the counter. "Let's go find Morgan."

CHAPTER SEVENTEEN

THE SUN WAS sinking below the horizon as they pulled into Neill's yard. They both clambered out of Neill's SUV, their eyes searching the shadows created by the trees near the back of the lot. Sherri had hoped they might see Morgan walking along the street toward home, but there hadn't been any sign of her. If Morgan was *her* daughter, there'd be consequences for behaving this way, but she wasn't the girl's mother. It wasn't up to her to decide.

"She didn't answer her phone, so she must have turned it off. She had better be in the house," Neill said.

"We'll find her," Sherri said, touching his arm as they stood at the back door.

"Why would she not go to Mom's when she knew I planned to pick her up there?" he asked, exasperation adding a sharp edge to his words.

"Let's check the house."

Just then, the door to the barn opened, and the girls came out, their heads close together. They were carrying a large red watering can.

"Morgan! What are you doing here? Why didn't you tell your grandmother or me where you were going?"

Morgan's face went white and her lips formed a big O. "Dad, I'm sorry." She rushed over to him, wrapping her arms around his waist. "We were done studying and decided we wanted to come here. I wanted to show Kirsten the barn."

He hugged his daughter to him, pressing his lips to the top of her head. Sherri's heart lurched in her chest. The sight of the two of them made her long for the child she'd lost. Patrick would have been eleven this summer...

"It's okay, sweetie, but from now on you have to tell me or your grandmother where you are at all times. That's why you have your own cell phone, so that you can call either of us whenever you need to." He tilted her chin up. "Got that?"

"Got it, Dad. I wanted to show Kirsten all the stuff in the barn, how awesome it is with the upstairs room and the funny little window that looks out into the trees. I want to clean out that room when we do the rest of the barn. Can we, Dad?"

"What did you have in mind to use it for?" he asked.

Sherri watched as Neill smoothed the long curls from Morgan's face, his touch loving and gentle. She wanted to be a part of their world, a part of Morgan's life. She missed not having a family of her own and the opportunity to enjoy moments like this, to experience a life that included a child.

Kirsten came and stood next to Sherri. "That barn is amazing. Totally." She glanced up at Sherri. "Could I get a drink of something? It was a long walk over here."

Sherri looked at Kirsten, at her straight blond hair and her big, round eyes, and smiled. Kirsten looked just like her father, Matt Seymour, one of the park wardens. "I'm sure you can. Why don't we go inside?"

She glanced at Neill, who nodded and linked his arm with his daughter's. He led the way into the house. Morgan hadn't looked in Sherri's direction yet, which was a bit disconcerting to say the least. Covering her discomfort, Sherri got each of the girls a glass of apple juice from the refrigerator and was relieved to hear them talking in animated tones about the barn and making plans to hold a yard sale.

Later, Kirsten and Morgan went upstairs to Morgan's room and Sherri put the glasses in the dishwasher. "Would you like a cup of coffee?" she asked.

"Sounds great," he said, and she could feel his eyes on her as she filled the coffeemaker with water.

She was getting the cups from the cupboard when she felt his body close to hers. He lifted the hair off her neck and pressed his lips to her skin, sending a cascade of need flowing through her body. "Neill." She sighed, leaning back into his embrace.

"I've missed this so much. Remember how we used to slip into your mother's house after school and get a can of pop and sit on the back step? Do you have any idea how much I wanted to make love to you back then? How hard it was to sit on that step and keep a conversation going when the pressure of your hand on mine was enough to make me want to carry you off to your room?" His arms tightened around her.

It all seemed so long ago. "I do," she said. She turned in his arms and looked up into his eyes. He was looking at her the way he used to all those years ago when they were so in love, so completely in sync with each other. Feelings of need, of confusion and of longing for the past surfaced. "We were so close, so incredibly aware of each other back then."

"And now?" he asked, kissing her slowly while his hands moved gently up her back and came to rest at her collarbone. Her pulse leaped beneath his fingers. His dark eyelashes framing his hazel eyes stood out against his pale skin; freckles still topped the edge of his cheeks. Everything about him was so much what she needed, and she wanted to forget the past and simply be in the present moment with this man.

She clung to him, her breath coming in short gasps, her head thrown back as he kissed her throat, the touch of his lips both demanding and tender.

"Dad!"

Neill's arms released her. He stepped back, his gaze going to his daughter. "Morgan, I didn't know you were there."

"No kidding!" She marched past them, over to the fridge, opened the door and got out two cans of pop. "Kirsten and I are making signs for the yard sale," she said, staying as far away from them as possible. "My father kissing someone I don't even know. This is so embarrassing!"

"Morgan, wait," Neill said. "I want you to come back here and apologize to Sherri. That is no way to behave."

Morgan stopped at the door, turned her angry gaze on Sherri and mumbled, "I'm sorry."

It was clear she didn't mean it, but Neill didn't say anything.

"Morgan, I hope you and I can get to know each other better," Sherri said in an attempt to make peace with the girl.

"What for?"

"Morgan, what's gotten into you? We talked about this, and you were all right with it. What's going on?" Neill demanded.

Morgan's face contorted, and she scrunched her lips together. "I wish she wasn't here," she said.

Silence shrouded the room. Neill went over to his daughter and put his arm around her.

Morgan stepped back, clutching the two cans of pop in front of her, shielding her from his touch.

"You're not being nice. We'll talk about this later," Neill said.

They both watched as she left the room, her voice rising as she called out to Kirsten to come downstairs and go out to the barn.

Neill sighed, his expression apologetic as he reached out his arms for Sherri. "I'm sorry." He put his arms around Sherri and rested his forehead against hers. "Nothing cools things off faster than an angry kid," he said, his hands moving back up to her neck.

But the moment had been lost. "Neill, this isn't working," she murmured, easing out of his arms.

"What's wrong?" he asked, his eyes telling her that he already knew. He joined her at the table.

"You want Morgan to be happy. And it's clear that she doesn't like me or want me in your life."

He rubbed his hands on his thighs. "Does anyone ever get this parenting thing right?"

Pain settled near her heart. "What do you mean?"

"I feel so guilty about so many things where Morgan's concerned—my divorce, her epilepsy. She'd been doing fine until we moved here."

"Has she had another episode since the one when we met?"

"No, but Dr. Reynolds says that if she does he wants to see her."

And if Neill went back to Boston with Morgan, and the doctor wanted them to stay…

"Then there are all the adjustments she's had to make since moving here. Mom's been a great help. Still, I feel guilty that I maybe haven't been around as much as I should have. And now there's you."

"She isn't happy about me being in your life. She thinks I'm trying to replace her mother."

"Possibly." Neill sighed.

"We can't put our relationship on hold because of her, though. It wouldn't be fair to us," Sherri said, regretting the words as soon as they came out of her mouth.

"And I don't want to put us on hold. I love you, and I want us to be together. Please don't ever doubt that, but I feel responsible."

Did Neill expect her to drop out of his life until he and Morgan resolved their issues? Old feelings of rejection, of having her feelings come second, flooded around her heart. She leaned back in her chair. "But that doesn't mean you have to let Morgan behave so rudely toward me, or make your decisions for you, does it? She has to learn that you have a full life, a busy schedule, and that life includes being with someone who loves you."

"I know." He rubbed his hands over his thighs. "But I'm worried about her. This is the second time she's disappeared on me."

Neill couldn't seem to see what was happening, that he was refusing to see the problem Morgan was creating with her behavior.

"I realize how frightening that had to have been for you. But what did you say to her that first time to get her to understand that taking off is not acceptable behavior?"

"What could I say? She was sorry, and I was relieved that she was okay."

She'd hoped he'd talked to her after the incident. "That's all?"

He stared at his hands. "Seeing her safe, knowing she hadn't had another seizure, was all I could think about."

"Neill, I realize that none of this has been easy for you, and I wish I could help. But until Morgan accepts me as part of your life—accepts that I belong here with you—this isn't going to work."

"Don't say that."

"I'm not going to come second in your life again. Watching Morgan behave so badly toward me tells me she needs to change her behavior or…" She couldn't finish the thought.

"Sherri, I don't know what to say."

"Then I'll say it for both of us. You have to decide how you want Morgan to behave, and then insist that she follow through."

Neill's head shot up, his gaze riveted on her. "I think she got that message today."

Sherri was quite certain that Morgan's attitude toward her was a long way from being changed. "Are you sure about that?"

"Morgan has had a lot of things to deal with in her life, and she usually copes well with them. Can we just give her a little time?"

Resentment flowed through her. As irrational as it might seem, Sherri was tired of being the one who had to adjust. The one who had to accept what others wanted even when it wasn't what she wanted at all. There was no doubt that Neill's daughter called the shots when it came to his personal life. She could understand a child being upset if her parents had recently divorced, but it had been two years. Two years during which Sherri had had no role to play and had given Morgan no reason not to like her.

What was happening with his daughter wasn't fair to her or to him. "Neill, I think it's about time you sat down with Morgan and told her the truth about me, about us."

"I did," he said. "I told her that you and I were in love years ago, and she seemed to be okay with it. I don't get it. One minute everything is fine, and the next she's acting like this." He scrubbed his face in frustration. "Sherri, I can't seem to get her to understand about us."

"What's to understand? You and I are getting back together, and as much as she might be angry about it, she has to get over it."

"She will. I promise."

"What does your mother say about this? About her behavior around me?"

"Mom would rather we took it slow," he said softly, reaching for her hand. "But that's how Mom thinks, and she's been so good to Morgan and me. She really wants us here and has rearranged her life so she can take Morgan when I need her to," he said, his eyes dark pools of misery.

She wanted to put her arms around him, to console him, to back off and let the situation work itself out. But from what she could see, that wasn't about to happen anytime soon. Morgan was a headstrong little girl who was used to getting her own way. Sherri understood how easily that could happen when a child had a serious health problem and the parent was feeling guilty. She wished there was an easy solution.

"Neill, until you get things straightened out with Morgan where we're concerned, I think we should take a break. I can't… I just can't see what chance we have if every time we see each other around your daughter, we end up with a situation like this. I realize that she's had a difficult time, but so have a lot of other kids and they don't all behave this way. Some of them just want to see their parents happy."

"What are you saying?"

"I'm saying that I've already watched you choose your career over me. I won't sit around and watch you give in to the unreasonable demands of a child. I deserve her respect, not her anger and jealousy. Under the circumstances I...I think it would be better if you drove me home." She got up and went to the door.

He came after her, the expression on his face one of disbelief. "You can't mean that. We'll work this out. Morgan will come around, you'll see. Why don't we plan on the three of us going out to dinner? We need to spend an evening together, give Morgan a chance to get to know you better, and for you to know her."

"That's a wonderful idea, and I really appreciate you offering. But I'm not willing to be subjected to a confrontation in a restaurant in front of other people, and you know that's a very real possibility. Morgan seems to feel that you're hers and hers alone. Is she the reason you haven't dated since you and Lilly divorced?"

He looked into her eyes and wished she could cuddle in his embrace and spend the night with him. She wanted him to make love to her, but that wouldn't happen tonight or any night soon.

He put his hands on her arms, his face close to hers. She desperately wanted to forget what had taken place earlier. "Neill, I'd like to go home now."

His shocked expression gave way to resignation. "I'll drive you. But I want you to know that you don't need to worry about a scene in a restaurant now or at any other time. I promise."

She was sure he meant it, but he was only half of the equation. She was not willing to do battle with a nine-year-old every time she had a date with Neill. They drove back to Sherri's condo in silence. A few days ago, she had been so excited about finally having the prospect of a life with the man she loved. But she realized that until he worked things out with his daughter, there was little chance of their relationship going anywhere. No matter how strong her feelings were for Neill, she didn't intend to be competition for Lilly in his daughter's eyes.

She'd lived this long without him. She'd manage without him once again if he couldn't convince his daughter to accept her. Sherri had an aunt who'd loved a married man most of her adult life, who'd carried on an affair with him in secret. Her mother had been in love with her boss, but hadn't acted on those feelings until after his wife died. Waiting for a man was in her genes.

But she didn't plan to wait much longer.

FOR THE NEXT WEEK, Sherri concentrated on her job while trying to avoid Neill where she could. Her condo was immaculate, thanks to her determination to remain occupied and in charge of her life.

Evenings were the hardest because she felt tired, at odds with herself as she focused on staying with her diabetic regimen and going for long walks to ease her stress. In spite of her efforts to stay positive during the long hours before she finally fell asleep, she couldn't help but fear that she and Neill were never going to get back together.

Where had it all gone so wrong? What if they hadn't gone back to Neill's house that afternoon after Charlie's accident? Morgan had been very upset, and she couldn't blame her. If she were nine years old and found her father with a woman she didn't know, she'd be angry and afraid, too. Had she been too hard on Morgan? Was that why Neill hadn't called? Had he decided that Sherri was being unreasonable and that his daughter deserved more?

She didn't want to accept that he could walk away from their love for each other because of his daughter. Yet they'd lived separate lives for a long time, and if she were completely honest, she didn't really know Neill anymore. Her understanding of him was based on the relationship they'd had when they were in high school. And she didn't know very much about his relationship with Morgan at all, except that they were very close and he worried about his daughter.

Had they rushed headlong into their relationship without considering the consequences? If his concern over Morgan's health forced him to rethink his decision to live in Eden Harbor, would he tell her? Was that why she hadn't heard from him? Was he making plans to return to Boston? A hollow sensation started in her stomach, moving up her chest into her throat. What would she do if he moved away? He could do it so easily, given his medical qualifications.

She gripped the counter, steadying herself, while the realization that she didn't want him to go anywhere without her ever again lodged near her heart, a wish that seemed less attainable with each day that passed.

Would it have been different if she'd stayed at his place, reasoned with him about Morgan in a more caring way? Her feelings of betrayal and fear had driven her behavior that evening, which may have been her downfall. She had let a child dictate her response to the man she loved. Had she been the one who had turned her back on their relationship this time around?

NEILL PICKED UP the phone at least a dozen times a day, intent on calling Sherri to apologize for what had happened at his house. But an apology wasn't what she was looking for, and he had to accept that. If they were ever going to have a relationship, he needed to resolve his problems with Morgan. Unfortunately, his problems now included his mother, too, because she'd listened to Morgan's version of things and was supporting her granddaughter's position—Sherri and Neill needed to wait.

But Neill wasn't willing to wait any longer. He'd called his mother to say he was coming over when Morgan got home from school, and they were going to work this out. He'd never told his mother the truth about what had happened with Sherri twelve years ago, and it was time he did.

He pulled into his mother's driveway, got out of the car and walked over the cobbled patio stones to the backyard, where his mother had told him she and Morgan would be waiting. This was beginning to feel like a showdown in some B-rated Western. He could feel his chest tighten as he reached the corner of the garage and followed the path out to the gazebo. He could hear laughter, his daughter's full-throated squeal of delight. One of the best parts about coming back to Eden Harbor was the close relationship his mother had formed with his daughter, and he was about to discover just how strong that relationship was when he said what had to be said.

The minute Morgan saw him she called out, her voice filled with pleasure at seeing him.

"Morgan and I were just talking about her school day, and some of the antics the boys in the class were up to. I remember when you were that age," his mother said, her voice cheerful as she let Neill slip past her to a chair near the teak table where Morgan's backpack rested, her books and lunch box spilling from the zippered opening.

"I remember, too, Mom. In fact, it's the same school. I don't know if I told you that, Morgan," he said, settling onto the chair.

"Yes, you did, Dad. The first day you took me to class." Morgan came around the table and hugged him, her hair sweeping his cheek. "Don't you remember?"

"Sure I do," he said, although he didn't. He'd had so much on his mind that morning. He'd been focused on getting his daughter to school while avoiding a meltdown over the fact that she "hated"—her word—the pants and top she was wearing that morning. It had been a clear sign of Morgan's anxiety, as the outfit was one her mother had given her.

His thoughts had also been preoccupied with the surgery he was scheduled to perform after he dropped Morgan off. Cedric Keating was his father's cousin and a man whose cancer had spread, leaving surgery as the only option. He'd known Cedric all his life, had played with his two sons growing up, and he'd been worried about how they'd accept what was happening to their dad.

"How was your day?" his mother asked as she sat down in a chair across from him.

"Busy." He drummed his fingers on the table, his thoughts clear as he faced his mother and his daughter across the teak surface. "Mom, Morgan, I have something I need to explain to both of you."

His mother clasped her hands, her gaze shooting to Morgan before settling on him. "We're listening."

"Okay. I'll start at the beginning so Morgan understands everything." He focused his eyes on his daughter. "I went through school with Sherri Lawson, from first grade until we graduated. We started dating in twelfth grade, and we…spent a lot of time together. On graduation night we made love."

His mother tucked in her chin, a surprised look on her face, but she said nothing.

"When I went away to Boston and started my pre-med studies, I got a call from Sherri in which she said she was expecting a baby—our baby."

His mother gasped. "You never told me that!"

"No, Mom, and that was my mistake. I let everyone think my son was Sam Crawford's child."

"Did Sherri not want you to be part of your son's life?"

"Yes, she did, but I was busy." He looked down at his hands as remorse flooded through him.

"I can't believe you'd do that. You weren't raised that way."

"No, I wasn't." He glanced over at Morgan, who seemed almost too calm. "I put what I wanted ahead of what was best for the people I loved. I let Sherri face the arrival of our child without my support."

"Is that why we moved back here, Dad? So you can make up for what you did to Sherri?" Morgan asked, her words guarded, her shoulders hunched.

"No." Hadn't he vowed to tell the truth? "That's not quite true. Yes, I wanted to come back to Maine, to find Sherri again. But I didn't know she was working here in Eden Harbor." He looked directly at his mother, who quickly lowered her gaze.

"I needed to see if there was a chance Sherri and I might still love each other. But I also wanted to come back for my own personal satisfaction. Being here is rewarding. People need me. They know me and my family. Being here has made me see how important it is to be at peace with yourself, and I want you to someday feel the same way about this place that I do," he said, his attention on Morgan.

Morgan looked away. For a few seconds, the only sounds that could be heard were a goldfinch twittering in the trees and the muted roar of a truck in the distance.

"What about Sherri? What does she have to say about all this?" his mother asked.

"At first she wanted nothing to do with me."

His mother's glance pierced him. "I have to say I can't blame her for that. How could you have walked out on her and your baby?"

"I…" He rubbed his face, his determination to tell the whole truth to two of the people he loved most in this world wavering. "I was so wrapped up in my new life, and I was so shocked by her announcement that… that I just couldn't deal with it." He stared at his hands, his stomach churning with shame. "I took the coward's way out."

Donna Brandon placed her hands over his. "No, dear, you lacked good judgment. You should have come home and told your father and me. We would have helped you. After all, it was our grandchild, and we really liked Sherri."

He rubbed his head and rotated his shoulders to ease the tension gripping him. "I didn't want people to see how stupid I was. When Sherri didn't tell anyone, and you told me that she was marrying Sam, I tried to call her, but she wouldn't take my call."

"I wouldn't have, either," his mother said.

"But, Dad, why didn't you go and find Sherri and

talk to her?" Morgan asked, her voice just above a whisper.

"Good question. I don't really have a good answer. I guess I figured that she was married and she was happy. And because she hadn't told anyone, I assumed her husband didn't want anyone to know who the father of her child was."

"But before that. When she first told you, why didn't you go talk to her?" Morgan insisted.

He saw the look in his daughter's eyes, the one that said he had hurt her with his words. He wanted to wipe that look from her face, to once again see the adoration in her eyes. "Because I was a stupid young man who didn't really want the responsibility of a child," he said, his heart breaking at the sight of the crestfallen expression on Morgan's face. "I've wanted to tell you the truth about my life, about Sherri, for a while now."

"As well you should," his mother said, rubbing her hands gently over the wood of the table. "I can't change what you did. No one can. But I plan to have a long chat with Sherri and tell her how sorry I am for what happened."

"Dad, if you had to do it over again, what would you do?"

How could he answer that? "Sweetie, I honestly don't know. All I know for sure is that I made a couple of really stupid mistakes, and I'm really sorry for all the pain I caused everyone, especially Sherri. She didn't deserve what I did to her, and I'll never be able to make it up to her. I do intend to have her in my life from now on, and that's what I wanted to talk to you about today."

His mother and Morgan stared at him in total silence.

"I love Sherri. I plan to marry her. Morgan, I want you to give her a chance. What happened at the house a couple of weeks ago was upsetting for you. But we'd had a very difficult day, and our emotions got the better of us."

"Are you sure about all this?" his mother asked. "You've hurt Sherri before."

His mother's words dug into him. "I'm positive. I love Sherri Lawson, and I won't hurt her ever again."

The old need to placate his daughter pushed against his heart, nearly blocking the words that had to be said. "Morgan, I want you and I and Sherri to have a life together. Lilly will always be your mother, but Sherri will be part of our lives from here on."

"Dad! What about how I feel?"

"Morgan, listen to your dad. It's so important for you to do that." Donna's gaze moved over her granddaughter's face. "Your happiness means everything to me, and your dad is trying to explain how he feels. Give him a chance." She turned her gaze to Neill. "And you're the greatest blessing I could ever have in my life. I wish your father could have been around to see you come home to practice medicine and to meet Morgan."

The love Neill felt for his mother tightened his chest, flooding his throat. His eyes met his mother's. "Dad would have loved her, wouldn't he?"

He turned to Morgan. "We both love you so much. Would you be willing to try to like Sherri, for my sake?"

"I guess I could try," Morgan said, mollified.

"That's all I ask," Neill said, feeling that he'd done the right thing by talking to the two of them together.

"It might be fun," Morgan said, her eyes meeting Neill's. Morgan put her arms around her grandmother. "I love you, Gram. And Dad needs us." She rolled her eyes. "Dads are so high-maintenance, aren't they, Gram?"

Neill chuckled as relief flowed through him in one long wave of release.

"What would I do without you?" his mother said, her voice muffled by Morgan's shoulder as she returned the hug.

"Thanks, both of you," he said.

His mother pulled away from Morgan's embrace and focused on him. "What are you and Sherri going to do now?"

Her question caught him off guard. "About what?"

"About how you feel about each other," she said with a quizzical frown.

"Well, we were dating."

"Dad, it's more than that!"

"Not at the moment."

"Why not?" Morgan persisted.

"Because we both feel you need more time to adjust to our relationship," he said.

"What will Mom say?"

"Your mom is not involved in this."

"But—"

"No, Morgan. Your mom and I are not getting back together—ever." Had none of what he said made an impact with her?

"It's not fair!"

"Life seldom is fair," his mother interjected. "But that doesn't mean we stop trying. Your dad is doing his best to make you see how he feels."

"I guess so." Morgan sighed, raising her shoulders in an exaggerated shrug.

"Thanks, Mom." Determined to make amends to Sherri for how badly he'd handled his daughter's issues, he turned to Morgan. "We're going to go see Sherri now, and we're going to make a few changes in how we both behave toward one another. Agreed?"

Her eyes dark, her lips poised to say something, Morgan instead came around the table and hugged her dad. "Sometimes I don't understand you at all, Dad. But I'm willing to be nicer to Sherri."

So his daughter was going to try a little harder, but was that enough to keep her from resorting to her old tactics? "You won't disappear on me again?"

"I didn't disappear. You didn't understand."

"Morgan, it's me, remember?"

She hugged him again. "Yeah, I do."

"And you owe me."

"Why?"

"Because you made someone I love very unhappy, and you owe her an apology."

Morgan's eyes bored into his, and a pout started to form on her lips.

He answered her look with a frown. "You're going to apologize to Sherri. Understood?"

She shrugged. "Okay."

He stood up, holding his daughter close to him. "We're off to see the woman I love."

"I'll be waiting right here to learn how it turns out," his mother said.

CHAPTER EIGHTEEN

FRUSTRATED AND FEARFUL that she hadn't heard a word from Neill, Sherri had taken everything out of her kitchen cupboards in preparation for cleaning them. Cleaning was cheap therapy for how she was feeling. All the cleaning hadn't worked so far, but what else did she have to do? Gayle had heard her sad story over and over again. Her other friends were married and busy with their families. Besides, she didn't really feel comfortable talking to them about something that didn't make sense unless the whole story was told.

She pulled her scrub bucket out of the laundry room, filled it with soapy water, pulled on rubber gloves and got to work. She forced herself to concentrate on the job at hand, as she climbed the step stool and started cleaning. Her version of therapy worked for the first four cupboards, and then her worry returned. Her arms aching, she glanced around at the mess from the remaining cupboards. She had at least another hour of cleaning before her kitchen would be back together. What a mess. And for what? She dumped the sponge into the bucket in disgust.

Face it. You've blown your chances with Neill by asking him to side with you against his daughter. What right did you have to do that?

She should have encouraged him to seek professional help in resolving Morgan's issues, or talked to

Morgan herself to see if she could ease the child's concerns. Instead she'd let her emotions rule her behavior. She peeled off the rubber gloves and put the kettle on to boil. She might as well have a cup of tea and a snack while she wallowed. Glancing around, she realized there wasn't an empty space where she could sit and enjoy her tea.

She was leaning on the counter, waiting for the kettle to boil, when the doorbell rang. Who would be at her door this time of day? She wasn't expecting anyone, and her mother would have called first. Colleen was convinced that Neill would show up and sweep her off her feet any day now. She'd taken every opportunity to tease Sherri about how she didn't want to be the next one to find them in bed together. She'd had lots of time to regret confiding in her mother and her sister.

She grabbed a paper towel from the dispenser, wiped the tears edging her eyes and checked her face in the mirror in the front hall on her way to the door. When she opened it, Neill and Morgan were standing there.

"We've come to invite you to our place for dinner tonight," Neill said, his eyes on her, his smile causing her heart to swell.

She muffled her surprise as her mind raced over what this could mean. "I…" She cleared her throat. "Would you like to come in?" she asked.

"We're on our way to the grocery store," Morgan said, curling her fingers into her father's hand as she looked up at Sherri. This time Morgan looked straight at her, her expression contrite. "You… I mean, I have something to tell you." She peeked at her father. "I'm sorry for being rude the other day."

"You had your reasons, I'm sure. Apology accepted."

Morgan squeezed her father's hand even tighter. "Does that mean you'll come?"

"I would love to have dinner with you tonight," she said while her heart did a funny little dance in her chest. "What can I bring?"

"Just you. We both want to spend some time with you. Don't we, Morgan?" Neill asked, his eyes never leaving Sherri's face.

"Yes," Morgan confirmed.

"Then we're off to get the groceries. Do you have any special requests?" he asked, his smile forcing her to grip the door frame to keep from dashing out the door and into his arms.

"I'll be happy with anything, anything at all."

"Dad and I are going to choose healthy foods for you. He told me about your diabetes on our way over here."

"Everyone's working on making sure you stay healthy," Neill said happily.

"Well, I appreciate that. What time should I come over?"

"Whenever you want."

She glanced behind her at the pile of pots visible from where she stood. "I need to finish up here," she said.

Neill glanced around her, spying the same pile of pots. "So, we were working out our frustrations, were we?" he asked, a knowing gleam in his eyes.

"We were." And suddenly she was laughing so hard she could hardly stand upright.

"Is she all right?" Morgan asked her father.

"She's better than all right. She's damned near perfect," he said, putting his arms around Morgan's shoulders. "I'll explain on the way home."

"See you once I clean up my kitchen."

"Why bother?" Morgan asked. "Dad doesn't do housework until he has to. You don't have to clean your kitchen before you come over, do you?"

"No, I suppose I don't," Sherri said, delighted that Morgan wanted her to come sooner than she'd planned.

"Then let's go," Morgan said, tugging at her father's hand, then heading for the car.

Neill leaned close to Sherri and kissed her lips. His cologne wafted around her, setting off a trembling sensation in her tummy. He let his lips wander over her cheek toward her ear. "I call her the action kid," he whispered.

No words passed her lips, no thoughts formed in her mind—they were blocked by the slow burn of need rising through her. She clutched his shirtfront. "Is she always like this?" She heard her voice over a strange feeling of weightlessness.

"Most of the time. Takes a little getting used to, I have to say." He placed his hands on hers. "But that's one of the reasons I love her. And you."

She drew in a deep breath as his words dropped into her heart ever so gently. "I love you, too."

"Dad! Come on!"

"See what I mean?" he said, taking her head in his hands and kissing her one more time.

"Yes," she breathed, wishing she could close her eyes and let the moment be hers. But there was a kid standing a few feet away, waiting for her father. Besides, she was anxious to have dinner with the two people who would be part of her life from here on. "See you soon."

"Wow! We're here together. We're all hungry, and I'm not on call," Neill said, to a chorus of cheers from

Sherri and Morgan. "Now all I have to do is get the barbecue going."

"What's on tonight's menu?" Sherri asked, resting a hip on one of the stools at the kitchen island.

"We're having salmon steaks with cucumber and dill sauce and veggies, followed by a scrumptious dessert of baked apple," Morgan volunteered.

"Sounds delicious," Sherri said. She came around the island to stand beside Neill as he brushed a mixture of oil and spices over the orange-pink flesh of the salmon steak. She gave him a kiss.

"What can I do?" she asked, tempting him to drag her off to his room—except that his daughter was there, washing asparagus at the kitchen sink.

"A few things come to mind, but they wouldn't do much to help get dinner going," he murmured, putting down his brush and pulling her into his arms for another kiss. "I'd like to pursue all my thoughts where you're concerned, but we are in the company of a minor."

"Dad! Would you and Sherri cut it out," Morgan groaned and rolled her eyes.

Sherri touched his cheek as she returned to her stool. "She has a point. Dinner will never be ready at this rate," Sherri teased.

"And I'm starving," Morgan said. "And, no, I don't need a lesson on sex or STDs or any of that stuff."

"Morgan, who have you been talking to?" Neill asked, only half kidding.

"Tara's mother has all these books in her bedroom—"

"And you've been reading them?" He wondered if he should have a chat with Tara's mother.

"Dad, you need a reality check. It's the twenty-first century. Sex has been around for eons," she stated with a no-nonsense look on her face that made him want to chuckle.

"That's enough, young lady," he said firmly, putting the final dab of oil on the fish. "Are you two ganging up on me?"

"No. Never," they chorused before breaking into giggles.

Just then the phone rang. Because he wasn't on call, he'd turned his cell phone off. He checked the caller ID on the house phone. *The hospital?*

"Is it for me?" Morgan asked.

"Don't think so."

"It's probably Gram wanting to know what we're up to, whether or not we're all still speaking to each other."

He answered to hear the anxious voice of the doctor in Emergency. "Neill, I hate to ask this, but we've got both ambulances out, and Dr. Fennell is on-site triaging the victims of a four-vehicle pile-up on the highway south of Eden Harbor. I tried Dr. Sanderson first, but he's out of town. You're the only one with the kind of trauma experience we're going to need. It doesn't look good. A hell of a mess, and I'm working alone."

As much as his heart went out to the families of the victims, and to his colleague faced with such a horrendous situation, he didn't want to have his evening end like this. He had earned the chance to be with Morgan and Sherri. And just when things were going so well…

But this was his life, and he couldn't deny his colleague's request. "You need me right away." Neill exchanged a glance with Sherri across the granite counter.

"The hospital?" she whispered.

He pressed the phone to his chest. "Car accident."

She shrugged. "You'd better go."

He put the phone to his ear. "I'll be there in a few minutes."

"Thanks, Neill." The call ended before he had a chance to say more, a perfectly normal response for a doctor who would be working to clear all other urgent cases out of the emergency department in preparation for the incoming trauma cases.

He explained the situation to Sherri and Morgan.

"So a lot of people are hurt?" Morgan asked, her tone subdued.

"Yeah. I'm sorry about this."

Morgan hurried to her father's side, her hand grabbing his. "Don't be, Dad. This is what you're good at. And remember how you explained to me before we moved here that it wouldn't be like Boston? That you'd be one of only a few doctors?" She smiled across the counter at Sherri. "Besides, we've got a bunch of girl talk to do."

"That we do," Sherri said, delighted at Morgan's attitude.

"Nice to know I'm not needed," Neill said, eliciting a smile from both of them. He felt a warm sense of belonging and being part of a family. "But I promise you I'll be back as soon as possible."

"Which could be a while, so Morgan and I will probably go ahead with dinner, and we'll do your salmon steak when you get back."

"I may be all night," he said. Sherri came around the counter and hugged him. "I'll stay here with Morgan until you get back, whenever that is."

"We'll miss you, Dad, but I'm sure we can find a movie on TV, one I haven't seen yet."

"You mean one you're not supposed to see." Neill

turned to Sherri. "Watch this kid. She's always trying to get past my rule about only watching PG-rated movies."

"Dad, don't spoil my fun!"

He placed his arms around the two females in his life and walked them to the door with him. "I'll be back. In the meantime, you two ladies have a good evening without me."

"We'll be waiting," Sherri said, her concern for him written in the way she caught her lip in her teeth. The action brought back a memory. They'd been in the school library and he hadn't been able to make sense of some of the phrases in *Macbeth*. She'd watched him quietly from across the study desk with the same expression.

Feeling the tension building from the sure knowledge of what his evening would hold, he opened the front door. He climbed into his SUV and roared down the highway.

INSIDE THE HOUSE, Morgan stared at Sherri. "So how are we going to cook the fish? Want me to get out a frying pan?" she asked, her gaze moving back to the door and the sound of Neill's vehicle backing out of the driveway.

Morgan's smile was her father's. As a matter of fact, there was a whole lot of Morgan that was her father's. Now that they were alone, Sherri wondered how they'd make out. She so badly wanted this evening to go well, for them to restart their relationship. She didn't want to blow this opportunity to spend an evening with his daughter. "I'm quite handy with a barbecue, actually."

Morgan's eyebrows arched in skepticism. "Where did you learn to barbecue?"

"I call it life skills for those living alone. Single gals like us need to develop our cooking skills."

Morgan leaned over the granite counter, toying with a large ceramic chicken painted in bright shades of red and yellow. "You think so?"

"I know so. I've been living a single girl's lifestyle for a long time, and I've learned a few things." She dug a package of matches out of the drawer near the sink and proceeded down the back steps to where the barbecue sat, reassured to see that Morgan was following her. She wasn't sure the child would go anywhere with her, but going to the barbecue was a start. She opened the barbecue, turned on the propane tank and set the burner knob to ignition before lighting a match over the burner.

With a soft whoosh, the burner lit, eliciting an awed sigh from Morgan. "How did you do that?" she asked.

"It's not hard at all."

"My mom isn't good at anything that's practical." She glanced quickly in Sherri's direction. "She's a great mom, but she's not handy."

"Handy at doing things around the house or yard, you mean?"

"We didn't have a yard in Boston. We lived in a condo downtown."

"Did you like that?"

"Not really. I couldn't go out like I can here. I only saw my friends at school or on play dates or at basketball practice. Here I can see Tara or Kirsten anytime." She picked up the spatula resting on the table next to the barbecue. "What else can you do?"

"Well, I've learned to change a tire and top up windshield washer fluid. And I've gotten used to eating in a restaurant alone."

"What's to learn about that?" Morgan edged closer.

"Well, let me see. Whenever I'm going to be eating alone in a restaurant, I always make a reservation for two."

"Why?"

"I don't eat out very often, but when I do, I find that with a reservation for two, I get a better table."

"Are you serious?"

She nodded. "That's been my experience."

"But why make a reservation for two when there's only you? Isn't that dishonest?"

"In a way, I suppose. But if I make it for one, they will give me the most undesirable table, usually the last table before the restroom or the back exit."

"How do you know that?"

"Again, experience," Sherri said, heading back into the house for the salmon and the vegetables.

"Is living alone hard? Do you get lonely?" Morgan asked, following along behind her.

Sherri passed her the platter of fish and a pair of oven mitts. "Sometimes, but most of the time I'm too busy to notice. And, of course, living alone means I get to make all the decisions about what I eat. And I don't have to wait to take a shower or share the closet."

"But you always have to take out the trash and do the chores, right?"

Sherri picked up the vegetable tray and headed back outside. "True, but one person doesn't produce much trash, and the chores aren't as time-consuming when they're being done for one."

"You make it sound like living alone is a good deal. Does that mean you don't plan to move in with Dad and me?"

Was that hope Sherri heard in her voice? "Living alone is neither good nor bad. It's a lifestyle. But when the right person comes along that you'd like to share your life with…"

"Do you want to share my dad's life?"

"Yes, I do. And I want to get to know you, too, and maybe we could get to be friends after a while."

Morgan studied her hands. "I don't know."

"I'm not pressuring you on this," Sherri hastened to add. "I love your dad, and I never expected to ever have another chance with him."

"And now you think you might?" Morgan asked, her brown eyes studying Sherri.

Sherri considered her answer. Morgan didn't want a new woman in her father's life, and she had to try to understand her position if the three of them were going to be part of a family. She could appeal to Morgan's sense of fair play. Morgan wouldn't be her father's daughter if she didn't have a keen sense of fairness. "Your father and I not only love each other, we share a history. We loved each other a long time ago."

"I wasn't even born back then," Morgan said in a tone that told Sherri that she believed that all adults were slightly dull.

"That's right. You weren't. But now there's you and your dad, and me. And it looks like we'll all be together eventually. All I want is for you and me to be able to enjoy being a part of each other's lives and to get to spend time together. I think you'll discover I'm not a bad person."

"Dad says you're great. So I guess…maybe."

Morgan stood there, a shy smile on her face. Sherri wanted to hug her she looked so ill at ease.

What have you got to lose?

"So, you think you'd be willing to get to know me?" Sherri asked.

Morgan nodded.

Sherri took a chance and hugged Morgan, prepared to let go if the child showed any resistance. Morgan's arms crept around her—awkwardly at first—and Sherri responded by simply holding her. Suddenly Morgan was clinging to her, squeezing so hard she could barely breathe. "I'm sorry. So sorry," Morgan sobbed into Sherri's shirt.

"You have nothing to be sorry for, nothing at all."

Holding Neill's child made Sherri realize how much she had to offer this girl who had seen so many changes in her life, changes she had no control over. Sherri understood only too well how difficult it was to be set adrift by the actions of others. "Right now, I really need your help to get the salmon steaks on the barbecue."

Morgan stepped back and pulled on the oven mitts. "See?" She waved her mitted hands around. "We can help each other. And when Dad gets back, we'll make his dinner for him. You and me."

"You and me," Sherri echoed, feeling the first tentative threads of a bond forming between them.

Their conversation was stilted as they began working on the dinner together, but by the time they finished eating, they were talking more comfortably.

"Do you think I should be allowed to wear lipstick?" Morgan asked, her assessing gaze so much like her father's.

How should she answer? In her mind, Morgan was too young, yet if she said so, it might send Morgan off to her room in a huff, and Sherri didn't want that. "I'm not sure about lipstick, but what about lip gloss in a color you'd like?"

Morgan brightened. "Really?"

She could remember wanting to wear lipstick and

having to accept her mother's decision that she was too young. But that was years ago, and almost certainly parents' approaches to such things had changed. "What can it hurt?" she asked.

"My mom says I'm way too young to wear lipstick, but she might think that lip gloss is okay." Morgan hung the dish towel over the towel rack near the sink.

Sherri saw the slump of her shoulders, and she began to understand how difficult it must be to be nine years old and not to have your mother around to talk to when you needed her. "Maybe you could ask her the next time you call her."

"How about now?" Morgan asked.

Sherri turned to see Morgan fidgeting with the edge of her shirt. Did she want her approval to make the call? Or was she worried about what her mother might say? "Calling your mother is a great idea. Maybe you could suggest a clear lip gloss to start with."

"Okay!" Morgan scrambled around the table and scooped up the phone before heading into the living room.

Sherri waited to hear how the call went, hoping Lilly would agree to some type of gloss.

When Morgan returned, she appeared dejected. "Mom wasn't there. Someone else answered the phone, someone who works for my mom. She says Mom left for China this morning. I called Mom's cell phone, but it went to her voice mail." Morgan slid into the chair across the table from Sherri. "I wish she'd told me."

"Maybe it was an urgent meeting and she didn't have time to call," Sherri said, surprised that Lilly wouldn't have called to let her daughter know that she was leaving the country. "Maybe she'll call tonight."

Morgan toyed with the hem of the table runner. "Do you think so?"

She hadn't a clue and didn't want to speculate further. Morgan was clearly disappointed. In a hurried attempt to change the subject, she said, "I imagine you'll be having a big shopping trip with your mom to get ready for summer, won't you?"

"Yeah. I guess so. But I don't want to wait that long. If Mom was here, we'd be going on a shopping trip now," she said wistfully.

"Would you like to go shopping with me? I'm not your mom, but between us we could probably manage to get a few things you'd like. What do you think?"

"Can I get lip gloss?"

"Only if you tell your mom about it the next time you talk to her. And only the clear stuff."

"Okay," she said, but her expression was still downcast.

"We can go get you a clear lip gloss and pick out some nice clothes."

Morgan edged around the table, closer to Sherri. "Is Dad coming with us?"

"Do you want him to?"

The girl's smile was hesitant at first, and then, as if a floodgate had opened, she gave Sherri a huge grin. "No. We need a girls' day out. Maybe we can drive to Portland and hit the mall."

Morgan chatted eagerly about all her plans for their shopping trip, and Sherri felt a sense of accomplishment. She'd managed to get Morgan to warm up to her enough to go shopping with her. And Morgan hadn't asked if a friend could come with them, which meant she was willing to spend time alone with Sherri.

Once they'd finished cleaning up the kitchen, she and

Morgan watched a movie together. Morgan insisted that they make popcorn to go with the show. Sherri wasn't surprised to see Morgan fall asleep about an hour after the movie started. It had been a long day for everyone. She managed to get her upstairs, and after sleepily brushing her teeth, Morgan climbed into bed.

In the soft light of the bedside lamp, Sherri realized that underneath all her bravado, Morgan was trying really hard to fit into her father's new life.

Feeling at peace for the first time in ages, Sherri turned off the light and tiptoed out of the room and down the stairs. She finished cleaning up in the kitchen while she waited to hear from Neill.

Finding the hours dragging by, she picked up a book and began to read. One word morphed into another as she tried to keep her eyes open. Around midnight, the phone rang.

"Sherri, I won't be home for another couple of hours."

She heard the exhaustion in Neill's voice. "I'm sorry. Are you okay?"

He didn't answer at first. "I will be when I get away from here."

She heard the tension in his voice and realized that something must have gone really wrong for him tonight. "I'll be waiting for you whatever time you get here."

A long sigh slid past his lips, increasing her fear. "I needed to hear you say that. I love you. I'll be there as soon as I can."

CHAPTER NINETEEN

WORRIED, SHE WAITED for him, all thoughts of sleep having vaporized. She tidied up the rooms on the main floor, her hedge against her dark thoughts. Fraught with concern, she went to Neill's computer in his office and surfed the internet for a while, searching for a distraction.

When she finally saw the headlights of his SUV flash across the office windows, she went to the door, holding it open for him. He didn't get out of his vehicle right away, and she was about to go to him when the car door opened and he stepped out. His gaze fixed on the ground, he made his way to her and, without a word, grabbed her, pulled her into his arms and sobbed into her neck.

Frightened, she patted his back, a pointless gesture, but the only thing she could do under the pressure of his crushing embrace. "Neill, what's wrong?"

He didn't answer, only tightened his grip on her.

"Why don't we go into the house, and you can tell me what's going on," she said, relieved to feel his grip ease.

"Are you hungry? Morgan and I—"

He shifted her in his arms, maintaining a tight grip on her as he walked through the kitchen and past the living room toward the stairs. "I need you to stay with me tonight—or what's left of it. I can't be alone."

She looked up into his haggard face, to the dark pools

of his eyes and the remnants of tears. "Neill, I'm not sure I should stay," she whispered. "What will Morgan say if she wakes up and finds me in your bed?"

"I don't care. All I care about is having you with me. Please," he begged, his hands moving through her hair, his body tense.

What could she do? Leaving him like this was out of the question. "Okay."

He took her hand and they walked up the stairs, across the landing and down the hall to his bedroom. Determined not to wake Morgan, Sherri eased the door closed behind her.

Neill crossed the room, peeled off his clothes and tossed them in a pile by the window before turning to face her. "Undress for me."

Mesmerized by the look in his eyes, she did as he ordered. Before she'd managed to get out of her pants and top, he was standing in front of her, pulling her shirt over her head as he kissed her lips. The fury of his kiss caught her by surprise. Out of breath, she pressed her hands against his chest. "Neill!"

His fingers shook as he undid her bra. "Sherri, trust me. I need to make love to you…to stop…" A shudder rattled through him. "I've waited so long…so long," he whispered, his hands palming her breasts as he kissed her again, gently this time.

Alive to his touch, she returned his kiss, her body melding with his, her heart pounding as if it would leap from her chest. He pushed her toward the bed until she felt the mattress behind her legs, then Neill was coming down on top of her, his body hard, his hands on either side of her to ease her onto the bed.

He moved beside her, while his hands slid down her body, coming to rest over her pubic area. With his eyes on hers, he whispered, "You are so beautiful." He kissed her neck and her shoulders while his fingers caressed her.

She closed her eyes, absorbing his touch as if it were his last, as if there were nothing left between them but a raging need to fondle each other. His lips set her body on fire as his fingers slid between her legs, causing her to melt. She pulled him to her, thrusting her body up to his, and felt him enter her. Her body rocked with his; his skin was slick with sweat against hers. His sudden intake of breath, the hammering of his body against hers, pulled her over the edge into the abyss of need that claimed her body and soul.

Her body shuddered with his, their breath blending together. His hands trembling, he brushed the damp hair from her forehead. "I… Don't leave me." He rolled off her and lay down next to her, his hands resting on her damp skin, his touch calming the wild beating of her heart.

In the dim light from the windows facing the backyard, she saw the way he was looking at her, as if he'd never really seen her before. "Neill, tell me what's wrong."

His fingers gently massaged her abdomen and then stopped suddenly. He pulled her into his arms and held her close, his lips near her ear. "I don't know any other way to say this." His arms tightened around her. "Charlie Crawford died tonight."

A tremor shot through her body. Her mind refused to process his words. "What?"

"I couldn't save him. I tried. The EMTs did everything they could. And still Charlie died." He swallowed hard. "He'd been trapped under his truck after the collision. God! Four cars, two transport trucks and Char-

lie's truck. He'd been drinking...." Neill turned on his
back and stared at the ceiling. "Charlie's injuries were
too severe. I couldn't save him," he said again, and once
again tears choked his words.

It didn't seem real. She could see Charlie's face that
last time she'd seen him in the clinic. He'd assured her
he would get help. He wanted to get better for himself
and his family. He'd said all the words that soothed her
guilt and hadn't been able to follow through on any of
them. "Are you sure he'd been drinking?"

"He reeked of it! Even in death he smelled like a
brewery." Neill rolled away from her, his fists pounding the bed as he lay on his side. "Damn it! I knew
he was an alcoholic, and I didn't confront him on it. I
even tried to stop you from getting involved. If I'd done
something, he might still be alive."

She turned toward him. His body was silhouetted by
the early dawn light. "Neill, don't do that to yourself.
Remember we gave him the number for that psychologist. He could have gone to AA, and he didn't. You
have no way of predicting how Charlie would have responded, even if he had gotten help."

"You didn't see his wife's face when she got to the
hospital. I had to tell her that Charlie didn't survive,
that there was nothing we could do. Then his parents
arrived. Damn!"

She pulled him into her arms, the deep tremors shud-
dering through his body leaving her feeling completely
helpless. "His family, his wife and children, all left to
grieve," he whispered against her throat.

She hugged him close, remembering another death
and how close it had brought her to losing her mind.
"Neill, try to remember that you did what you could to

help Charlie. That some things are simply beyond our ability to fix."

He snuggled closer to her, his breathing slowing a little. "How did you manage to get through Patrick's death?"

"He only lived fifty-two hours, and he died peacefully in my arms. I tried to comfort myself with that."

"Did it work?"

She hesitated, afraid even now to show him how vulnerable she felt over what had happened years ago. "No. When I lost him, I lost my ability to cope. There are whole weeks I don't remember." She rubbed her finger over the faint scar on her wrist where she'd dragged the knife to end her agony. "The pain was unbearable. And if it wasn't for Sam coming into my hospital room…"

The sadness evident in his eyes, he whispered, "I've said I'm sorry for what happened to you so many times, and yet I know how inadequate those words are. Still, that's all I can think of to say, even now."

"Neill, tonight was a terrible accident, and so many lives have been forever altered. Yet we can't let that change our belief in how good life can be. We've found each other again. I had a wonderful evening with Morgan, and I'm looking forward to spending time with her. Can we try to concentrate on the good in our lives? I've been through enough of the bad."

She could feel his eyes on her. "I never want you to leave me," he said. "Never. I am the luckiest guy on this planet, and we have everything two people could ever wish for."

She remembered Morgan's face, a mirror for her insecurity. "But maybe I shouldn't sleep here. I don't want to wreck my new relationship with Morgan, and regardless of how difficult tonight's been I'm not sure she'd understand. It's nearly light outside, and you need to sleep."

Neill rose up on his elbow, his eyes looking directly into hers. "There is nothing I want more than for you and my daughter to get along, but I meant it when I said you and I are staying together from here on out. Morgan will just have to accept that."

She wanted to argue with him, but his expression told her it would be a wasted effort. "Then, it's about time we got some sleep."

In less than ten minutes, Neill was snoring softly, his body wrapped around hers, warming her as she tried to sleep. But her mind still niggled away at her worry over Morgan's reaction. What would Neill's daughter do when she found her in bed with her father? Should she simply get up and leave now that Neill was asleep? She moved a little bit away from Neill, only to have him pull her back against him and snuggle closer.

Watching the dawn light spread across the bedroom, her mind cruised over all the events of the past few months, stopping on that moment in the emergency room when she woke to see Neill's anxious face. The day she'd come to believe that they would be given a second chance, and it had turned out to be true.

Whatever Morgan's reaction, she couldn't leave Neill. With that thought uppermost in her mind, she drifted off into an uneasy sleep.

CHAPTER TWENTY

SHERRI WOKE TO a sense that someone was watching her. She turned, only to come up against Neill's arm. Craning her neck, she looked out the bedroom door into the hall. The door had been closed. She'd closed it behind her when they'd come up to the bedroom.

The only person who would have opened it was Morgan. Was she up?

Ever so gently, she got up from the bed, grabbed her clothes and pulled them on without waking Neill. In the hall, she debated whether or not to check Morgan's room. She decided against it, as she was quite sure Morgan had been the one to open their door, which meant she knew that Sherri had stayed the night. Creeping down the stairs, she went into the kitchen to find Morgan sitting at the kitchen table, the expression on her face one of apprehension. "Good morning," Sherri managed.

"Is Dad okay?" Morgan asked. "I heard him crying last night."

Sherri sat down across from Morgan, her heart opening to the child whose concern for her father was written on her every feature. "Yes, he was crying. There was an accident last night, and someone we both knew and cared about died."

"Someone from school? When you were grow-ing up?"

"Yes. Charlie Crawford went to school with us, and he was my husband's brother."

Morgan looked surprised. "Are you all right? I mean, I've never had someone die like that. How do you feel?"

Sherri wanted to take the girl in her arms and hug her. With a complete sense of relief, she shared with Morgan what had happened and how it made her and Neill feel.

"I'm glad you were here for Dad last night. He doesn't often tell me about patients who died, and I wouldn't have known how to help him."

"Morgan, I'm so relieved to hear you say that. I wor-ried last night that you would be upset when you real-ized I'd stayed the night."

Morgan bit her lip. "I was at first. After I heard him crying, I tiptoed to his door and heard your voice. I was angry with you, but then I heard you being so kind to my dad. I went back to my room and fell asleep for a little while. I woke up around dawn. I saw the two of you together in the bed."

Sherri held her breath. "And?"

Morgan shook her head. "Dad was holding you close to him, and he was sound asleep. The two of you looked so peaceful. Dad and Mom had a huge king-size bed, and I used to come into their bedroom sometimes early in the morning. I never saw Dad with his arms wrapped around Mom the way he had them wrapped around you."

This nine-year-old child could piece that all together for herself. "I'm sorry—"

"Don't be. I wanted my parents back together. Mom

didn't have a boyfriend. When Dad didn't have a girl-friend, I thought he still loved Mom, that all they needed was more time together to work things out between them." She rubbed her arms and looked away. "I guess I was wrong."

"Morgan, I realize how difficult it's been for you to find your father in love with me, and it's all happened so fast. We've done so many things wrong in the past, which nearly caused us to give up on each other, but now we have another chance. Only this time we have you in our lives."

Morgan looked at her, her gaze searching, assessing. "Is that… I mean…" She rubbed her cheeks vigorously. "Are you okay with that?"

"I am. I truly am. I love your father with all my heart. I would do anything for him. His happiness means everything to me."

Morgan's eyes swam with tears. "I never heard my mom say that about my dad."

Feeling Morgan's agony like a physical force, she pulled her into her arms, hugging her close, smoothing her curls. Somehow, she had to relieve this child's pain. "Tell you what? Why don't we have a bite of breakfast and let your father sleep. He's tired and probably won't surface until noon. We could even go shopping in Port-land at the outlet malls. What do you think?"

Morgan gave her a slow smile. "I might want to look at lipstick."

"Looking is good. Buying might require a little ne-gotiation."

"I do need some clothes, and with Mom away in China…"

"I could sub in for her, if you'd like."

Morgan high-fived her. "It's a deal. Can we hit the road now? I really want to go to L.L.Bean. They have cool sports things, and I'm starting soccer this summer."

"We could grab a bite at the Sage Bistro on the way out of town," Sherri offered, excited and thrilled to be taking Morgan shopping.

With a smile transforming her face, Morgan went to the counter. "I'll write a note and leave it for Dad. He doesn't like to shop, so he'll be glad we went without him. Besides, he needs his beauty rest." She gave Sherri a crooked smile.

"We'll have to stop at my place so I can change my clothes and take my insulin."

"What about a car? You came here in Dad's car."

"Put in your note that we'll leave his car at my place until we get back from Portland. I doubt he'll be going anywhere today, and we'll be back this afternoon."

"Great. I'll wash my face, comb my hair and put on clean jeans. I showered yesterday," Morgan said on the way out of the kitchen. When she came back down the stairs, they left the house quietly so as not to wake Neill.

They stopped at Sherri's house before heading to the bistro. It had just opened, and they were the first customers. They ordered two morning glory breakfasts consisting of an omelet, toast and juice, only to discover that they were both starving.

The drive to the outlet malls was filled with Morgan's excited chatter about her friends, her school and how much she hoped she could get the barn fixed up as a hangout for her and her friends.

After a few hours of intense shopping, they had filled the backseat with parcels and Morgan was hungry again. They stopped at McDonald's on the highway heading back to Eden Harbor.

"This has been so much fun. Maybe we can bring Tara next time," Morgan said.

"Do you think Tara's mother would agree?"

"Oh, yeah. Tara gets to do pretty much everything she wants. She has a boyfriend." Morgan bit into her hamburger as Sherri nibbled on her chicken Caesar salad, remembering how Neill had expressed his concerns about the preteen dating scene. She had thought nine was way too young to be worrying about dating. Talk about being wrong!

"Sherri, do you think I'm too young to have a boyfriend?"

"That's a tough question. I think that maybe you should focus on your friends, your schoolwork and sports for now."

"Why can't I have a boyfriend?"

"You're asking me? I didn't have a boyfriend until grade ten."

"Was there something wrong with you?" Morgan covered her mouth, her eyes round. "Sorry. I didn't mean that the way it came out."

Sherri chuckled. "Most of the boys in my class were my friends. I liked having friends who happened to be boys. Do you have friends who are boys?"

"Yeah, I do." Morgan put her hamburger down. "They're fun some of the time."

"Well, your dad and I were friends before we started dating."

"So you think I should just be friends with boys for now?" Morgan frowned.

How was she going to get herself out of this discussion? She was a long way from being an expert on anything having to do with relationships. "Try it and see. You've got lots of time to decide."

Morgan sighed. "I guess you're right."

They chatted about Morgan's classmates, her cell phone and her friends. "Morgan, I want you to know that being out with you today has helped me a great deal."

A suspicious frown appeared on the girl's face and then vanished. "How?"

"Charlie Crawford was my friend, and I feel really bad for him and his family. But being with you has made it easier."

A pleased expression settled on Morgan's face. "Why?"

"Because you kept me from being sad. I need to be there for your father, to help him get over what happened, and because of you I feel I can do it."

"Really?" Her voice was eager.

"Yes."

Morgan's hug caught her by surprise. "You're so cool."

NEILL WOKE UP around noon. When he went looking for Sherri and Morgan, he found the note his daughter had written. He smiled at the message, written in his daughter's large, carefully printed letters. So the two of them were out shopping and would be home in a few hours.

He wasn't hungry, so he settled for coffee. Feeling restless, he went out to the front veranda and brought in the newspaper. The headlines were all about last night's accident. There were the usual comments about speeding and highway issues, and a short piece from the officer in charge of the accident scene. No mention of the victims until all family members had been notified.

Feeling a profound sense of sadness, he put the paper down and finished his coffee. He didn't want to think about Charlie today, at least not until Sherri came home. The sense of failure still haunted him, despite his pleasant memories of Sherri staying over at his home the night before.

Home. Would they be sharing this house together? They hadn't discussed it, but he hoped this would be where they'd start their new life together. There'd been so many little things he'd wanted to do around the house and precious little time to do them. He glanced at the clock. He might have a few hours today to knock some of the things off his list, and he needed physical exercise to ease the stress from the hours he'd spent in Emergency.

There was no point in doing anything in the barn until he had a crew to help him, as there were old farm implements, worn-out lawn mowers and years of junk piled everywhere. He had planned to paint the railing on the front veranda. He even had the paint and brushes he'd bought at the hardware store the other day.

Gathering what he needed, he went out to the front porch into the sunshine. The bright light made him feel much better, much more upbeat than he had last night. He stood staring out across the wide expanse of lawn and across the street to where the ocean was visible through the trees, and he felt so grateful to be living in this community.

The scent of the pine trees off to the side of the house filled his nostrils as he opened the white paint and spread his painting tarp on the veranda floor. Dipping the brush into the paint, he began the back-and-forth strokes required to paint the posts, the movement soothing in an odd way. He brushed carefully but with determination. He could finish the railing before Sherri and Morgan returned if he really pushed himself.

A couple of hours later, his shoulders aching with the strain, he put the top back on the paint, cleaned the paintbrush and went to sit on the top step. The veranda was done.

He was sitting there, basking in the heat of the June sun, when a car slowed down and turned in his driveway. Sherri was driving his SUV, with Morgan in the front seat beside her, and both of them were smiling. His heart filled with love at the sight of them. An overwhelming sense of need for them arced through him as he watched them emerge from the car and come toward him. "Well, by the look of the number of bags, you gals cleaned out a few stores," he teased.

"That we did," Sherri said as they approached the steps.

Dumping the parcels at the foot of the steps, they sat down on either side of him, happiness radiating from them. He enveloped them in his arms.

Morgan leaned into her father. "Dad, Sherri is so cool. She let me shop wherever I wanted. We bought a whole bunch of stuff, and you owe her a lot of money."

"I do?" He kissed Sherri—a warm, heartfelt kiss. "Do they still have debtors' prison?"

"I don't think so," she said, kissing him back. "But something could be arranged, if you'd like to be imprisoned."

He grinned. "Maybe I'll have to find another form of payment."

"Like what?" she asked, giving him a gentle poke in the ribs.

"Like maybe you come here to live...with us. I would buy your groceries, provide the heat and electricity. A lot of heat?" He arched his eyebrow in question.

She kissed his neck. "Would I have my own room?"

He fought the urge to drag her upstairs. "Definitely not. You have to share mine."

Sherri glanced past him to Morgan. "What do you think, Morgan? Should I accept your dad's offer?"

"It's up to you. But if I were you, I'd take it."

"Why?"

"Because Dad isn't getting any younger. And someday I won't be here to look after him."

"Hey, wait a minute! I'm not *that* old!"

Morgan gave him a wide smile. "Gotcha, Dad."

Neill could see that Sherri was struggling not to burst out laughing. "See what I have to put up with?" he said, trying for an injured tone.

"I'd say you're pretty lucky." Sherri pressed her body into his.

If ever there was a moment—one worth remembering forever...

"Sherri, will you marry me?"

Her eyes glowed as a smile transformed her face. "I will."

"What about me?" Morgan asked. "Do I get to say anything here?"

"Sure, but make it fast."

Morgan moved away from her father's embrace and wagged her finger at the two of them. "If you're getting married, I want to be a bridesmaid. I want a light green dress with tiny flowers." She rambled on about what she wanted to wear and how soon could they go shopping again. How if they were really going to live in this house, they needed a dog so Neill and Sherri could get exercise in their old age. She stopped her chatter just long enough to check for a response.

It was clear to anyone who looked at them: Sherri and Neill had heard none of what Morgan had said.

"Dad, pay attention. I'm talking about our future— the three of us. About your wedding."

"Wedding plans can wait," he said, gazing at his beautiful fiancée, his eyes brimming with love.

* * * * *

COMING NEXT MONTH FROM

H HARLEQUIN®

super romance®

Available October 1, 2013

#1878 HIS BROWN-EYED GIRL • by Liz Talley

Lucas Finlay is completely out of his league looking after his two nephews and niece. Luckily assistance is next door. Addy Toussant manages to make order from the kid chaos. She's also sparking an out-of-control attraction in him!

#1879 A TEXAS FAMILY
Willow Creek, Texas • by Linda Warren

Jena Brooks returns to Willow Creek, Texas, to find the baby who was taken from her at birth. Will Carson Corbett stand in her way...or does he hold the key to solving the mystery?

#1880 IN THIS TOGETHER
Project Justice • by Kara Lennox

Travis Riggs is a desperate man. So he does something a bit crazy: he kidnaps Elena Marquez. His only demand is that Project Justice review his case, but things get complicated when Travis starts falling for his hostage!

#1881 FOR THE FIRST TIME • by Stephanie Doyle

Mark Sharpe has been torn about JoJo Hatcher since he hired her. Yes, she's a great investigator. Yet she tempts him to cross the line between boss and employee—something he's never done. But when his teenage daughter is threatened, JoJo is the one he trusts to find the truth.

#1882 NOT ANOTHER WEDDING
by Jennifer McKenzie

Poppy Sullivan intends to stop her friend from marrying the wrong woman. Problem is her first love—and heartache—is the best man, and he wants a second chance. But there's no way she's giving Beck Lefebvre the opportunity to break her heart again, no matter how charming he is!

#1883 BECAUSE OF AUDREY • by Mary Sullivan

Audrey Stone and her floral shop are thorns in Gray Turner's side! All he wants to do is wrap up his family's business holdings in Accord, Colorado. But every move he makes, she's there...in the way. Worse, now he can't get her out of his mind!

YOU CAN FIND MORE INFORMATION ON UPCOMING HARLEQUIN® TITLES FREE EXCERPTS AND MORE AT WWW.HARLEQUIN.COM.

HSRCNM0913

Poppy Sullivan's teenage fling with
Beck Lefebvre happened so long ago it isn't
worth remembering...until she runs into him
at a wedding she's trying to stop. He's still
good-looking, but her pride takes a hit when he
doesn't seem to recognize her! What's a girl to do?
Pretend she doesn't recognize right back....
Read on for an exciting excerpt of

Not Another Wedding
By Jennifer McKenzie

"So?" Beck's voice drew Poppy's attention, caused her to turn before she thought better of it. "Aren't you going to ask how we know each other?"

Oh, he'd like that, wouldn't he? Though she might not have seen him for years, she knew his type. He prided himself on being unforgettable to women. Well, it was time he learned a lesson.

"No." She couldn't help noting how good he looked. Really good. However, she'd give up chocolate before admitting it.

She turned on her heel, intending to return to the party and find someone—anyone else—to talk to, but his hand caught her bare arm above her wrist. His fingers were warm.

"I guess I've changed. You're as gorgeous as ever, Red." His blatant appraisal of her body should have ticked her off. She was not his to behold, but the attraction sizzling through her was impossible to deny. Poppy shook the thought off. She did not want him looking at her. Not even a little. He'd lost that privilege years ago and a bit of sexy banter and warm hands didn't change anything.

"If you'll excuse me." She pulled her arm free and hurried away before he got a chance to stop her again. As she made her way through the crowd, Poppy did her best to ignore the knocking of her heart. When she sneaked a glance back, Beck was still watching. He even had the audacity to raise his glass toward her as though to toast her running away.

Fabulous.

Will Poppy be able to avoid Beck?
Or is he determined to renew their acquaintance?
Find out in NOT ANOTHER WEDDING
by Jennifer McKenzie, available October 2013 from
Harlequin® Superromance®.

REQUEST YOUR FREE BOOKS!
2 FREE NOVELS PLUS 2 FREE GIFTS!

HARLEQUIN

super romance®

More Story...More Romance

She's as voluptuous as Elizabeth Taylor, yet as classy as Jackie Kennedy

Audrey Stone and her floral shop are thorns in Gray Turner's side! All he wants to do is wrap up his family's business holdings in Accord, Colorado. But every move he makes, she's there...in the way. Worse, now he can't get her out of his mind!

Because of Audrey
by Mary Sullivan

AVAILABLE OCTOBER 2013